A LEAGUE OF EXILES

A SHADE OF VAMPIRE 56

BELLA FORREST

ALSO BY BELLA FORREST

HOTBLOODS

(New paranormal romance series!)

Hotbloods (Book 1)

Coldbloods (Book 2)

Renegades (Book 3)

Venturers (Book 4)

THE GIRL WHO DARED TO THINK

The Girl Who Dared to Think (Book 1)

The Girl Who Dared to Stand (Book 2)

The Girl Who Dared to Descend (Book 3)

The Girl Who Dared to Rise (Book 4)

The Girl Who Dared to Lead (Book 5)

The Girl Who Dared to Endure (Book 6)

THE GENDER GAME

(Completed series)

The Gender Game (Book 1)

The Gender Secret (Book 2)

The Gender Lie (Book 3)

The Gender War (Book 4)

The Gender Fall (Book 5)

The Gender Plan (Book 6)

The Gender End (Book 7)

A SHADE OF VAMPIRE SERIES

Series 1: Derek & Sofia's story

A Shade of Vampire (Book 1)

A Shade of Blood (Book 2)

A Castle of Sand (Book 3)

A Shadow of Light (Book 4)

A Blaze of Sun (Book 5)

A Gate of Night (Book 6)

A Break of Day (Book 7)

Series 2: Rose & Caleb's story

A Shade of Novak (Book 8)

A Bond of Blood (Book 9)

A Spell of Time (Book 10)

A Chase of Prey (Book 11)

A Shade of Doubt (Book 12)

A Turn of Tides (Book 13)

A Dawn of Strength (Book 14)

A Fall of Secrets (Book 15)

An End of Night (Book 16)

Series 3: The Shade continues with a new hero...

A Wind of Change (Book 17)

A Trail of Echoes (Book 18)

A Soldier of Shadows (Book 19)

A Hero of Realms (Book 20)

The Secret of Spellshadow Manor (Book 1)

The Breaker (Book 2)

The Chain (Book 3)

The Keep (Book 4)

The Test (Book 5)

The Spell (Book 6)

BEAUTIFUL MONSTER DUOLOGY

Beautiful Monster 1

Beautiful Monster 2

DETECTIVE ERIN BOND (Adult thriller/mystery)

Lights, Camera, GONE

Write, Edit, KILL

For an updated list of Bella's books, please visit her website:
www.bellaforrest.net

Join Bella's VIP email list and she'll send you an email reminder as
soon as her next book is out: www.forrestbooks.com

NEW GENERATION LIST

- **Avril (vampire):** adopted daughter of Lucas and biological daughter of Marion.
- **Blaze (fire dragon):** son of fire dragons Heath and Athena.
- **Caia (part fae/human):** daughter of Grace and Lawrence.
- **Fiona (vampire):** daughter of Benedict (son of Rose and Caleb) and Yelena.
- **Harper (sentry/vampire):** daughter of Hazel and Tejus.
- **Scarlett (vampire):** daughter of Jeramiah (son of Lucas Novak) and Pippa (daughter of Cameron Hendry).

FAMILY TREE

If you'd like to check out the Novaks' family tree, visit:
www.forrestbooks.com/tree

1

HARPER

Despite the constant pushback from a planet whose dominant species wanted us in chains, and eventually dead, we'd actually made some progress. After we found that Darius of House Xunn was still alive, and actively engaged in an intricately designed plan to subdue us and bring more of our people to Neraka for the sole purpose of feeding on their souls, it sufficed to say that we had our hands full.

The rest of our team had barely escaped from Azure Heights with a mind-bent Blaze and horrific truths. The Four Lords, aided by the majority of their own people, had been conspiring with the daemons to bring more "soul food" to Neraka. The Imen population was dwindling, and they were bound to die out. From what Amund, Eristhena, and Ledda—the elders of the Imen village where we'd camped for the night—said, the Exiled Maras and daemons' plan to breed Imen for blood and soul consumption didn't work out too well.

Worst of all, the Druid delegation could still be on Neraka, after thousands of years—or at least some of its surviving members. The swamp witch was still alive, held captive and forced to spill her magic secrets. The daemons and Exiled Maras had managed to build a detailed plot, a theater play of sorts, complete with magic tricks and mind-bent Imen, to convince us that the Exiled Maras had truly started a new, better life here. They hadn't. Not only were they still draining the blood of innocent supernaturals, they'd upgraded to consuming their souls, too.

Despite this stark painting of life on Neraka, there was still hope. We still had allies on the Imen's side, as well as some Exiled Maras, and even daemons who didn't want this kind of existence, and didn't want their world to thrive on the backs and the suffering of others.

Arrah, the only Iman girl we knew to be resistant to the Maras' mind-bending ability, had helped my team get out of Azure Heights. Cadmus had turned on his people, just as Caspian had done. Even more surprising was Zane, one of the seven daemon princes, the son of the king himself—he'd helped us out of Shaytan's palace, and he'd also assisted Avril and the others in escaping from the Maras, who had finally revealed their sickening and despicable nature.

The planet was cloaked in some kind of magic that restricted our ability to communicate with GASP and Calliope via Telluris. If we could get to the swamp witch, we could put an end to that. The moment we could reach out to Draven and our families again, it would be over for these Nerakian overlords. At least we knew what we had to do, although we had a complicated road ahead.

Both daemons and Exiled Maras were out to get us, and we

lacked strength in numbers. We were, however, much smarter and more resourceful than they'd given us credit for—and I sure as hell wasn't going to give up as easily as they thought. Besides, I had a score to settle with these exiled bastards, for the blood oath they'd put Caspian under, and for destroying his family. He couldn't reveal the swamp witch's location without setting himself on fire, but Caspian was on our side, and desperate to restore order and peace on Neraka.

Most importantly, he'd become one of the most significant people in my life over a surprisingly short period of time. My heart fluttered whenever we got close, and, given the hunger with which he'd kissed me, the feeling was mutual. I'd come to Neraka to kick some ass and solve a mystery, and wound up falling for a royal-blooded Mara.

After we caught up with the rest of our team, we managed to get some sleep in the small teepees that the Imen had prepared for us. I didn't want to leave Caspian alone in that cage, where the elders were still keeping him, but Jax and Hansa convinced me that I needed to get some rest, and that Caspian would probably be released in the morning. The Imen were simply traumatized by the Exiled Maras—I figured it would take some time for them to accept that not all of the Maras were evil and bloodthirsty.

My dreams weighed heavily on me throughout the night, and I found myself constantly running from red-eyed daemons and sneering Maras. I felt a presence near me, at some point, and immediately opened my eyes—I wasn't sure if I'd dreamed it. Caspian was sitting next to me with his legs crossed, and his black hair tousled over his forehead. The faint light of dawn was visible through the teepee's front slit. It was still very early, but Caspian had been freed.

I sat up, and gazed at him for a while. He didn't say anything, either, but his smiling jade eyes told me everything I needed to know.

"I see they finally let you out," I breathed.

"They're just scared. I don't blame them," Caspian replied with a soft shrug.

A couple of moments went by in heavy silence. Last night's urgency had worn off, and we were now sitting in front of each other with only a few inches, and the resurfacing memory of our kiss, between us. I didn't know what to do with that. It was as if my courage had flown out of the teepee sometime during the night.

"So, what now?" I asked, feeling my heart pump faster as his gaze dropped to my lips.

"I don't know. I guess... good morning?" he replied, slowly inching closer.

"Yeah, we could start with that, I suppose," I murmured.

"I've got the perfect follow-up, though," he said, then pulled me in for a kiss.

His lips were soft and warm, and I welcomed the taste of him. We were both hungry for each other. He wrapped his arms around me and held me tight as he deepened the kiss. With no iron bars between us, I could finally feel his body against mine, and it was truly an experience that ignited my inner-sentry. His aura turned gold as he trailed soft little kisses along my jawline, then found the side of my neck.

His hot breath raised my temperature, making my spine tingle. I raked my fingers through his hair, prompting him to look up. Losing myself in his jade gaze, I brushed my thumb over his lower lip as he struggled to recover his breath.

"I'm afraid you're going to be the end of me, Harper," he

whispered, then took me for another spin, kissing me deeply. His tongue tasted mine, and I found it difficult to control myself when he devoured me like that.

"Well, then, you're free to run, now," I chuckled, my lips pressed against his. He laughed lightly, then dropped a kiss on my forehead and gently laid us both down on the soft blankets. He held me close, his fingers tracing the curve of my waist.

"Why would I ever want to leave your side?" Caspian replied, then sighed. "When all I've been trying to do was to get closer to you."

"I don't know how to handle this, Caspian," I said, my brow furrowed. "I've never been with anyone. I mean, dating and stuff. It's not my forte, I guess. So, I... I have no idea how this is supposed to work."

"Do you think *I* know?" Caspian smiled. "I'm as baffled by this as you are, Harper. But I know I'm not letting you out of my sight again. I'm constantly drifting toward you, and it's time I stopped avoiding the inevitable."

"What's that, exactly?"

"The fact that you've become a central part of my existence, and I don't mind it one bit."

He floored me with that statement. His aura glowed gold, and he rolled us over. He pinned me down with his massive frame, while his hands found mine and slowly raised my arms over my head. I was putty in his hands, my pulse racing. Our hearts thudded in wonderful unison. He then guided my arms around his neck. His thigh slipped between my legs, and his fingers traveled down my arms, his thumbs brushing against my sides. He kissed me again, this time with fierce hunger, and I parted my lips, welcoming him in.

I was getting lightheaded, and I had no intention of coming

down from this little flicker of bliss anytime soon. Caspian's hands slipped under my lower back, his fingers digging into my skin through my suit's layer of leather. I moaned against his lips, and he responded with a low growl as he gently bit and suckled at my lower lip.

"And I'm also genuinely terrified of you," he whispered.

"Now you tell me?" I replied, and we both burst into laughter. He pulled himself back up into a seated position, and I joined him, with my arms still locked around his neck.

"You do. I can barely control myself when I'm with you," he said, his index finger tracing the contour of my cheekbone.

I let out a heavy sigh. "You're not the only one with that problem."

"But you're the only one who can read my emotions. While I have no idea what you're thinking."

My cheeks caught fire, my lips still tingling from his kiss. "That might change once... once we... you know."

"Once we what?" he asked, cocking his head to the side. There was a twinkle of amusement in his eyes. My temperature was rising, which was both delightful and unnatural—further testament to his impact on me, both physically and emotionally.

"You know. Once we... I mean, you know what I mean. It's just..."

"Once we make love?" he replied, raising an eyebrow.

And boom, there goes my heart.

"I was going to say 'once we get intimate', but yeah," I stammered. He narrowed his eyes at me, not buying it for a second.

"Were you, really?" He smirked.

My shoulders dropped, and I admitted defeat. "Okay, no. I just... Man, this is hard to talk about."

"You mean to tell me that once we take this to the next level,

I'll be able to read your feelings the same way you read mine?" Caspian asked, going back to the full statement and sparing me another minute of awkwardness.

"Theoretically speaking, you'd become a sentry, like me," I replied. "A Mara sentry, to be precise. But only theoretically. It didn't really work with a Druid, for example. A Mara may be different..."

He nodded slowly, processing that information. "Sounds fun. We should try it."

I blinked several times, not sure I'd heard him right. "Wha—What?"

"For the sake of... science. We should definitely find out if your sentry abilities get passed on like that. I'm more than happy to act as your test subject. Mind you, *yours* and yours alone," he said, giving me a playful smile.

"What if you grow a second head, instead?" I replied, pursing my lips.

"Could that really happen?"

"What if it does? Will you still be happy to act as my 'test subject'?"

"And have two heads to kiss you with? Sure," he quipped, then tightened his arms around my waist, and pulled me in for another dizzying kiss. He filled me with warm, golden light, his emotions so powerful, so pure, that I could almost feel them as a part of my very fabric.

"You're... different," I said, taking a deep breath and putting a few inches of distance between us. If I didn't, I knew I'd lose control, and we didn't have the time, nor the privacy we needed, to test the whole Mara sentry theory, as much as I wanted to.

"Define 'different'," he replied.

"I think you're more relaxed now, for some reason. There's

still a cloud of concern weighing over you, but, I don't know, you don't seem as dark as before," I murmured, trying to interpret the accents of color in his aura.

He gave me a soft smile, tucking a lock of black hair behind my ear. "It's probably because we're here, in the open. I don't have to hide from you anymore. Sure, I can't tell you much, either, but at least you know why. You're still here, and not running as far away from me as you possibly can. I guess I have more to look forward to now than I did before."

"Speaking of which, what do you think of our plan, so far?" I asked. He took my hands in his, and looked me in the eyes.

"Whatever you set your mind to, Harper, you *will* achieve it. There's absolutely no doubt in my mind about that," he replied. "But I've had the whole night to think about ways to help you without setting myself on fire."

"I don't want you to risk it, Caspian," I said, shaking my head. "We'll handle it our way."

"No, listen. Neraka used to be more diverse, as you probably know. There were other species, powerful and feared, though vastly outnumbered by the daemons and nearly driven to extinction. They're still out there today, just not in large numbers. Enough to cause some serious disruption."

"What do you know about them?"

"There are three species you'll want to focus on, somewhat scattered across this side of the continent. You might have to rethink your strategy to cover more ground in as little time as possible, on top of looking for the—"

"Swamp witch," I interrupted him. "Don't say it." I couldn't bear to see his face turn red and literally burn, due to his blood oath. Whatever I could do to spare him the suffering, I did. His gaze softened, and that warm golden glow returned, further confirming my suspicion of how he felt about me. *The L word.* "What are these three species?"

"The Adlets have higher numbers," he replied. "Once you meet them and talk to them, you'll understand why. They're double spirited, so to speak. Like the Druids and the Lamias. In one form, they look like us. In another, they're beasts, much like the pit wolves but with thick red fur."

That sounded eerily familiar. "Like werewolves," I breathed. "They can turn from humanoid to beast."

"Yes," he nodded, "though I don't know what a werewolf is."

"It's a supernatural species we have back home. Once we get out of this mess, I'll introduce you to some," I quipped, then kissed his cheek and waited for him to continue. He smiled, squeezing my hands.

"The Adlets were last spotted in a region to the northeast of here," he continued. "Once we're all gathered around a map, I can show you. To the northwest, closer to the second daemon city, is a suspected settlement of Manticores. You'll have to be careful with them. They're rare, but deadly. They're hybrids of sorts, with bodies mostly like ours, but their hands have long claws, and their tails sting with lethal venom. They're extremely territorial, and word has it they've been able to hold onto a few patches of desert land."

It was my turn to nod, as I processed the information, and quietly built a map in my head, reassigning tasks in a way that best matched our priorities. "And the third species?"

"The Dhaxanians. Few of them remain, but they're nearly impossible to kill," Caspian said. "They've secured a mountain chain farther to the northeast, where they have full control over the terrain. Where daemons thrive on heat and fire, the Dhaxanians are harbingers of cold and frost. Everything they touch freezes, and that can be lethal when aimed at an enemy."

"How are you allowed to tell me all this?" I asked, relieved to hear him talk so freely without suffering from the blood oath. In all fairness, we had a pretty good idea of how the spell worked already, but it was still fascinating to discover the limits of revelation before the burns kicked in.

"These creatures are not a secret. They're part of Neraka," he replied. "I'm not allowed to talk about the... conspiracy, and everything that involves this collaboration between daemons and Exiled Maras..."

He hissed from the pain as several red blotches appeared on his face. "Stop it," I whispered, and pulled him close. He instantly responded, holding me tight, and his lips found mine. We lost ourselves once more, my heart aching for him and my soul beaming.

The burns healed fast, but it didn't mean they weren't painful. Judging by the outbursts of red in his aura, the blood oath took its toll, and I suffered, too.

"I have to admit," he muttered against my lips, "if this is how you're going to react whenever I set this curse off, I'll put up with the pain just so I can experience this, over and over."

"You're a masochist," I chuckled, then gently bit his lower lip.

He let out a low growl from his chest, tightening his grip on me. "And you're playing with fire, Miss Hellswan. Careful, or you'll get burned."

"It's too late for that, Lord Kifo," I replied, using his dignified tone. "I'm already in too deep."

He exhaled, then kissed me again. We couldn't get enough of each other, and, the more time we spent together, the more difficult it became to envision a future in which he wasn't present.

My stomach was tied up in deliciously painful knots as he ran his fingers through my hair and deepened the kiss.

It *was* too late. I was already burning up, like a rock hurled onto the surface of the sun, and I could no longer have it any other way.

2

SCARLETT

I had nightmares about Azure Heights and Jack throughout the night. The city was burning to the ground, and I was running around, the flames licking at my skin as I desperately looked for the pit wolf I'd rescued during our first mission in the Valley of Screams. His gleaming red eyes chased me all the way back to consciousness. I gasped and sat up, a thin sheet of sweat covering my face.

What a nightmare.

We'd left Jack behind during our escape from Azure Heights, and I hadn't seen him since. I was genuinely worried about him —he'd saved my ass more than once, after all. He'd chosen to stick around, even though he had his freedom back, no longer subdued by that charmed iron collar.

He's a giant beast with claws that could slice a daemon in half. Surely he made it out of there in one piece, unlike anyone who might've tried to stop him.

A couple of deep breaths later, I pulled my hair up into a ponytail, geared up, and left the teepee I'd been given for the night. Dawn was breaking in lazy purples and pinks across the sky, but the sun was still somewhere beyond the gorges, and the Imen's camp was surrounded by trees with thick crowns. There was no need to cover my face yet.

The Imen had left a large stone bowl filled with water and flower petals next to my teepee. I washed my face, welcoming the sweet taste of freshwater on my lips. The camp was quiet, with just a few Imen females buzzing around, carrying baskets filled with clothes to a nearby spring to wash them.

The rest of my team were still in their tents, except for Patrik —he sat quietly in front of the dying campfire in the middle, his legs crossed and his eyes closed. A faint shimmer enveloped him, and I instantly recognized it. Patrik was deeply submerged in a connection with nature. It was a process the Druids used for focus and clarity, becoming one with the very forces that fueled their magic. It was called Resonating, and it pretty much meant exactly that—similar, in many ways, to meditation.

I quietly walked over, watching him. His hands rested on his knees, and he took deep breaths every other second. His curly black hair covered his forehead, his jawline sharp and clenched. *I'm pretty sure you need to be fully relaxed to Resonate properly.*

Equal parts curious and fascinated, I sat down next to him and gazed at him for a while. It was one of those rare moments in which I could just look at him and take in every feature, while the last embers of the fire crackled on the ground in front of us. My lips tingled with the memory of our kiss, and my heart ached a little as I wondered what was going through his head whenever he looked at me—did he think of Kyana at all? Was I anything like her? I couldn't stop myself from thinking about it.

He'd spent a long time suffering as a Destroyer, just so she could be spared by Azazel. That was, by all possible definitions, real love.

Was I the rebound girl, or did we have a shot at something more profound? Patrik had been through enough. He deserved a chance at a fresh start, and every fiber of my body and soul wanted to be a part of it. I'd fallen for him—so fast and so deep, I doubted there was a way out for me. My only fear was that I wasn't enough to heal his broken heart. That I wasn't Kyana.

His lips parted slowly, and I instinctively did the same with mine, reacting to him in a way I'd never thought possible. He suddenly opened his eyes and looked at me—I froze, entranced by those steely blues. Patrik didn't give me a chance to react, just firmly pulled me into his arms, nearly crushing me against his chest, and kissed me.

I instantly surrendered, sizzling like a droplet of water on a hot stone, gradually disintegrating. His lips caressed mine slowly, and I couldn't stop a moan from escaping my throat. Patrick tasted like the honeysuckle blossoms covering the trunk of my parents' treehouse back in The Shade.

He held me close and paused for a couple of seconds to look at me before he kissed me again. Patrik was disruptively handsome, and there was a fire blazing beneath his cool surface. I could almost hear the blood rushing through his veins, his heart thudding in his chest as he pulled himself back, breathing heavily. His Resonating shimmer was gone, his gaze darkened and so intense. I couldn't help but wonder what it would be like once we got closer to each other.

"I'm sorry I interrupted you," I breathed, brushing my fingers over his slightly swollen lower lip, which was all flushed and tender.

"Nonsense," he replied, giving me a warm smile. "I was just killing time, waiting for you to wake up."

"You could've just woken me up," I said, shrugging. "It's not like I need seven straight hours of sleep."

"Scarlett, if I were to go inside your tent in the morning, I doubt we'd be out before the sun came back down." Patrik chuckled softly. My face burned, the mental image of him waking me up taking over my feeble brain. My breath hitched, and he seemed to enjoy that sound. "Clearly, you don't understand the extent of your effect on me."

"I don't. Care to explain?" I murmured, stifling a smirk while my heart jumped backward with sheer delight. "Since I'm having such a hard time understanding, that is."

His fingers drew invisible lines down my back, gently digging into the leather as they reached my hips. It felt like a massage of sorts, only it set my senses on fire, instead. We were out in the open, where anyone could see us, and yet the intimate nature of his touch made the entire world disappear. It was just me and him, and a dying campfire, as he kissed me again.

"I'm not sure I can find the words to explain it, Scarlett," he whispered. "All I know is that I have a hard time controlling myself when you're near me."

"Should I feel sorry for you?" I quipped, dropping a kiss on the tip of his nose.

"Not at all. Though I'm worried that if you let your hair loose in front of me, I'll come undone," he replied, his lips stretching into a seductive smile. *Oh, my days, this Druid sure knows how to get a girl all worked up.*

"Now I'm curious," I giggled, then reached up to the back of my head to pull the hairband off. Patrik caught my hand and brought it back to his lips, kissing each of my knuckles while his gaze penetrated my very soul.

"Don't, Scarlett. We have a long day ahead of us, and I doubt I'll be able to focus if I see you with your hair down," he said softly, then kissed me again. "It's too early in the morning for you to devastate me like that."

I cupped his face in my hands, speechless and overwhelmed by the flurry of emotions coursing through me. My insecurities were still grumbling somewhere in the back of my head, but, for the time being, I relished the way he looked at me—as if he worshipped me. As if I was the single most important creature in his life. And it felt so good that I pressed my lips against his, trying to transfer everything I felt back into him, just so he could experience the same.

An Iman female's scream made us both jump to our feet. Shortly after that, she was joined by a few others. We turned around toward the south side of the camp, where several Imen had huddled to the side, visibly terrified by the presence of a pit wolf.

Oh, crap.

The beast was massive, its black skin stretched over bulging muscles, its claws and fangs sharp and ready to slice. There were several cuts on its chest, and a wary glimmer in its red eyes as it lowered its head and trotted deeper into the camp. The Imen scrambled for the nearest sharp objects they could find, but the beast wasn't interested.

Patrik instinctively moved in front of me, muttering spells under his breath. Blue fires gathered in his palms. The pit wolf saw us and cocked its head to one side. "Jack," I breathed, gripping Patrik's shoulder. "It's Jack!"

"Kill the beast!" one of the Imen shouted, rushing toward Jack with a broadsword.

"No! Wait, don't!" I cried out, and ran forward.

Jack glanced over his shoulder, noticing the armed Iman, and bared his fangs at him, snarling defensively. I reached them just in time, positioning myself between Jack and the Iman with my arms stretched out. "Stop, please! He won't hurt you!"

"*He*? It's a pit wolf! Vicious flesh-eaters, all of them!" the Iman spat, angered and terrified at the same time—not to mention confused, given that he didn't know Jack's history.

"Please, don't!" I shouted, hearing Jack growl behind me. I glanced over my shoulder at him. "Tone it down, Jack!"

He huffed, then shut his fanged trap. It made him look less threatening, despite his massive size. Patrik reached us, his hands up in a defensive gesture, helping me keep the other Imen away from him—more of them had picked up weapons, and were glaring at poor Jack.

"He's friendly, sort of," Patrik said. "There's no need for violence, trust us!"

"His name is Jack. We freed him from the daemons!" I explained, my heart throbbing. "He won't hurt you. He won't hurt anyone unless he has to defend himself. Or me."

"What are you talking about? Pit wolves tear our people to shreds without hesitating!" Vesta interjected, emerging from a nearby tent with her sword drawn.

"Not Jack. The collars, remember? They're charmed with swamp witch magic," I said. "That's how the daemons control them. Once you set them free, the pit wolves run off. They didn't ask for any of this. Jack... He didn't ask for this."

"Then what is *it* doing here?" Vesta replied, raising an

eyebrow and pointing her sword at Jack, who kept growling, visibly agitated.

"He came looking for me." I sighed. "We have a bit of a bond, I guess. He killed daemons for me. He even helped us get into the tunnel and away from Azure Heights. And look at him: he's wounded. Trust me, he's not going to hurt anyone."

The Imen stared at Jack in disbelief for a while, then at each other, exchanging the occasional shrug and shake of the head. Vesta clicked her teeth, clearly dissatisfied with the pit wolf's presence in her camp, but eventually relented and motioned for the others to put their weapons down. "You are directly responsible for this beast; do you hear me?"

"Yup." I nodded.

"If it so much as looks at any of my people in a way that makes me feel uneasy, I'll chop its head off," Vesta continued.

"That's a bit harsh. I mean, look at him. It's not like he can pull off big, soft puppy eyes," I muttered. It was true, though. Even in his gentlest moment, Jack still looked like a lean, mean killing machine. His size alone was enough to make people tremble. His black skin and blazing red eyes didn't help, either, not to mention the gruesome size of his claws and fangs.

"Okay, fine. Just make sure it doesn't chomp down on my people!" Vesta retorted, crossing her arms. Even she couldn't take her eyes off him.

I turned around, and Jack immediately sat on his hindquarters, like the good, oversized hound of hell that he was. "Hey, buddy." I smiled, then reached out to touch him. He lowered his head so I could pat the top, following up with a good old-fashioned scratch behind his right ear. He stuck his tongue out, breathing heavily but definitely enjoying my touch, and licked my forearm a couple of times.

"Those cuts look deep," Patrik said, slowly moving around to get a better look at the gashes on Jack's ribcage. He fumbled through his belt satchels for some healing powders and took a few steps toward Jack, who instantly growled at him. "Whoa, there. Just trying to help."

"Jack, let him take care of you," I said, and looked deep into his big, round red eyes. I used both hands to gently stroke his neck, while Patrik mixed the powders with water and applied the mixture along the cuts. Jack whimpered, but I held his head so he could look at me. "It's okay, Jack. He'll make the pain go away. You'll be okay."

Meanwhile, Imen gathered around us, both wary and curious as they watched us interact with a pit wolf—a creature they'd known their whole lives was bred for one thing and one thing only: killing them. I couldn't blame them for being afraid, but Jack really was different. He was free.

I was pretty sure that other pit wolves would act the same, but Jack was the only living example I had to work with, at this point. For the time being, he was a wonderful breakthrough.

"I think these were caused by daemons," Patrik said, covering the last of Jack's cuts with healing paste. "Judging by the width and depth, someone really wanted Jack dead."

I inched closer and noticed the dried blood around Jack's mouth and on his chest. "Something tells me they got the short end of the stick on that one. Good boy, Jack."

The pit wolf seemed pleased to hear me say that, though he still wasn't comfortable with Patrik, given his grumbling protests. Nevertheless, I was happy to see him. After everything we'd experienced in the Valley of Screams and in Azure Heights, Jack was my little glimmer of hope that Neraka wasn't inherently evil

—just stuck under the dark influence of greedy, horrible creatures.

And we were going to restore the balance in this world. Realistically speaking, there was no way for us to get off the planet without defeating the bastards who had put Jack under a spell in the first place. Luckily, Jack was eager to help us with that.

3

AVRIL

The growls of a pit wolf got all of us out of our teepees with lightning speed. Nevertheless, I instantly relaxed when I saw Scarlett defending the beast from the terrified Iman—it didn't take long to put two and two together and identify the pit wolf as Jack.

"Is that—"

"Scarlett's pet. Sort of. Yup." I cut Heron off, just as he reached my side.

"His name is Jack," Scarlett interjected.

"Oh, good, she named him," he replied sarcastically. "I tell you, he is freakin' huge. No wonder they're all scared of him."

Jax, Hansa, Caia, Blaze, and Fiona joined us as we walked over to Scarlett, Patrik, and Jack. Vesta kept a few feet's worth of distance from the pit wolf, but I could almost see the tension dissolving from her shoulders. Harper and Caspian came out of the same tent, flushed and wide-eyed as they, too, figured out the pit wolf's identity.

"How did *you* sleep?" I quipped, giving them both a playful grin.

"Like a baby," Harper replied bluntly, ignoring my innuendo, then nodded at Caspian. "They let him out this morning."

"Good for you, Lord Kifo," Jax interjected, then shifted his focus to Jack. "I take it this is your new beastly friend, huh, Scarlett?"

Scarlett smiled, scratching Jack behind the ears, while Patrik wiped the healing potion and dried blood from his hands with a wet cloth. "Yeah, I'm genuinely impressed by the fact that he made it, after last night's insanity."

"Just goes to show what resilient creatures the pit wolves are," Jax replied. "I think we should focus on setting them free from those collars going forward."

"They would come in handy against their daemon overlords, for sure," Hansa said. "Anyway! Now that we're all gathered here, it's time to get organized."

"Speaking of which, Caspian shared some insights—as much as he could, anyway," Harper replied. I knew for a fact that the two of them were getting closer. It was written all over their faces, especially in the way Caspian's gaze softened on her. I couldn't help but feel a little pang in my stomach, wishing I could muster the courage to tell Heron about my feelings toward him.

Watching him as he inched closer to Jack just made my heart swell and ache. He looked like a kid, eager to pet the big pit wolf —who towered a couple of heads above him. Jack sniffed his hand, then lowered his head, allowing Heron to touch him.

"Ah, look at that." Scarlett chuckled. "He likes you."

Heron grinned. "Yeah, he recognizes awesomeness when he sees it."

"Be careful, though," Patrik suggested. "He's still a little cranky because of his wounds."

As he said that, Jack looked at him and growled, prompting Patrik to take a couple of steps back and away from Scarlett. "I think he's just cranky when you get too close to his adoptive mom." Heron laughed.

"Can you kids focus a little bit?" Hansa muttered, frowning at us.

"Okay, okay," Heron sighed, dropping his shoulders and putting his hands behind his back, like the soldier he was. "We're just enjoying these scarce moments of peace, that's all."

"I know, Heron, and there's nothing I'd love more than to relax with you all," Hansa said, "but right now there are daemons and Exiled Maras out there looking for us. Once we get to the swamp witch and reach out to GASP, this nightmare will be over."

Hansa was right. We couldn't really enjoy much of anything —not until we broke the daemons and Exiled Maras down. The damage they'd done to Neraka was horrific, and it was now spreading to our people, too. We had to stop them from bringing more Shadians and Eritopians over here. No one deserved to suffer like the Imen had over thousands of years.

"You mentioned insights," Hansa said, looking at Harper and Caspian. "What insights, exactly?"

"Caspian said there are three other species worth looking for," Harper replied, briefly glancing at Vesta, who'd joined our circle. "The Adlets, the Manticores, and the Dhaxanians."

"That's worth a shot, actually," Vesta muttered, then snapped her fingers at her two trusted scouts, Dion and Alles, who were busy gawking at Jack. "Boys, bring out the maps from my tent. We'll need them."

The Imen scouts nodded and darted to the side, then returned with armfuls of rolled paper—rudimentary maps of the region, which they carefully spread out on the ground, pinning the corners down with rocks.

"I thought the Imen were on their own," Jax replied, his brow furrowed as he analyzed the terrain maps, which showed the Valley of Screams, the isolated coastline of Azure Heights, the western plains, and the world beyond—a colorful array of deserts, wide fields, hills, and snowy mountains. Various pigments had been used to mark the geographical features, along with curves for the hills and sharp angles for the mountains.

"They are, for the most part," Vesta said. "There are rumors of other species still surviving, but their numbers are downright negligible, and they're isolated in parts of this continent where not even daemons dare to venture. For example," she crouched, and pointed at a desert area on the northwestern part of the map, "this is where Manticores were seen, just a few months ago. Over here, toward the east, there is at least one pack of Adlets still standing, and there are rumors of a handful of Dhaxanians using the mountains as refuge, farther to the north."

"Can you show us where in the daemon city they're keeping the Druid delegation?" Hansa asked.

"It's here, on the north side, past the desert," Vesta replied, her hand traveling across the map. "This is Draconis, a prison city. The one beneath the Valley of Screams, the capital of Shaytan's kingdom, is called Infernis. Draconis is where all their prisoners go, Imen or otherwise. Each daemon city keeps a steady supply of Imen to feed on, but they're all processed through Draconis first and transferred via subterranean tunnels."

"Okay, so, if it's all the way up here, we could pass through this desert and look for Manticores, right?" Hansa asked, joining Vesta in a crouching position before the map.

"Yes, but the Adlets and Dhaxanians are farther to the east," Vesta explained. "Maybe if we put two teams together, we could reach that side, too," she added, then sighed. "If we spread out like this, I'll forfeit my request for the dragon to stay here and look after my people. We'll need all hands on deck for this. My tribe will stay on high alert in the meantime."

Vesta had initially requested that we left Blaze to look after the tribe but, given our circumstances and the possibility of gathering allies in this fight, it was no longer a viable option.

"That actually makes sense, though I dislike splitting our team up again," Jax replied. "We don't have much time and have a lot of terrain to cover, however. I suggest we break up into two groups, one large and one small. Harper, Caspian, Fiona, Caia, Blaze, Hansa, and I can take Draconis and the Manticores, for example, and Avril, Heron, Patrik and Scarlett can handle the Adlets and Dhaxanians."

It sounded reasonable, but I did have some concerns. "How do we communicate, then? How do we know who has done what? Do we meet back here in the camp? How would this work?" I asked.

"Here," Vesta replied, pointing at a solitary mountain smack in the middle, roughly one hundred miles north of the camp. "This is Ragnar Peak. We could all go together up to this point, then go our separate ways and meet back here in, I don't know, seven days, tops? It'll take a couple of days, at least, to reach the mountains, for example, and the same goes for Draconis. And that's with indigo horses."

"You have enough of them here?" Jax asked, raising his eyebrows.

Vesta nodded. "Yes. I strongly recommend using Ragnar Peak as a marker. This camp will move in a couple of days. Hansa is right: there are daemons and Exiled Maras looking for all of us, not just you. They will, eventually, track us here, and our swamp witch magic tricks are not enough against a full-scale attack. I'm hoping that once we get to Draconis, we can get our hands on that cloaking spell that the daemons use to conceal their entrances into the city. My people sure could use that."

"Okay, that works. Let's consider seven days to be the absolute maximum. If either team gets back to Ragnar Peak sooner, they'll stay there and wait for the others," Jax said. Then his gaze darkened, and his tone dropped. "Should the other team fail to return in seven days, it will mean that the worst has happened, and you'll have to regroup and continue the mission—which, right now, is to find the swamp witch."

"I think we'll be okay over on the northeastern side," I said, "especially with a Druid and a pit wolf. I'm more worried about you guys, dragon or not."

"I'll go with Jax and his team," Vesta replied. "Dion and Alles will guide your team through the plains on the northeast. We have better odds now than we did before, I'll tell you that. Up until a few days ago, I didn't think we had any allies left."

"You said you know people in Draconis last night, didn't you?" Hansa said.

Vesta nodded. "Two daemon pacifists, to be precise. I've been in touch with them via secret messengers. One will be waiting to get us into the city, and the other will help us move around, as well as answer some questions."

"Good. Sounds like a plan," Hansa replied.

I felt like we had it somewhat easier this time, but I also didn't want to keep underestimating this world. We knew little to nothing about what lay beyond the camp, and even less about these potential allies. I couldn't help but draw some parallels back to Serena and her group, back when they were first abducted and brought to Calliope.

They'd had trouble finding trustworthy allies, and the last thing I wanted was a repeat of what happened with the Sluaghs, who had joined forces with Azazel's Destroyers and incubi soldiers. We lacked strength in numbers. The least we could get were quality friends.

4

CAIA

Patrik had Dion and Alles help him prepare healing potions and a couple of other spells with the supplies he had left in his backpack. "Unfortunately, I don't know enough about Neraka's flora and minerals to choose suitable replacements for some of these spells," Patrik muttered, "so we'll have to be careful with how we use these."

"That's fine," Vesta said. "Dion and Alles know how to cook up some of *our* swamp witch spells, if needed. They won't work as well as yours, but they'll do the trick."

"Tell us about these creatures we'll be looking for," Avril said, while sharpening her sword with a diamond rock. There was a pile of them left for us to prepare our weapons, and we were all busy doing the same, along with restocking our belt satchels and backpacks. Ledda had been kind enough to have the Imen females prepare some dried breads and fruit, as well as water, for our non-vampire and non-Mara team members.

"The Manticores are thought to have a nest here, in the Akrep Gorge," Vesta replied, pointing at the map. "It's a cluster of tall red rocks in the middle of the Harvaris Desert. It's a dangerous territory, and few of us venture there. The wild animals are mostly night hunters, and extremely hostile. To be honest, the Manticore nest is more of a rumor, but it's worth a shot."

"What are they like?" I asked, then stole a glance at Blaze, who was still refusing to look at me. I had a feeling he was still struggling with guilt after Rewa had mind-bent him into strangling me. I knew dragons were kind of hard-headed, so it would take some time for him to loosen up and understand that it really wasn't his fault.

"The Manticores were always vicious warriors," Vesta replied. "Their culture was tribal and violent, and the strongest and fiercest of their fighters were always honored with precious stones and other riches. Their tails have a needle-like extension, and it injects deadly venom with incredible speed. We don't have an antivenom, so we'll have to be careful not to cross them. If they sting us, we will die."

"I wonder if vampire blood can heal that," Harper muttered.

"Mara blood definitely can't," Caspian replied. "We tried, a long time ago."

"How many of them do you think there are left?" I asked.

"Honestly, I have no idea," Vesta said with a shrug. "A nest could hold up to fifty of them in the old days, but I don't know what it's like for them these days. *If* they're still out there, that is. They would be thriving in the desert, though. They like it hot and dry. It's one of the reasons the daemons went after them first when they started conquering the surface territories. They didn't want the competition—the Manticores eat raw flesh, too. They never got along with the daemons because of that. They're also extremely territorial, but, then again, so are the Adlets."

"Caspian said they're two-spirited creatures," Harper replied, then looked at me. "They're like werewolves. They shift from humanoid to wolf."

"No way!" I gasped. "Nerakian werewolves! Who would've thought?"

"They're huge, though," Vesta said, then nodded at Jack with a smirk. I followed her gaze and found Jack lying on his back, his belly up as he watched Scarlett sharpen her sword and knives. "As big as pit wolves, to be precise."

"They have red fur, though," Harper added.

"Bright red, yes. Long before the Imen understood the Adlets' nature, back in more primitive days, they used to call them 'fire spirits'," Vesta explained. "They usually live and hunt in packs of ten and more, each covering up to ten miles' worth of land. They were spotted in the Plains of Lagerith, here," she said, pointing at the map again. "It's covered in tall grass, perfect for the moon-bison to graze. The Adlets take cover in the neighboring forest patches and hunt during the day. They used to rule the nights, until the daemons came to the surface and pushed them into changing their hunting habits."

"You know for a fact they're still there?" Scarlett asked, sheathing her sword.

"Yes. I know of one pack, for sure. They mark their territory with the skulls of their fallen brothers. The daemons like to crush them, just to show everyone else that they've taken over, but this area here," she replied, her index finger circling a particular spot on the map, "is still Adlet territory. Dion and Alles passed by a few nights ago, and the skulls were still there. Intact."

"The daemons don't like that region much," Dion added, while holding a small leather bag for Patrik to fill with a mixture of crystal powders and herbs. "It rains a lot in those parts, and, since they like hunting invisibly, it doesn't work for them. They just hijack the fringe cattle when their meat source runs low near Draconis. Infernis covers the southeastern plains, so the Adlets were left with Lagerith. For now, anyway. It's only a matter of time before either the Exiled Maras or the daemons decide it's time to wipe the red wolves out, too."

"What about the Dhaxanians?" Harper asked. "I'm told they're quite the opposite of daemons."

"Yes, literally." Alles chuckled, then got up and passed healing bags around to each of us, while Patrik and Dion moved to prepare the rest. "They're ice people. Everything they touch is taken over by frost. They're pale and skinny, barely a wisp, but boy, don't let them touch you!"

"They were last spotted in the Athelathan Mountains, farther north from the Lagerith Plains," Vesta added. "We know for sure there are some of them still living there because the mountain peaks are always covered in snow, even in the middle of summer. No daemon dares to go up there, anyway. They thrive in fire, but the Dhaxanians like it cold. The low temperatures will slow a daemon down. I'd bet you'll find plenty of them frozen up there."

"I hope so," Avril muttered. "I've never rejoiced in the deaths of others, but, man, I'm okay with making an exception for daemons. May those mountains be loaded with their corpses. At least it'll be proof that the Dhaxanians can do some serious damage."

"Speaking of which," I said, "why haven't they tried to get together, between species, and fight the daemons?"

Vesta sighed, then rolled the maps into two tubes, which she then tied with leather strings. She kept one and handed the other to Patrik. "They tried, thousands of years ago. But when the Druid delegation crashed and the daemons got their claws on the swamp witch, it was game over. The Manticores went down first. The Adlets managed to retreat and survive in small packs, keeping to secluded patches, particularly where it rained a lot. The Dhaxanians didn't stand a chance, either, but they were able to secure a couple of mountain peaks, and the daemons stopped trying to go after them. They couldn't leave the mountains, either."

"Yes, we'll have to be careful when we reach the Athelathan Mountains," Dion said. "Daemons will probably be stationed there. They're always there, even after, what, seven thousand years?"

"More or less," Alles replied with a nod. "They're quite persistent in making sure the Dhaxanians don't try to come down. Chances are they'll have fires constantly burning, just to remind them of their fate."

About an hour passed as we finished planning and stocked up on supplies and spells. Patrik wrote down the swamp witch spell incantations we needed for the pouches he gave us—fire starters, water detectors, and invisibility paste, the last made with local ingredients. We had to be prepared for everything on our end, even the worst-case scenario in which Blaze and I couldn't use our fire abilities.

Dion and Alles then brought over the indigo horses, one for each of us. They were all strong, muscular males with long white manes and sparkling violet eyes that reminded me of the Daughters of Eritopia. My heart twisted itself up in a painful knot as I patted a stallion's neck—I missed Vita, my parents... Hell, I missed Bijarki, Draven, Serena, the whole gang.

Blaze seemed to notice my sadness. He inched closer and briefly squeezed my shoulder. "It'll be okay, Caia. We'll get this done, and we'll go back home."

"Damn straight!" Heron grinned, and gave him a hard, albeit friendly, slap on the back. "I can't wait to go back to Calliope. White City is gorgeous during the summer. All white and sparkling beneath the moonlight. You haven't seen it, have you, Avril?"

Avril shook her head. "I haven't had the chance, no."

"Well, I'd be happy to take you there when we get out of this hellhole," Heron replied, the shadow of a smile flickering across his face. Vesta then smacked him on the shoulder. "Ouch!"

"Show some respect!"

"Sorry," he mumbled, then scratched the back of his head. "Though, technically speaking, you're not from around here, either."

"I was definitely born here, so it's my home," Vesta replied.

"Fair enough," Jax said, then smacked Heron on the shoulder again, prompting him to mutter a curse under his breath. "Be kinder to the locals, Brother."

"Wait till we get back to Calliope," Heron shot back. "I'll kick your ass in the training hall until you beg for mercy."

"I'd like to see you try," Jax replied with a smirk.

"And I'd love to watch," Hansa interjected with a dazzling smile, before she dragged Jax back by his hood, "but we have a long road ahead of us, so cover up and let's go. The sun is coming out."

Vesta chuckled lightly, then got on her horse, while the vampires and Maras covered up with hoods, masks, goggles, and gloves. The sun was coming out from behind the gorges in the east, casting its vibrant light across a watercolor-blue sky. It looked so beautiful and tranquil, the very opposite of what was going on beneath.

We all got on our horses and bid the Imen goodbye.

"We'll travel to Ragnar Peak together," Vesta said. "Then we'll be off to Kerentrith via the Akrep Gorge, while Dion and Alles will take your friends to Lagerith, as planned."

"Wait, Kerentrith?" I asked, frowning. "I thought we were going to Draconis, the prison city of daemons."

"We are," Vesta replied, putting on a sad smile. "Draconis is beneath Kerentrith, the abandoned citadel of the Imen. It's still beautiful, with its white marble walls and towers, but it's empty. The Imen were driven out eventually, when the daemons decided to become conquerors and disregard all other creatures in this world."

I nudged my horse with my heels and followed the rest of my team as we shot through the woods to the north. The trees whizzed past us in shades of dark brown and green, and birds flew out above, startled by hooves thundering across the hard ground.

This was it. Our most dangerous endeavor yet, and the most important one. Our lives depended on its success. One way or another, we *were* going to get that swamp witch back. Neraka was not going to hold us hostage for much longer.

5

HARPER

The horses were ridiculously fast, reminding me why I loved their species so much. These beauties could cover a hundred miles in less than an hour at a smooth and steady gallop. Once we reached Ragnar Peak, we noticed how the landscape was slowly beginning to change.

We'd left the woods behind, flat green plains now spreading all around us. Before us stood Ragnar Peak, a tall but slender mountain—mostly bare stone with thousands of stairs carved into its ridges, leading all the way up to a fortress at the top. There were patches of trees here and there, but they didn't do much to soften its rough appearance.

"This used to be a lookout point," Vesta said, looking up at the fortress. "We still use it now and then, to check our surroundings for daemons."

"No need this time," I replied, then used my True Sight to

briefly glance around. "It looks pretty clear for at least five miles in each direction."

We hugged and said our goodbyes to Scarlett, Patrik, Avril, and Heron, who had Jack, Dion, and Alles with them. "We'll see you here in seven days," Patrik said, giving Hansa and Jax a warm smile. "Try not to get yourselves killed, please. By the Daughters, you have a dragon!"

"Same goes for you, Druid," Jax replied with a grin. "You've got a pit wolf and the fastest vampire in the world. Make it count."

I couldn't ignore the hole in my stomach as I watched my friends leave for the northeastern Plains of Lagerith. Caspian guided his horse closer to mine, enough to gently brush his knee against mine and make me turn my head to look at him.

"They'll be fine, Harper," he said softly. Even with his leather garments, head and face fully covered, I could still make out the warm gold aura of his emotions. "That pit wolf will make all the difference in the world for them, especially with the Adlets."

His aura turned red for a brief moment—pain, as he stopped himself from telling me more.

"Are you okay?" I asked.

"Yes," he grunted, "don't worry. Just testing my limits here. It seems like that's all I can tell you about the Adlets and the pit wolf."

"Don't overdo it," Jax interjected. "We need you in one piece. And so does Harper."

I couldn't see Jax's face, but I could still sense the softness in his tone. He'd already figured out that Caspian and I were getting closer—though, to be honest, we didn't really hide it, either. My cheeks were flushed, nonetheless, as our horses continued on their frantic sprint toward the northwest.

Over the span of three hundred miles, the terrain shifted around us. The green plains faded into dried-up dirt, and reddish sand dunes rose ahead. The horses didn't seem to have much trouble, though, as they continued to gallop with impressive speed.

As the scorching emptiness engulfed us, I realized that the temperature was reaching some critical hot points. It was beginning to feel uncomfortable. The sun shone brightly above us, the sky too clear. There wasn't a single wisp of cloud anywhere in sight, just an endless blue overlooking wave upon wave of red sand. It was beautiful, but incredibly cruel to creatures such as myself.

"Is anyone else getting hot, or is it just me?" I asked, my throat feeling parched.

"Nope, we're all feeling it," Jax replied. "It is getting way too hot. I've been in deserts before, but this... this is something else entirely."

"Speak for yourselves. I'm doing fine, for the most part," Vesta said. "But, then again, you vampires and Maras can't be out in the sun for too long, can you?"

"I'm okay, too," Caia added. "I mean, it's hot, but I'm comfortable."

"That's because you're made of fire, you adorable weirdo," I shot back. "Something tells me Blaze is just peachy, too."

Beads of sweat were gathered above Vesta's eyebrows as she looked at me. "I think I know why," she said. "It's the lava."

"Huh? What lava?" I asked, briefly glancing around.

"There are lava lakes beneath this desert," Vesta replied. "Stretching for hundreds of miles all around Draconis. It's a prison city, and it was built with that in mind. No prisoner can easily get off it. It's basically an island surrounded by liquid fire, reducing possible escape routes to a few, potentially deadly ones."

"It must have an impact on the environment, for sure," I muttered.

"Oh, it definitely does. I just never traveled with a vampire or a Mara before. You guys seem to really feel its effects. I've gotten used to it, and your fae and dragon are both fire creatures, so they definitely wouldn't be affected by it," Vesta explained. "But that's why we have a desert in these parts. We're quite far up north. It should get colder, not hotter. The daemons did something beneath the crust, worked some swamp witch magic for sure, in order to get that much lava collected around Draconis."

"It's ridiculously hot," I gasped, searching for my water bladder. I'd gotten used to living exclusively off blood, but I still packed water whenever I went out on longer trips—a reflex I was grateful for at this point, because my throat was in desperate need of a soothing liquid, and I didn't make a habit of carrying blood over long distances, as it spoiled fast.

I carefully lifted my mask and drank some water, welcoming its freshness into my stomach. For a few minutes, it felt good, before the heat came back, almost twice as bad.

"The Akrep Gorge is right ahead," Vesta said, pointing at the massive formation of sharp, red rocks rising over the dunes, less than twenty miles away. "We should get you into the shade for a while so you can cool down a little."

"Fabulous idea!" I quipped, and pushed my horse to go faster.

Soon enough, we were all racing toward the narrow gorge opening, a crevice just fifty feet wide. "I'm practically steaming," Fiona said, then got ahead of me.

"Okay, clearly the horse with the smaller load is faster!" I chuckled, watching her go.

"Elegant way of calling me 'tiny', Cuz!" She laughed.

Five minutes later, we reached the Akrep Gorge. It towered over us with sharp peaks and ridges as the sun headed west across the sky. "Look, a cave." Vesta nodded toward a small, round hole in the wall. "Might be worth staying there for a bit."

"Once again, I love how we're on the same page," I replied, then got off my horse and looked into its beautiful violet eyes. "You stay here, gorgeous, and keep the others with you."

My stallion was now under my mental control, and I knew it wouldn't go anywhere. I went inside the cave, followed closely by Caspian, Jax, Hansa and Fiona. Vesta, Blaze, and Caia soon joined us. I took deep breaths, removing my mask, hood, and goggles, relishing the flow of cool air through my lungs.

The darkness was absolute, and downright perfect. I could feel my temperature gradually dropping back to its normal level. We stood there for a while, leaning against the cold walls of the narrow tunnel, enjoying the chill.

The murmur of water at the other end caught my attention. "Do you guys hear that?" I asked, and Caspian nodded. I used my True Sight to look deeper into the cave, and nearly yelped with delight. I shot through the darkness. "Come on!"

A gorgeous cavern unfolded at the end of the tunnel, in the form of a huge, red stone bubble with smooth walls. It was filled with sapphire-blue waters, dimly lit from within. My guess was some species of phosphorescent algae. But it was truly stunning. The pool was deep, and the air was colder than in the tunnel.

"I don't know about you, but I'm definitely in the mood for a dip," I said, removing my gear. My hand reached for the zipper, but I quickly changed my mind about taking the suit off, too, suddenly way too self-conscious in Caspian's presence.

I briefly glanced at him.

"By all means," he replied, slightly amused. He took off his gear and boots, but kept his suit on, like the rest of us.

"Beat you to it!" Hansa laughed, and jumped into the water, screeching with sheer joy. "This is amazing!"

"Tell me about it." I somersaulted headfirst, and as soon as the waters swallowed me, my skin tingled with relief. I couldn't help but laugh once I got back to the surface. Jax, Caspian, and Fiona joined us, while Caia, Blaze, and Vesta sat down on the edge and washed their faces.

It was a much-needed break in the middle of a scorching desert. Neraka could be merciless, but it sure knew how to reward those with enough patience to find hidden gems like this cave. The dim glow from the water flickered across the red walls, and, for a brief moment in time, just as Caspian swam up to me and took me in his arms, it felt perfect.

6

HANSA

I needed this, badly. It wasn't just the desert heat taking its toll on my body, but the cumulated amount of awfulness that had taken over our lives in such a short period of time. The water was cool, and it instantly relaxed my muscles. My skin rejoiced beneath the leather suit, and, as soon as it permeated my hair and scalp, it felt as though all those deadly problems we were dealing with simply went away—even if for just a handful of minutes.

Caia and Blaze stayed on the edge of the water for a while, washing their faces and necks, then moved closer to the grotto entrance to keep watch. Vesta, on the other hand, seemed to enjoy watching us frolic in the water. She sat on the stone lip, removed her sandals, and submerged her feet. She then started playing with the water, pulling out crystalline streams and manipulating their swirling motions with gentle flicks of her wrists. It was always a pleasure to watch a fae at work, so deeply connected to the natural elements.

Fiona was giggling and swimming around like a happy little frog, and my heart swelled a little at the sight of her smile. I hadn't seen much of it during our stay on Neraka, and I had been missing it, since it always brightened me up. Harper and Caspian were busy chasing each other around, looking more relaxed than ever. Come to think of it, this was the first time I was watching Lord Kifo simply being himself—and most likely in love, judging by the way he beamed whenever he heard Harper laugh. There was more good inside him, hidden deep beneath the darkness and secrets he'd been forced to carry for so long. We were lucky to know him. If it weren't for him, we would've been daemon chow by now.

They made their way behind one of the large rocks poking out of the water on the other side—not by plan, but rather by how they "hunted" each other as they swam. They didn't rush back out, either, and I wondered where my responsibilities as the "adult" in the grotto ended. Then Jax popped out of the water right in front of me, startling me. I stifled a yelp, he laughed, and I completely disconnected from the idea of a "responsible adult".

His jade eyes twinkled with delight, as his body temperature had lowered. As a nightwalker who had been riding for hours in the desert sun, with no shade other than what his gear offered, Jax needed this cool water more than the rest of us non-blood-drinkers.

"I didn't peg you for being so easily scared," he quipped, then wrapped his arms around my waist and pulled me closer.

"Whoa, using bold words there, Lord Dorchadas." I grinned, resting my hands on his shoulders, while we constantly moved our feet to stay afloat.

"Back to official titles, now?" he replied with a smirk, then inched forward and kissed me, deeply, reminding me of why my heart throbbed for him, and him alone. We'd met during a war, and we both carried our worst memories with us, at all times— and yet, we fell in love, albeit in the middle of a world ruled by soul-eating daemons and Maras.

"Nah, I'm just playing hard to get," I chuckled, my lips still pressed against his.

"Sorry, succubus, but I've got my sights set on you now," he breathed, his jade gaze darkening. "Play as you wish; you won't get rid of me that easily. As a matter of fact, you won't get rid of me at all."

The second time he kissed me, my senses went haywire. He was hungry and passionate, in desperate need of more—and I was the same, if not more so. We lost ourselves in each other as the water lapped gently at our shoulders. For just a few minutes, we were all we had to worry about. There weren't enough words to describe what I felt for him, but it was deeply embedded in my system. Over the span of a few months, Jax had snuck into my soul and had taken a firm hold of me, while trying to deny his own feelings about me.

His lips moved along the side of my neck, dropping kisses until he reached the collar of my leather suit. He growled. My temperature was spiking already, and my breath was cut short— it was surprisingly difficult to keep my wits about me, while staying afloat and glued to his powerful frame. "I'm a horrible person, Hansa."

My heart skipped a beat, and my stomach dropped. I worried that Jax was still weighed down by the tragedies in his past. "What are you talking about?" I asked, caressing his sharp cheek with the tips of my fingers.

"We're in the middle of a Nerakian desert, looking for our only way off the planet, and all I can think of is getting everybody out of this cave so I can have you all to myself. Even though that would delay our mission by a couple of days, at least, and earn me the ire of GASP," he replied, a smile tugging at the corner of his mouth.

Relief washed over me, promptly followed by the urge to laugh out loud. Instead, I pressed my lips tight and did my best to keep cool. "A couple of days, *at least*?"

He shrugged, giving me his most charming and seductive smirk, and tightened his grip on me. "Well, what do you think will happen when I finally get you out of this gear, Hansa? I already can't get enough of you as it is."

Just when I thought I couldn't love him more, he went ahead and demolished the last of my defenses. I giggled, lighting up like a silvery flame as I blushed in his arms. He loved that look on me; I could see it in his eyes. I was about to kiss him again, when I caught movement somewhere below.

A shadow darted through the water several feet beneath us. My instincts kicked in with lightning speed. "What is it?" he asked, immediately noticing the shift in my expression.

"I'm not sure. I thought I saw—"

Fiona's short but sharp scream filled me with dread. She vanished beneath the water, pulled down with abrupt force.

"Fiona!" I heard Harper cry out, as she and Caspian emerged from behind the rock. They'd both heard her. Jax let go of me and dove after her, just as more shadows gathered, crisscrossing through the water. I went under as well, then stilled, my blood freezing. Slick, black creatures swarmed beneath us—at least six feet in length, each. They looked like thick snakes, with intense blue scales covering their bodies and black spikes emerging from their spines. Their beady black eyes glistened in the turquoise water, and they were incredibly fast.

Three of them had gotten hold of Fiona, and were tightly coiled around her legs as they pulled her down. Jax was the first to reach her, grabbing her arms and struggling to pull her to the surface, while the creatures viciously held on to her. More swam around us, baring their sharp fangs.

Harper and Caspian swam toward Jax and Fiona, but I waved them away. The water snakes moved toward them, and I knew we all needed to get out of the water, *fast*. I rose to the surface for a quick breath. Harper and Caspian tried to make their way to the edge, though they, too, were quickly surrounded by the creatures.

"Stay out of the water!" I shouted. "They're trying to get Fiona!"

"What are those things?" Caia cried out, her voice trembling with angst. Blaze held her back. Her first instinct had been to jump in, but the dragon's self-preservation instinct had kicked in.

"You don't want to know," Vesta gasped, and readied her bow and arrows, her gaze flickering across the water as she tried to get Fiona's location. "Hansa, get out of the water! They won't settle for just Fiona!"

"No, I need to help Jax!"

"Get out! I'll help," Vesta replied, narrowing her eyes at Fiona's figure underwater.

I couldn't leave her and Jax there. I went back under, and instantly understood what Vesta had meant. The snakes had freakishly huge mouths, with an opening about three feet in width and razor-sharp fangs. Two of them were snapping at Caspian and Harper's legs. They both went primal as soon as the creatures drew blood. The vampires and Maras didn't shy away from using their claws and fangs when needed, so they both snapped and slashed back at the snakes, while others circled in.

Jax used his claws to cut through the ones tightening around Fiona's legs. She screamed underwater as the third snake bit deep into her thigh. Others came at me, and I knew that I wouldn't be able to fight them all back. I didn't have any claws, fangs, or weapons on me—I'd gone in for a swim, not a fight to the death.

Arrows shot in from above, several in quick succession. A couple struck two of the three snakes currently holding Fiona down. They let go and flailed away, leaving thick trails of black blood in their wake. Jax managed to tear the third snake off, then pulled Fiona back to the surface. I swam as fast as I could, kicking and punching the creatures that came at me.

But it wasn't enough. Sharp pain burned through my right calf as one of the snakes took a bite. The water then trembled and moved around me, and the next thing I knew, I was being sucked upward by a small whirlwind. I landed on the edge of the pool with a sloppy thud, and gasped with relief when I saw Blaze pulling Fiona and Jax out of the water. Caia had joined forces with Vesta to conjure up another whirlwind, and they were now sucking Harper and Caspian out.

"Thank the Daughters," I breathed, feeling a little lightheaded.

My leg throbbed with pain, and I broke into a cold sweat. I felt weak, in the most literal sense of the word. We'd all made it out, but none of us seemed well. Harper and Fiona were the worst, far too pale—even for their vampiric complexions—and unable to stand.

Jax and Caspian seemed more alert. They had minor bites on them, but Harper and Fiona's thighs and calves were covered in puncture wounds. "What the hell are those things?" Fiona murmured, her eyes drooping. She was close to passing out.

"They're called Anguiles," Vesta replied, checking her vitals. "They don't just bite, they suck blood. You're weakened... You need blood. You all need blood to recover fast; otherwise, we're stuck here for hours."

"Take some from us." Blaze offered his wrist, as did Caia.

I was able to get up, though my legs were unstable. Vesta pulled out a small knife and cut her forearm. She pushed the bleeding wound against Fiona's lips, while Blaze took care of Jax and Caspian, and Caia looked after Harper. I made my way to their side and took Jax in my arms. He welcomed me with a shuddering embrace, pulling me closer and kissing my face, while being careful not to touch the silver blood oozing from my calf wound.

"Next time, don't wait around and get yourself killed just because I'm still fighting," he whispered, then bit into his wrist and offered me a few droplets of his blood. "Yours might kill me, but mine can heal you, and I need you at full strength, Hansa. So drink."

I nodded slowly and licked his wound. The salty taste of his blood filled my mouth, and I could feel its soothing effect almost immediately. The bite marks on my calf were gone, with just a couple of holes left in the leather as a reminder of how close we'd all been to disaster.

7

FIONA

The grotto, with its reddish ceiling and walls, and the turquoise reflection of the water, came into focus. The mind-numbing pain in my legs was gone, and my heart recovered its pulse. Vesta's fae blood wasn't just incredibly delicious; it also sped up the recovery process. Human blood wouldn't have brought me back this fast.

"Do these Anguiles wait in underwater caves for unsuspecting suckers such as ourselves to show up?" I asked, pushing myself up into a seated position. Vesta was kneeling by my side, holding her bleeding wrist. "Here, swallow a little bit of this. It'll heal that faster," I said, then bit into my thumb, enough to draw a little blood. I smeared some on her lower lip so she could ingest it. She gave me a thankful smile, which I returned, along with a wink. "Least I could do."

"I didn't think there were any Anguiles in these parts. They usually stick to lakes and swamps. They're freshwater creatures,"

Vesta replied, then glanced at the water. They were all gone, and the surface was eerily peaceful and smooth. It didn't even look like it held dozens of Nerakian bloodsuckers.

"Jeez, even your eels are trying to suck the life out of us," Harper muttered, regaining her senses. Caspian held her in his arms, breathing heavily.

"Oh, my days, you're right," Caia replied. "They did look like eels. Sort of."

Harper sighed, then raised an eyebrow. "Did you see their mouths, though?"

"They could swallow any of us whole," I said, then looked at Vesta, Caia, and Blaze. "Thankfully, we had you to save our asses. I was literally about to tell you guys that you were missing out on all the watery goodness when those things grabbed me."

They chuckled lightly. "The upside is that they're not venomous, just vicious and sneaky," Vesta replied with a shrug, then frowned. "It's still strange that they're here. I mean, this pond is definitely coming from an underground spring, but how could the Anguiles have traveled up here on their own? They're usually confined to other regions, and there are hundreds of miles of desert between this place and the nearest swamp."

"What are you saying?" Hansa asked, while gearing up.

"I'm saying that this isn't natural," Vesta replied, pointing at the water. "They really aren't supposed to be here."

"So, what, someone brought Anguiles here?" Jax muttered, tying the leather strings of his scabbards back on his belt.

"Basically, yes. Think about it. If you were a creature nearing extinction, like, say, the Manticores, wouldn't you go out of your way to protect your territory?" Vesta said. "As outsiders, the first thing we did, after hours in that scorching desert, was literally jump into the first body of water we could find. This one. Just in time for the Anguiles to try and eat us."

"The Manticores brought Anguiles to the cave to further protect their gorge," I murmured, my heart skipping a beat. "They're trying to keep outsiders away by all possible means."

"And you know what that suggests, right?" Harper smirked.

"That there are definitely creatures hiding in this gorge," I concluded. "Not necessarily Manticores, but if the rumors are true, then they're the most likely culprits."

"We're on the right track then," Hansa replied, pulling her long, rich black hair back into a loose bun. "How is everyone feeling?"

We were all back on our feet, geared up and ready to go. "I think we're good," I said, feeling the strength come back to my limbs. "Though I must say, it was pretty weird to be on the receiving end of a bloodsucking fang."

"Yeah, who would've thought, huh?" Harper chuckled. "Do unto others and so on."

"A taste of our own medicine," I continued, laughing lightly. Soon enough, both Harper and I were doubling over to the point of tears, while the others watched, equal parts confused and amused. Of course, they didn't know this little inside joke that Harper, Scarlett, Avril, and I had, as vampires in The Shade.

"We laughed about something like this about a year ago," Harper explained. "Fiona, Scarlett, Avril, and I spent a lot of time together, especially after I turned. We used to talk a lot, about life, death, and how we could possibly die. We came up with the freakiest scenarios, like something out of a slasher movie, but the most ironic and, at the same time, amusing, was this. Sort of."

"It was exsanguination, basically," I completed her memory

of our long talks beneath the pearly moonlight, surrounded by rustling redwoods and darkness. "Vampires getting their blood drained."

"Technically speaking, it wouldn't kill us right away, but still. The irony made us laugh out loud then," Harper said, a tinge of sadness added to her voice.

"It's still making you both laugh now, it seems." Caia grinned.

I sighed, slightly overwhelmed by the nostalgia of days gone by, long before the madness of Neraka. "Yeah, it brought back memories, I guess. I miss The Shade. My family. Those nights we spent talking about nothing."

"We wanted this, remember?" Harper replied softly. "We wanted to come here."

"I'm not walking back on this, don't get me wrong," I said. "Sure, we wanted to come here. But we didn't plan on not going back. I don't like being stranded here—not having the option to go back home."

That hit all of us on a deeper level. They all nodded slowly—they knew and felt the same. We'd come here on a mission, and, aside from the fact that the mission was far more complicated than originally anticipated, we couldn't even leave. We were stuck here.

"We'll find the swamp witch, and we'll all be able to go back home," Hansa reassured us. "But before we do that, we need some allies on our side. So, how about we all go out there and meet some Manticores, huh?"

A couple of seconds went by. We all looked at each other, allowing ourselves the luxury of a confident smile. "Sounds like a plan," I replied, then followed Hansa and the rest of my team out of the beautiful but deadly grotto.

I covered my head and face, then stepped into the searing

afternoon sun. The air was uncomfortably dry, but the temperature was a little more bearable than before. The heat peak had passed, and we were ready to delve deeper into the Akrep Gorge.

We got back on our horses and quietly trotted through the reddish ravine, carefully analyzing our surroundings. I couldn't help but go back to my previous thoughts about going home. It hadn't been that long since I'd last seen my parents—it wasn't that I missed them yet, per se. I wasn't even homesick at this point. What hurt was the prospect of never seeing them again. I hated not having the option to return.

Soon enough, my mind wandered back to Zane. After he'd helped us escape from Azure Heights the night before, I worried. Was he okay? Did he get himself in trouble for what he did? Surely King Shaytan wouldn't just let that slide—provided someone recognized Zane, of course. Maybe nobody saw him.

Maybe I'd see him again. *Soon, hopefully.* I still had so many questions for him. Or so I kept telling myself, to avoid the truth —I wanted to see Zane, alive and well, wearing his arrogant smirk and reminding me that I was in over my head. It was much better than not knowing whether he was even still alive.

8

HARPER

After that epic scare in the grotto, my caution spiked as we advanced through the gorge. It was a beautiful but savage place. The red stone walls rose high on both sides, with jagged tips at the top and narrow crevices at the base. Patches of weeds were sprinkled across the hard ground, with clusters of palm trees bending overhead, their wide, waxy leaves providing temporary shade from the still-burning sun.

A narrow stream flowed to our right, snaking its way through the ravine. We spotted some of the local fauna—mostly deer-like creatures with big, vivid green eyes and a soft, pale orange coat—drinking water from the stream. There were plenty of reptiles creeping behind the rocks, such as brightly colored snakes and lizards.

Birds trilled from the tops of the gorge walls, their bright pink and yellow plumage making them stand out. They seemed to serve as some kind of natural alarm, as they squawked whenever the jackal-like predators emerged from their holes and rushed after the orange deer. One of them was bold enough to stop in front of our group and bare its fangs at us. It nearly spooked the horses, until Caspian hissed at it—it was a primal, guttural sound that both fascinated and scared me, as it brought out his own predator nature.

The jackal didn't stand a chance, and it knew that very well. It yelped, then scuttled over to the other side, hiding behind another rock formation.

"Don't let the snakes get too close," Vesta muttered, then shot an arrow at a ten-foot serpent that had been slithering toward her indigo horse. It was so quiet that even the stallion hadn't heard or seen it. "They're extremely venomous and can kill a horse in seconds."

The arrow missed the snake's head by half an inch, at most, but it was enough to send a message. The creature swiftly turned and made its way back under the rocks. With that in mind, I used my True Sight to scan our surroundings again.

"Oh, damn, there are so many of them," I breathed, feeling my skin crawl. I had never been a fan of anything that slithered —with the exception of my brother-in-law and the rest of the Druids—but this was a whole new level of creepy. There were literally hundreds of snakes moving through the gorge. Most of them were hidden beneath chunks of red stone, and not visible with the naked eye. "Are they all venomous?"

Vesta nodded. "Yes. The brighter the colors, the deadlier the snake, too."

That didn't comfort me one bit, because they were all covered in bold pink, green, yellow, and red scales, their reptilian eyes quietly following our every move. I looked ahead, my True Sight still on, and pulled the reins on my indigo horse. "Guys, stop," I murmured. "Thirty yards ahead. I think they're Manticores."

Perched on a natural stone ledge approximately twenty feet above ground, the two Manticores were watching an orange deer lapping at the stream. From that distance, I could tell that they were young and slender creatures, but their muscles were toned to perfection, and their skin was the shade of chocolate. Their vivid yellow eyes were fixed on the deer.

"We need to get out of sight, for now," Vesta whispered, then pulled her horse to the side. We all followed, and got off our horses.

I once more beckoned mine to keep the others in check. "Look after them, and don't go anywhere," I muttered, then shifted my focus back to the Manticores.

Vesta came to my side, one hand resting on her sheathed sword. "Where did you see them?"

"Up there," I said, pointing at a portion of the wall on the right side. It was crooked and angled outward, obscuring the actual ledge. The rest of my team couldn't see the Manticores from that angle, but I had a clear view with my True Sight.

They were beautiful, though clearly dangerous creatures, and they matched Caspian's description of them. Their bodies looked mostly humanoid, except for some key differences. Their hands were a tad oversized and covered in auburn fur, with a long, sharp claw extending from each finger. Their hair matched the color of the fur covering their hands, forearms, backs, and calves, and it was naturally styled into a rich, lion-like mane. What really caught my eye were the tails—nearly identical to scorpions', with well-defined segments across a length of ten, maybe fifteen feet, and a black spike, through which the poison was delivered, at the end. I shuddered, the sight of those tails reminding me of Cyrus Drizan, the fearsome jinni king who'd taken on a half-scorpion form. Though, from the stories my Great-Uncle Ben had told me about him, that jinni's tail hadn't been nearly as terrifying as these.

The Manticores wore strips of brown leather over their private parts and carried multiple short spears strapped to their backs. That was how they hunted from a distance—and they were impressively fast as they both threw two spears at the unsuspecting deer. The metal tips pierced the animal's neck. It gave out a short, sharp cry of pain, then collapsed.

The Manticores then rushed down from their ledge and reached the deer. One of them bent down and slit the creature's throat with one claw. At least the deer was spared an agonizing death.

"Don't move," Vesta whispered. She'd seen them as soon as they came down. She pulled her bow and prepped an arrow. "Just in case," she said, noticing my questioning frown. "We don't know what we're dealing with, for the time being. Let's observe and follow first."

"After you," Hansa breathed, her hand clutching the bejeweled handle of her broadsword.

We followed Vesta, sneaking along the side of the gorge as we got closer to the Manticores. They were both young males, and were quick to tie the deer's legs. One of them hoisted the animal over his shoulder, and then they both hurried ahead. I followed them with my True Sight, until the sound of a broken branch distracted me.

I glanced over my shoulder and noticed movement behind us—shadows rushing between the large rocks and palm trees. "Hold on," I whispered, and scanned the area we'd just left. "Oh, crap."

I didn't need to explain myself, as a split second later, we were all brought to a halt—we were surrounded by Manticores on all sides, not just from the back.

"Should've seen this coming," Caspian muttered, then pulled his sword out.

"We come in peace," Vesta announced, slowly raising her hands in the air, in a defensive gesture.

Judging by the looks on the Manticores' faces, they didn't really care. There were at least thirty of them, all strong and baring their fangs at us. They held spears up, their sharp tips pointed at us. My main concern revolved around the scorpion tails, the venomous spikes twitching, and also aimed at us. They seemed eager to poke us with something sharp, one way or another.

I held my breath and drew my twin blades. My instincts told me that we wouldn't be able to tell them much, and that we'd have to fight them into submission before we could explain our presence here—provided we didn't get our asses handed to us, of course.

The Manticores didn't give Vesta a chance to state our peaceful intentions again. They launched their spears at us first, from all around. We were fast enough to dodge them all, though one did graze my shoulder before stopping halfway through the trunk of a palm tree nearby. They then came at us with their claws and spiked scorpion tails.

I had two of my own to deal with. They were highly adept at using their tails in combat, and ridiculously fast. I couldn't stand still for more than two to three seconds, and used every angle at my disposal to launch an attack. I dodged a poisoned tail spike, then slashed both my swords out, before quickly withdrawing. The tails were, by far, the most dangerous part in dealing with

Manticores, so I figured it would be wise to keep at least ten feet between me and my opponents in order to avoid being stung.

A quick glance around told me that the rest of my team was experiencing the same difficulty. "Listen, we're not here to hurt you," I said to the Manticores attacking me—now four of them, with more coming from the narrow crevices in the walls on both sides.

I dodged another spike, then bolted between them. I spun around with my swords out and drew blood from two of them, then slid across the dirt and cut through the other two. I went for the thighs, hoping to slow them down. It would've been nice to have Blaze go full dragon at this point.

A loud thud made me turn my head. I froze for a couple of seconds, until Caia's scream pierced through my consciousness. Blaze had been stung. One of the Manticores was withdrawing his spike from Blaze's chest, and he'd fallen flat on his back.

There was no time, and no telling how long it would take for the venom to kill him. *Crap.* I shifted my focus back to my four opponents—still standing, but extremely pissed—while Caia shot fireballs at the Manticores that had surrounded her and Blaze.

"We're here to help you, dammit!" I growled, and went in for another double-bladed attack. The hostiles knew the trick this time. They were quick to study and remember my moves, and dodged the swords at the last minute. I wound up cutting through air. A faint rattle and swish coming from behind prompted me to lunge forward and roll on the ground. I'd avoided their spikes by just a couple of inches—too close, given what was at stake.

I immediately sprang up and put my swords out again. The Manticores grinned, then stalked toward me, worryingly confident. Jax and Hansa had cut two of their opponents down—cutting deep enough to maim, but not kill.

Vesta used water from the stream to confuse her opponents, while Caia continued to rage out with robust balls of fire. Fiona was hard on the defensive, until one of the Manticores got too close and left his waist vulnerable. Fiona swung hard with her left fist, and I heard the creature's ribs crack from the violent impact. That girl's left hook was freaking lethal.

Caspian was just a few feet away from me, dealing with his own set of four Manticores, swinging his sword left and right as best as he could. But my instincts kept telling me to run—we were woefully outnumbered, and our dragon was down. They'd probably been following us for a while now, and we'd been too focused on the two hunters to check our six o'clock.

"We're looking for the swamp witch. We want to bring the daemons and Exiled Maras down!" I shouted at the Manticores. "We're not from here! We've come to help! We can bring an entire army over here, of creatures you've never seen before, creatures that can end the daemons' reign for good!"

I heard a scoff before I was forced to dodge another spiked tail—a move I instantly regretted, as I watched it go right into Caspian's shoulder blade. He'd been keeping himself as close to me as possible, fending off backstabbers. "Caspian!" I cried out.

He grunted from the pain, then dropped to his knees and collapsed on the ground. Rage flared through me. That was the final straw. I pushed out a massive barrier and knocked all the Manticores around me backward. I rushed over to Caspian's side and turned him over. I used my True Sight to see his face beneath the mask and goggles—he was too pale, and thousands of dark purple capillaries became visible, spidering across his face.

The Manticores were dazed, but got back up and came at me again. I pushed another barrier out, followed by a second, much stronger one, that sent the others flying back, too. *Where is this much strength coming from?*

I'd never been able to produce such potent pulses before. Enough to knock some opponents down, sure, but certainly not on that wide radius, and not against dozens of Manticores at once. They were all baffled and hissing, while the rest of my team was stunned. Caia quickly slid to her knees next to Blaze, motioning for Jax to help him. The Manticores groaned and struggled to get back up.

"Help him, Jax, please!" she said, her voice trembling.

I held Caspian in my arms and turned him around so he wouldn't get direct sunlight on his face. I pulled his mask down, then bit into my wrist and pushed the open wound against his lips. Hansa, Fiona, and Vesta kept the Manticores at bay—Vesta started shooting arrows at anyone who dared come close. The Manticores were furious, their tails rattling and their chests swelling with every ragged breath.

Caspian wasn't drinking. In fact, he couldn't even hold his head up anymore. My heart thudded, and dread washed over me in freezing waves. "What... What's happening? Caspian, drink my blood... You'll be okay, just drink my blood."

Jax had the same issue with Blaze, who was equally unresponsive, his face covered in dark purple tainted blood vessels. "He's not drinking, either," Jax gasped, then looked at the Manticores. "Help us! Help them!"

To my surprise, the Manticores suddenly calmed down. I couldn't hear anything, but I could have sworn they were listening to something—their yellow eyes went pale and glassy for a couple of seconds, before one of the males regained focus and looked at me. "Your blood can't cure Manticore venom. Nothing can cure Manticore venom, besides another Manticore," he said.

"What do you mean? Please, help us! We're not here to harm anyone. We're here to offer an alliance!" I cried out, losing my mind. I couldn't even focus with Caspian literally dying in my arms. It was too much, too fast, and I didn't know how to cope. Not after we'd just found each other...

"If you agree to meet with our queen, we will cure your friends," another Manticore spoke.

"Yes. Hell yes!" Hansa retorted. "Obviously it's what we're here for. Now help them!"

Two Manticores came forward, while Hansa, Vesta, and Fiona motioned for the others to stay back. One of them stopped by Blaze's side, and the other came to Caspian and me. There was a twinkle of curiosity in his eyes, and only then did I realize that I could read his emotions—I could read all of them, as a sentry. They were worried, and fearful. There were waves of red-hot anger emanating from some of them, particularly the ones we'd injured. But they weren't aggressive toward us anymore.

"How did you do that?" the Manticore asked, as he crouched in front of me, cocking his head to one side. He was a good-looking male, with strings of leather braided into several tails of his rich, reddish mane. His amber eyes scanned me with visible interest.

"What are you talking about?" I breathed.

"How did you push us all away like that? No one can do what you just did," he replied.

"Sorry, my boyfriend is kind of dying here." I nodded to Caspian in my arms. "Can we leave my combat skills for later?"

My sarcasm and angst weren't lost on him. He chuckled

lightly, bringing his tail up from behind. "Don't be alarmed, and hold him still. This will sting."

It hit me then, by how the spike of his tail was positioned, that he was going to use it again. I instinctively put my hand out, my fingers trembling. I was ready to launch another barrier. Whatever new strength I'd found, it wasn't going anywhere.

"What are you doing? Trying to finish the job?" I growled.

"Like I said, only a Manticore can cure Manticore venom," he said, and didn't even flinch. I didn't scare him at all. If anything, I fascinated him. "One shot poisons, and, eventually, it kills. The second shot counteracts the venom's effect, and stops it from rotting the body from the inside out."

"Holy crap, it rots?" I murmured, my eyes wide. The Manticore replied with a nod, and I mirrored it to signal my permission for him to sting Caspian. The spike went right into his chest, the tip plunging deep into the muscle as it pushed the venom inside. *Fighting fire with fire, I guess.*

He withdrew the spike, and I briefly glanced over to Blaze, who'd just been given the same "treatment". "It will take a while for them to recover," the Manticore in front of me said. "Expect some turbulence."

"Turbulence? What turbulence?" I asked, my stomach knotting.

Before the Manticore could reply, Caspian started shaking in my arms, his convulsions violent. He groaned in pain, and I held him tight, whispering in his ear. "Shh, you're okay, Caspian. It'll be okay. Ride it out, baby."

The Manticore raised an eyebrow, watching him struggle in my firm embrace. "Well, *that*, mostly. His body is reacting to the venom purge. It's actually a good sign. It means he'll be up and running soon."

The sound of hooves on the ground made me look up. The Manticores brought our horses out from the shade, then motioned for us to get up. The one standing next to me lifted Caspian up from my arms and hauled him over his shoulder as if he weighed nothing. "I'm Kai, by the way," he said, irritatingly jovial given everything that had just happened. "And this is your mate, I presume."

I had just referred to Caspian as my boyfriend, after all. *Oh, damn.* Good thing Caspian was unconscious when I said that, since I wasn't sure he was ready to receive such a title from me. Not in these wretched circumstances, anyway. Kai smirked, visibly amused by my expression for some reason. "He'll be fine, don't worry. Maras are resilient creatures. Now, come. Our queen wishes to hear what you people have to say."

"Oh, *now* she wants to listen," I muttered, picking my swords off the ground and sheathing them.

"Be thankful," Kai replied. "We would've killed you by now, had she not been curious about you, outsiders."

Should I be thankful, though? They had nearly killed Blaze and Caspian. They had clearly followed us around, and hadn't backed down when we specifically said we'd come in peace. My stomach churned as I followed Kai and the others deeper into the gorge.

The Manticores were not going to make this easy on us. That, I just knew.

9

FIONA

W e moved forward through the gorge for about a hundred yards, then made a sharp turn left through a side crevice. There were two Manticores between us at all times, their spears aimed at our backs. They didn't speak, and they didn't take their eyes off us, either. Blaze and Caspian were out cold, but at least they were still alive and not rotting on the inside.

Neraka was all so wild and beautiful, but damn, some of its creatures were downright terrifying—and I was tempted to put the Manticores right up there with the daemons, based on what I'd just seen. No wonder the daemons wanted them out of the way in order to dominate this world!

They let us keep our weapons, at least, though they held on to our horses. We were fast and strong, but we were no match for their numbers, especially without horses and proper knowledge of the Akrep Gorge. This place seemed a lot more intricate than what I remembered from the map.

The sun was slowly setting in the west, to the point where its rays no longer reached this part of the ravine. We took our hoods, masks, and goggles off, but it was still uncomfortably hot. I could feel the cotton underlayer of my leather suit soaked with sweat, but at least that sensation came with a temporary hint of coolness.

The crevice then opened out into an enormous bowl structure neatly carved into the red stone. The bottom in the middle was an arena, and the curved walls were riddled with tiny, round gaps, from which Manticores emerged. It looked like a massive hive, in a way. They led us down a set of narrow stairs leading to the arena, while the rest of their people trickled around, all of them curiously eyeing us.

I could hear murmurs and hissing, but I couldn't make out any words, and I figured it was part of some distinctive language or dialect. My heart skipped a beat when I recognized their queen waiting for us at the base. It was impossible to miss her— she was fiercely beautiful, and significantly taller than all the other Manticores.

Thin strips of black leather hugged her curves, and layers of gold and unpolished gemstones covered her neck, chest, hips, and forearms. Her reddish mane was fully braided into a mohawk, with the sides neatly shaved, and she wore a gold band on her forehead as a crown. Her scorpion tail was larger than the others', too, twitching behind her. But it was the pair of slim, iridescent wings on her back that really set her apart from the rest—they reminded me of a dragonfly, and carried a distinctive shimmer.

Kai, the Manticore who'd helped Caspian, moved to the front

of our group, while the others lined up behind us in a semicircle. The queen of Manticores gazed at us, her expression firm and unyielding as she measured each member of our team from head to toe. When her amber eyes met mine, I felt my stomach tighten. She certainly knew how to make her presence known.

As soon as she looked away, I could breathe again. I exhaled sharply, then glanced around at the dozens of Manticores gathered around us. There were about two hundred of them—more than we'd expected, but still not enough to raise a solid army against the daemons. They were mostly males, while the females were kept separate, in an aisle behind the queen, and covered in soft, white linen hoods. There were several female Manticores among the hunters who had brought us in, so I assumed there were some gender-based hierarchies in this nest. Needless to say, I had plenty of questions at this point.

"Our Queen Neha wanted to hear what you have to say," Kai finally spoke, taking his position by her side. "Since you were brazen enough to come to Akrep, that is. Even daemons are wise enough to stay away, after all."

Jax was the first to reply. "I'm Jaxxon Dorchadas, and these are—"

"Queen Neha wishes to hear what *she* has to say, in particular," Kai cut him off, and nodded at Hansa, who blinked several times, visibly confused.

"Me? Why me?" Hansa muttered, frowning.

"Because she knows a warrior queen when she sees one," Kai answered with a smirk. Queen Neha's eyes twinkled with genuine appreciation.

Way to go, Hansa!

I had to give the Manticore queen credit. She was betting on the right horse here, since Hansa was, by far, one of the most seasoned and experienced in our group—but so was Jax. My guess was that it had something to do with her gender, which brought me back to my many questions about the nest's hierarchy. *Hopefully, they'll be nice and answer. After they agree to help us.*

Hansa wore a proud glow as she took a step forward, holding her chin high as she spoke. "We come from another world, Your Grace. From a galaxy called Eritopia—the very birthplace of the Maras who have infested your planet. They were banished from our land thousands of years ago and given the choice to start a new life elsewhere, in exile. The idea was for them to be better and stop killing innocent creatures to satisfy their thirst for blood. They called us out here for help, but not long after we arrived, we began to peel away at the many layers of lies they used to lure us into a trap."

The Manticore queen listened quietly, her gaze fixed on Hansa. The other Manticores barely moved as the succubus told her the rest of our story on Neraka, beginning with day one.

"We've come here in peace, Your Grace," Hansa ended her plea, after outlining every action we'd taken and every discovery we'd made, all the way up to the moment of our arrival in the Akrep Gorge. "And we're on our way to Draconis to look for the swamp witch that the daemons and Exiled Maras are holding hostage. If we set her free, we'll be able to remove whatever shield is preventing us from reaching out to our people in GASP. It will allow our armies to come through, in thousands of balls of light, and lay waste to whatever army the daemons and Maras may conjure up. We have powerful creatures on our side, including dragons. It will be over for these fiends in a matter of hours, at most, and peace and balance will be restored to Neraka."

A couple of moments passed in absolute silence, until Kai and the queen exchanged knowing glances.

"And what makes you certain that the swamp witch is still alive?" Kai asked.

"We've had multiple confirmations up to this point, particularly from the Imen," Hansa replied. "The witch is clever, and isn't easy to persuade into giving away all of her secrets at once. She's far exceeded our expectations where her resilience is concerned, and she deserves to be saved. She is also the last of her kind, therefore extremely important to our world and, as it stands, yours too."

"And what would we gain, if we were to help you?" Kai said, crossing his arms.

Hansa glared at him for a second. "I'm sorry, can't the queen speak for herself?"

"She is speaking for herself," another Manticore replied.

"She speaks through all of us," a third chimed in.

"Queen Neha only uses her voice for those she deems worthy of her utmost respect and fealty," Kai said. "But she speaks through all of us for everyone else. We hear and feel her at all times."

It made sense now—that moment when they'd all blanked out earlier, just before they offered to save Caspian and Blaze. That was the queen talking to them. And to us, through them. The Manticore nest must have a hive mind, where the queen spoke and her subjects listened and communicated her wishes.

"A hive mind," Hansa concluded as well. "Does that mean you're all telepathically connected?"

"In a way, yes," Kai replied. "We're all connected to our queen."

Hansa nodded slowly. "I understand. Well, then, to answer

your question, Your Grace, the Manticores would regain their freedom of movement in this world. I thought that was obvious."

"You've taken quite the risk to come all the way here and tell us this," Kai said. "Have you not considered the fact that we might have settled our territorial disputes with the daemons already? That our settlement here in Akrep Gorge is a part of that settlement?"

My muscles tensed. I hadn't thought of that. I hadn't even considered the possibility.

"I've thought about it, yes," Hansa replied, unfazed. "But let me ask you this: are you okay with living here, confined between these rocks for the rest of your lives, or would you like your lands back? I see your numbers are slightly higher than we anticipated. Do the daemons know the size of your tribe? Do you think they'll just let you live and rebuild your armies?"

The queen smirked. "And what guarantee do we have that *your* people won't claim Neraka as their own once they arrive here?" Kai asked.

"Eritopia has twenty planets of its own, and we've recently overthrown our own version of an evil overlord," Hansa scoffed. "And GASP is an alliance between worlds, dedicated to supporting and protecting those who need help. We do not conquer. We do not claim. We simply restore, nurture, and assist, in pursuit of peace and prosperity. We live and die by that credo."

Kai and the queen looked at each other once more, before they both shifted their focus back to us. "Very well," Kai said. "And how could we possibly assist you in finding the swamp witch? We do not know where she is, or how to get to her. And the daemons will not take kindly to us raiding their city. They will wipe the Akrep Gorge off the map."

"We'll handle that part," Hansa replied. "We need to know that when we call, you *will* come. We do not have strength in numbers, but we are resourceful and organized, and we may need your help to create a diversion for us to get the witch out if we can't do it on our own. And, now that you've mentioned it, we'll need your word that *you* will not rise against us when we lead an attack against the daemons and Exiled Maras—if you do have some sort of agreement with them, that is. We *are* stronger than them with our armies here, and you *will* want to be on the right side of history here, not fighting for those bastards out of fear of losing this little patch of dry land."

Queen Neha chuckled softly, prompting the Manticores to smile in eerie unison.

"There is only one way for you to earn our allegiance," Kai said. "In order for the queen to trust you, she must see with her own eyes that you are strong, reliable, and capable of seeing this mission to the very end."

"What will it take?" Hansa asked, giving us a brief, slightly nervous sideways glance.

A grin slit Kai's face from ear to ear. "Your strongest fighter against our greatest Manticore warrior, in close combat. Use of weapons and whatever abilities you have included. The first to fall loses."

"That means your warrior can use the venom in an attack, and potentially kill our champion?" I gasped, then looked at Caspian and Blaze, who were slowly returning to consciousness, slumped on the ground next to Caia and Harper.

All the Manticores looked at me, including the queen. Suddenly, all eyes were on me, and I felt like a candle beneath a powerful spotlight, slowly melting from the heat. I really didn't like all that attention, particularly not in these circumstances.

"That is correct," Kai said, slightly amused. "Our queen will offer her support only if your fighter wins."

"What if we refuse to put our fighter at such a risk? Given our current situation, we cannot lose any of our people. We need all hands on deck to get our swamp witch back," Hansa replied.

"Given your current situation, your biggest concern should be getting yourselves out of this gorge alive," Kai hissed. "Your only choices are to stay and fight, and earn our support, or try and flee, and die before you reach the main passageway."

That didn't sit well with any of us, but there wasn't any time to waste worrying over our predicament. The choices were clear, and there was no way in hell we could get out of here alive—not with our dragon still recovering, anyway. We'd told Blaze to hold back earlier because we needed to speak to the Manticores, not kill them. Ironically, now that we did actually need him to go full dragon, he couldn't. He could barely sit up at this point.

"So, who will you nominate?" Kai asked, smiling and sizing each of us up.

Hansa turned to face us, frowning at the sight of Caspian and Blaze still sluggish and weak. She let out a heavy sigh, slowly shaking her head. "Blaze would've been perfect to shut them all up," she said. "I could give it a try."

"No way," Jax replied bluntly. "No. You're not even immortal. You can't heal as fast. No, I should fight."

"Guys," Harper interrupted them before Hansa could object, and stood up from Caspian's side. "I think I should take this. Hansa, you know I can hack it."

Hansa and Jax stared at her for a couple of seconds, then looked at each other. "She's ruthless," Jax said, shrugging.

"And she's got that barrier thing, plus her other sentry skills," Hansa added, a grin blooming on her face as she turned her focus back to Harper. "You've seen the Manticores fight already. What is your assessment?"

"They're fast, but so am I. Their claws cut deep, but so do mine. They're fierce and well-coordinated in one-on-one combat, and they pay attention to their opponent's attack techniques before they engage the second time around. They learn fast, and they are strong. But there's no way in hell I'm letting any of us die in this place today. Besides, I learned a couple of new tricks from Bijarki before we left Calliope, and I'm dying to put them to the test in a one-on-one."

Hansa and Jax both chuckled lightly.

"That's the spirit," I replied, giving her a friendly nudge.

"So it's settled, then," Hansa said, then turned to face the queen and Kai. "I nominate Harper Hellswan as our champion."

I moved closer to Harper and placed a hand on her shoulder, squeezing gently. "Be careful out there, Cuz," I whispered. "Watch the Manticore's feet."

"You noticed the foot shuffle, too, huh?" Harper replied with a wink.

"What foot shuffle?" Caia frowned slightly.

"They all use the same stance, using the left foot for support. They shuffle briefly before they charge," I explained. "It's that split second that can make all the difference."

Harper patted us both on the back, then took her backpack off and pulled her hair up in a tight bun. "Thank you, ladies. Now, allow me to kick some Manticore ass."

The crowd murmured as the females behind the queen moved to the side to let one of their own through. A young Manticore girl made her way to the front and joined Kai and the queen. She didn't look older than sixteen, and she was dressed in solid warrior attire—dark red leather garments covering her chest and hips, sandals strapped all the way up to her knees, along with wrist cuffs and knee and elbow plates made of silver, and a beautifully molded silver helmet that covered the top half of her head. Her mane was braided back in thick cornrows, the tips wrapped in red leather strips.

She carried a short sword and two long knives, along with her eagerly twitching scorpion tail. The young Manticore was slender and short compared to Harper, and had to tilt her head back in order to look her in the eyes.

"Very well," Kai said on behalf of the queen. "Meet our champion, Pheng-Pheng."

I didn't have too many years of experience under my belt, but one look at the young Manticore and I *knew* that her size had absolutely nothing to do with her title as champion. According to the painful churn in my stomach—my instincts reacting— Harper was in a heap of trouble.

10

HARPER

Pheng-Pheng was a spunky and spry little thing. My first reaction was to let out a chuckle, which I promptly stifled as I realized, by the look on her face, that she was going to be my opponent. Her expression was firm and cold, but her amber eyes burned with a fiery, quiet rage. The smirk on Queen Neha's face confirmed my suspicion: Pheng-Pheng was a potentially deadly opponent.

"Don't let her size fool you," Hansa whispered, then gave me a brief pat on the back and nudged me forward.

The crowd cleared a wide space in the middle of the arena for Pheng-Pheng and me, while the queen, Kai, and the rest of my team stepped back. I had my twin swords on my belt, plus two knives in my boots, and the metal plates on my chest, arms, and calves for protection. My heartbeat was erratic as Pheng-Pheng and I circled each other.

"This will be a simple fight," Kai said, raising his voice. "Like

I said, the first to yield loses. And Pheng-Pheng is not the kind of warrior to easily yield."

I looked at Pheng-Pheng, a chill running down my spine. I certainly couldn't afford to underestimate her based on her age. Not too long ago, I was just like her—surprising the seasoned officers of GASP in one-on-one sparring sessions, as they fell flat on their backs with the air knocked out of their lungs.

The way she moved, the way her hips swayed, and her fingers gripped the sword handle—they all told me the same thing. In many ways, Pheng-Pheng was a lot like me. Fierce. Determined. Lethal. I had a feeling her fighting skills were out of this world.

Just to cross certain dos and don'ts off my list, I briefly tried my mind control on her. It wasn't my strong suit, but I still had the ability to manipulate someone, provided they belonged to a species that was vulnerable to a sentry's abilities. *Crap.* I couldn't get in. I could see her emotions clearly, but I couldn't influence her actions. *So, mind control is out of the question.*

"Begin!" Kai shouted, and my muscles instantly stiffened.

Damn. Relax!

I was off to a bad start. Pheng-Pheng measured my stance, sliding her left foot back for hers. That was my first sign that I was in a bit of trouble. She used her right foot for support, and I no longer had that split-second advantage prior to an attack. I had to keep my distance and find another weak spot in Pheng-Pheng, since she didn't use the same fighting stance as the other Manticores.

"Are you going to make your move, or shall I get this over with and just kill you?" Pheng-Pheng smirked, drawing her sword.

"Oh, man, you're one of *those*," I muttered, and brought my twin blades out, bending my knees.

She frowned. "One of those?"

"One of those who can literally talk their opponent to death," I shot back with a light chuckle. Flames flared beneath her eyelashes, but she didn't move. She wanted me to attack first.

Okay, so be it. I couldn't play this waiting game. A quick in-and-out attack was enough for me to briefly assess her defenses, while she collected her own impressions of my offense. I darted toward her and brought one of my swords down.

She blocked it effortlessly, then brought one of her knives up, nearly nicking my ribs. I pulled back, my gaze fixed on hers. Pheng-Pheng was fast and observant. I wasn't going to repeat that basic move again—if she'd nearly cut me this first time, she was definitely going to poke me the next.

Pheng-Pheng came at me in an exploratory attack. She slashed at me multiple times, and I swiftly dodged each hit, then brought my swords up in a cross to block her blade, which came down surprisingly hard and heavy, given her muscle mass. I didn't doubt her technique or skill, but I had hoped that her strength wasn't as potent as mine. I was horribly wrong.

She grinned, noticing my surprise, and took a couple of steps back. The Manticores and my team quietly watched us—the latter were choked with worry. I could tell from their expressions, and from the deep yellow auras surrounding Blaze, Caia, Hansa, and even Caspian, the only Mara whose emotions I could read. He was awake and focused on me, as was Blaze. They'd finally come to.

I heard Pheng-Pheng's feet shuffle across the dirt, and instantly switched to defense mode. She came in like a boulder in an attempt to ram her sword through me. She missed me by inches, and I retaliated. She was letting herself loose, and it didn't bode well for me.

She was ridiculously fast, darting from left to right before each attack. Her sword strikes made my shoulders hurt whenever I blocked them, either with my blades or my forearm plates. She was relentless, too, not giving me more than one, maybe two seconds to breathe between blows. The worst part was that she was constantly studying my defenses and getting better and more accurate in her attacks.

Five minutes in, and it was becoming more difficult to keep up with her.

Why the hell am I so intimidated by her? I've fought daemons galore, and big-ass pit wolves... I couldn't let a little girl get the best of me, but I knew, deep down, exactly *why* she was getting to me. Pheng-Pheng was a younger version of me. *I was right.* She fought like me, and learned from me.

I couldn't employ my usual tactics on her. Every attempt to cut her ended in her sword clashing with mine, making my blades zing and tremble in distress. "You're too slow," she said, then brought her sword down—I blocked it, but didn't have the extra split second needed to stop her knife from puncturing my side.

The blade made it in several inches, and the pain was sharp, spreading through my torso like liquid fire. I gasped, and instantly kicked her in the ribs. She coughed, and withdrew her knife in the process. *Now I'm riled up.*

I got angry, and fast. I went in, releasing a flurry of double sword hits, which she expertly blocked and dodged, grinning with delight. I wasn't sure if it was a display of arrogance or if she was really enjoying this fight, but I knew that my only way out alive was to win this.

Pheng-Pheng wasn't ready to give up that easily, though, as expected. She slipped to the side and came back in with her sword. I blocked her hits once more, and used my legs this time to weaken hers, kicking her in the side of her knee whenever I could. She hissed from the pain, and made her first mistake, coming in too slow with the sword.

My right blade met hers, and my left blade slashed her wrist before she could bring the knife into my side again. She dropped her sword, then growled and instantly pulled back, blood dripping into the dirt in rich crimson droplets.

Though I expected retaliation, the sheer force with which she came back took me by surprise—she was pumped up by the adrenaline, and I had to work harder than ever before. The angrier she got, the more vicious her attacks became.

I gave it all I had, hitting back with all my strength. It was enough to rattle her a couple of times, but her speed still knocked me off my feet. She brought her knee up into my stomach, and I fell backward with a grunt. She didn't wait for me to get up, though. Pheng-Pheng was relentless, but I'd been holding back, too.

I pushed out a barrier, strong enough to send her sliding on her back through the dirt. She jumped back to her feet and came at me again. This time, she had both knives out, and her scorpion tail pointing at me. *Uh-oh, she's bringing in the heavy artillery.*

The sun was down, and the sky turned dark pink and purple over us. My eyesight adjusted, noticeably sharper in the absence of light. I could see the fluidity in her moves, and the nervous twitch in her tail before it went straight for my head. I dodged the hit and darted to the right, then attacked.

As long as I was the one hitting, and she was the one on the defense, I had a minor upper hand. I looked for weak points, but, for the life of me, I couldn't find one—not while she was focused on the actual fight. I needed to wound her again, to get her angry enough to lose her momentum for just a second.

Most importantly, I had to be unpredictable. She could see my hits coming from a mile away at this point. *Think! What wouldn't Harper do?*

It was time for a drastic measure, before she brought the tail in again. I deliberately delayed one hit, giving her the split second she needed to push back and attack me. She slashed at me with vicious strokes, going straight for my throat. I let her cut my shoulder, and hissed from the searing pain. I caught the flicker of a smile on her face, and made my move.

I dodged another strike and dropped to one knee as I brought my sword out at a tight angle, cutting into her side. "Argh," she yelped, and I instantly twisted and used my right knee for support to kick her ankles with my left leg. It was a straining move for me, but it got the job done.

Pheng-Pheng fell flat on her back, holding her bleeding side. I'd cut deep, judging by the amount of blood coming out of her. *Now comes the anger.* She was going to get up and—her scorpion tail came up, and she stung me.

Oh, crap.

My heart was pumping fast from all the physical effort. I only had one, maybe two minutes before the poison really kicked in —and I was already feeling lightheaded. The venom spread through my body, and I was burning from the inside out.

I briefly glanced at Caspian. The look of horror on his face as Jax and Hansa held him back broke my heart. I only had two choices, now clearer than ever: die from the venom, or beat this Manticore kid into submission and get her to yield, then sting me again to counteract the deadly toxin. *I'm not dying here, dammit!*

Pheng-Pheng must've guessed my thoughts or something because, despite her wounds, she got up and kicked me in the chest. I fell back, my limbs getting weaker with every passing second. Her grin made my poisoned blood boil.

I am not... dying... here...

"This is it," Pheng-Pheng said. "You're not strong enough for my mother's support."

"Your mother—" I breathed, then realized what she'd just revealed. Pheng-Pheng was Neha's daughter. *Why doesn't that surprise me?* "You should've waited until I was dead to tell me that."

"Why? You wouldn't hear me if I said it then." Pheng-Pheng chuckled, pointing both knives at me, and pushed her foot deeper into my chest. The pressure made me cough. One more push and my ribs would snap.

"Because now I have leverage, little Manticore," I growled, as I mustered the last sliver of energy left and pushed out a targeted barrier against her knees. I heard the bones crack from the impact.

She cried out in pain and collapsed on top of me. I instantly rolled us over, my left knee digging into her wounded side, and pulled one of the knives out of my right boot. I pushed the blade against her throat and looked over my shoulder.

It was becoming difficult to breathe, and the image before me was getting hazy, but I could still make out the terrified look on Neha's face. *That's what I wanted to see.*

"Yield," I told Pheng-Pheng. "Yield, and I won't slit your throat."

"Slit my throat, and you will die," she hissed, her expression pained from the pressure I was applying on her side wound. My knife blade nicked her, a thin line of blood drawing its way across her tan skin into the dirt beneath her.

"If I slit your throat now, *I* win, and your *mother* will have no choice but to help my people. It's worth dying for, as far as I'm concerned, Pheng-Pheng. Is your pride worth dying for?"

She thought about it for a second, her aura bursting in violent reds. She was furious and helpless, and she knew it. I just needed her to yield before I blacked out—and that was any second now. Her face turned into a puddle of watercolor splashes. *This is it.*

A sharp pain flared through the back of my neck. The Manticore sting.

"I yield!" Pheng-Pheng shouted.

I heard cheers behind me. And hurried steps coming toward me.

But I couldn't see them. I couldn't see anything anymore. My consciousness slipped through my fingers, and everything turned black.

11

AVRIL

Dion and Alles led the way from Ragnar Peak into the Plains of Lagerith. We covered hundreds of miles in the span of several hours at a steady speed. The plains themselves were truly beautiful—seemingly endless waves of tall, dark green grass swaying in the wind.

The more we advanced through the fields, the darker the skies. Rain eventually started to pour down, cool and heavy droplets weighing us down. We kept our hoods on as we moved forward, constantly checking our surroundings, especially the nearby patches of woods. I could see the snowy mountains rising in the distance, their white peaks obscured by charcoal clouds.

Heron and I were right behind the young Imen, with Scarlett and Patrik several feet at the back, accompanied by Jack. The pit wolf was large and heavy, as tall as we were on horseback, but impressively fast over long distances. He stayed close to Scarlett's side, his red eyes relentlessly checking the area.

"We're getting closer to Adlet territory, I think," Dion said.

"What makes you say that? Did you see them?" I asked, feeling somewhat nervous at the prospect of encountering a new species of Neraka. Not knowing whether they'd welcome us or try to kill us put me on edge. Jovi must've felt the same way during their trip to find the Lamias of the River Pyros, back on Calliope, during the rebellion against Azazel. I'd learned plenty from those endeavors, though—we had something that the Adlets wanted. We had a way out of the death and destruction handed out by the daemons. We had armies and dragons ready to come in, provided we got the swamp witch back.

"I told you they mark their hunting grounds," Dion replied, pointing ahead.

Several skulls were scattered across the grass—not visible right away, given the tall greenery. A herd of moon-bison rumbled somewhere to our right. There were hundreds of them grazing along the base of a distant hill.

Jack's growl emerged from behind us. Alles smirked, glancing over his shoulder. "And the pit wolf is getting anxious. He can sense they're nearby."

I looked back at the pit wolf and followed his nervous gaze to our left. Black smoke billowed close to the horizon, flames licking at the ashen sky. "What's that?" I asked.

"That... That was an Imen village," Dion replied, his voice trembling. "The daemons must've gotten to them."

"I thought this was Adlet territory," I said, frowning.

"It is. But I doubt it stretches that far. The Adlets keep their distance from everyone, Imen included," Dion explained, then exhaled. "I knew there were Imen living in these parts. I'd seen the caravans before."

"You knew it was only a matter of time before the daemons

got to them," Alles replied. "Ledda sent word to them, offered to join forces and strengthen our village, but they foolishly chose to stay here, probably thinking the Adlets would protect them."

"Why wouldn't the Adlets help them?" Scarlett asked, gazing at the threads of smoke. It didn't rain in that village area, specifically on the northern edge of the Lagerith Plains. A daemon attack didn't come as a shock, especially if they were able to use their invisibility spell to take the Imen by surprise.

"It's every creature for itself here," Dion replied bitterly. "That's why we're so pleased to see you people trying to bring us all together. For too long we've strayed on our own, little groups scattered across the continent, struggling to survive, while the daemons slaughtered our friends and families. Maybe GASP will bring back the old alliances."

"We'll do our best, that I can promise you," Heron said. I could see the pain in his jade eyes as he gazed into the distance, watching the village ruins burn. He'd seen this before on Calliope, before he was imprisoned by Azazel. I could only imagine the dreadful memories coming back to haunt him.

Another hour went by as we delved deeper into Adlet territory. We moved slowly, waiting for the moon-bison to come closer to our side. Adlets were bound to appear at some point, stalking the herd, since they preferred hunting during the day.

The silence between Heron and me was becoming uncomfortable—and that was mostly my fault. After everything we'd been through, my feelings for him were clearer and more profound than ever, and I needed to tell him. Death was constantly on our trail, and I didn't want to leave this world without him knowing how I felt about him.

Most importantly, it pained me to think that, once we got out of here and back to Calliope, he'd be back with all those lady friends of his. I couldn't bear the thought, actually. And the longer I held that in me, the more it hurt. I had nothing to lose, given our circumstances.

"What's up with you?" Heron asked, noticing my frown.

"Nothing," I replied, shaking my head.

"That look on your face doesn't say 'nothing'. It says 'I'm upset and I feel like kicking somebody in the face'," he retorted, giving me a half smile. The way his eyes lit up made me tingle all over. Man, I had such a crush on the wrong guy.

"That's not what this look says. You're reading it wrong," I said.

"Oh. My bad. What does it say, then?"

"It says you're terrible at reading people. Duh."

"See, now you're straight up lying to me," Heron replied, visibly amused.

"How can you tell?"

His gaze darkened as it settled on my face. "Your heartbeat, Avril. I can hear it. It's... frantic."

That shut me up fast. He still wasn't reading it right, though, because it wasn't my attempt to deceive him that was making my heart pound like a maniac. It was his very presence, the way he looked at me. The way his short black hair brought out the jade green in his eyes. Not to mention that five o'clock shadow that gave him this hot, rugged allure. *Snap out of it, Avril.*

I didn't say anything for a few minutes, and Heron didn't insist, either. But my nerves continued stretching, to the point where even my horse was sensing my emotional discomfort. It neighed and shuddered beneath me, prompting me to blurt out the truth.

"I like you, Heron," I said, my tone slightly pitchy. "Like, really like you. I didn't think I would. Honestly, just until we got here, I promised myself I wouldn't touch you with a ten-foot pole, though my body never listened. You're a serial philanderer with one too many girlfriends. You made a pass at me at a wedding, and even though I slapped you, I actually wanted to kiss you. I still do. Only now it's even more intense because I'm getting to know you better. And you're amazing. And I don't understand why you hide beneath the façade that got you slapped in the first place. You're smart, and strong, and resourceful... And I'm using too many 'ands'... Dammit. Point is, Heron, I really like you, though I hate to admit it because it goes against my promise to myself to never allow someone like you to break my heart. I don't know what to do with these feelings, given our circumstances, but I do know that if something happens, and one or both of us die here, I wouldn't forgive myself if I couldn't be honest with you, all the way."

Boy, that was a lot I'd been holding in. I felt like an agitated bottle of soda. The seal had just snapped, and the foam was overflowing—in my case, the words. The feelings. I didn't even look at him until after I finished my ramble.

My heart skipped a beat when our eyes met. Heron was stunned, his eyebrows raised and his mouth open, close to gaping. He didn't say anything, and that just made it worse for me because now the anxiety caused by not speaking my mind was being replaced by the anxiety of having bared my damn soul in front of him. And he was too quiet for my comfort. *Is it supposed to feel like this?*

Wasn't he supposed to say something? *Anything?*

He looked away for a few moments, and I crumbled on the inside. My face burned with shame as a million negative thoughts cut through my brain. *I should've kept my mouth shut. This wasn't a good time. But when would be a good time, given our constant movement and fighting to stay alive? No, it was good, even healthy, to let it out. He can ignore me if he wants to. Or he can say something. The ball is in his court.*

Then why do I feel so freaking awkward? And why the hell is he so quiet?

"Avril, I—"

"Adlets!" Dion interrupted Heron, and completely halted the conversation. He pointed at the herd of moon-bison. The animals cried out and ran to the south, their hooves thundering across the plain.

My stomach dropped, yet I had no choice but to focus on the task at hand. I shifted my focus back to the moon-bison herd, carefully analyzing their erratic movements. They worked very much like a swarm, outside influences swaying them off their usual course.

"There!" I said, and pointed at two patches of reddish fur darting through the tall grass on the west side of the herd, then noticed the other four, farther back. "And there!"

The Adlets hunted in a pattern similar to the wolves back on Earth, approaching the large herd and targeting the calves. We brought our horses to a halt and watched the creatures as they cornered a sturdy calf, separating it from the herd.

"Do we wait for them to have dinner, or what?" Heron asked, his tone dripping with sarcasm. He was beyond irritated after he'd been cut off earlier. *At least I'm not the only one in a foul mood now.* And at least I knew that he *did* want to reply to what I'd just said.

Jack's growls turned to whimpers, and he baffled us all when he shot across the grass, headed straight for the Adlets. "What the..." I murmured, then saw Scarlett rushing after him, her horse galloping at his speed.

"Jack, no!" she shouted after the pit wolf. "Jack, come back!"

"Ah, man, that mutt's going to get himself killed," Patrik grumbled, then nudged his horse and went after Scarlett and Jack. We had no choice but to follow.

"Jack," I called out. "Get back here!"

We all tried to get him to turn back, but the pit wolf didn't listen. He just ran, whimpering like an excited puppy, until the Adlets saw him. It took less than a second for them to forget about the moon-bison calf and bare their huge fangs at us, and at Jack, in particular.

They were gorgeous creatures, as big as the pit wolf, just like the descriptions we'd heard. Their fur coats were soft, thick, and brick red, curled upward along the spine as a sign of aggression. *Uh-oh.*

Jack came to a screeching halt when he saw the Adlets coming at him, snapping their jaws and growling viciously. "Ah, crap," I muttered, and beckoned my horse to move faster.

Scarlett was the first to reach Jack, and moved her horse in front of him, while the Adlets—six of them in total—charged toward her.

"Stop, please!" she shouted at them.

They didn't even acknowledge her, their orange-yellow eyes fixed on the pit wolf. Hate burned bright in them. Scarlett leapt off her horse and put her hands out in a defensive gesture, while Jack yelped behind her.

Patrik jumped off his horse and reached her side, while we slowed down and joined them on horseback. The Adlets stopped just a few feet away from us, snarling and shuddering with what I assumed was rage.

"Please, don't hurt him! He's with us!" Scarlett pleaded. "We come in peace. We don't want to hurt you!"

Jack sat on his hind legs, keeping his head down and his red gaze on the Adlets, who suddenly calmed down. They all blinked several times and cocked their heads to one side—I could swear there was a glimmer of recognition in their eyes as they curiously checked Jack out.

We all heard Scarlett's sigh of relief. She'd grown really attached to Jack, and, by proxy, so had we. Whoever joined our "pack" was with us until death, and the pit wolf was no exception, especially after he'd saved her during her last encounters with daemons and Exiled Maras.

"We've come to offer an alliance," Scarlett said. "We're not from this world, but we want to help. We have armies, and we can bring them here to fight the daemons and end their tyranny."

One of the Adlets took a couple of steps forward, then shifted into his humanoid form. The bones cracked beneath his skin as he got up on his hind legs, his arms stretching out. He grunted from the pain, then straightened his back and frowned at us.

He was a couple of heads taller than us, extremely well built, with ropes of muscle covering every inch of him. His hair was long and curly—the same shade of red as his Adlet fur. He was naked, of course, but the tall grass kept his nether parts hidden. *Thank the stars.*

His amber eyes settled on Jack, and the grief was instantly recognizable. I had a feeling they knew each other. The wheels started spinning in my head, and I started sniffing the air, looking for scent markers. The Adlets were territorial and feral, but still organized in packs. The others shifted into their humanoid forms as well, and I noted their different facial features. Two of them were definitely related, and they had a youngling with them who didn't look a day past thirteen.

"What are you doing here?" the first Adlet grumbled, unable to take his eyes off Jack.

"We need your help," Scarlett said. "We have friends who are on their way to Draconis to look for the swamp witch. Once we get her back, we'll be able to bring down whatever shield the daemons put up to stop us from contacting our people. When that happens, all hell will break loose for King Shaytan, and we'll need all the fighters we can get to protect us and her until our armies get here. We heard there were Adlets in these parts, and that you might want to be a part of this."

A few seconds went by in silence. Another Adlet came forward, also appearing stunned by Jack's presence. "Is that—"

"I think so, yes," the first Adlet cut him off.

"You know Jack, don't you?" I asked, noticing the pit wolf's gentle demeanor. Scarlett gave me a curious look, then glanced at Jack and the Adlets, and came to the same conclusion.

"You've seen Jack before?" she said, placing a hand on the pit wolf's head.

"We can't be out here like this," the first Adlet replied, his reddish brow furrowed. "I'll take you to our pack leader, Colton, in the woods there." He pointed at a patch of forest just a couple hundred yards off to the west.

"It's him," the youngling gasped, and moved to reach out to Jack, but the others stopped him and pulled him back. "It's him!"

My heart ached at the sight of tears running down his tanned face. There was so much pain in his amber eyes, I could almost feel it myself. They definitely knew Jack, and that just made room for a whole lot of questions.

"Quiet, Mahlon! Know your place!" the first Adlet barked, then looked at Scarlett. "Come with us. Daemons prowl on the edges of this plain. We can't have them see you here."

Scarlett and Patrik nodded, then got back on their horses. "Stay close to me, Jack," Scarlett ordered the pit wolf, her tone harsh and reprimanding. She'd had quite the scare with him just now, and she was clearly afraid she'd lose him if she didn't keep him close—not that I could blame her. "Please."

Jack's ears perked up, and he let out a soft whimper to acknowledge her demand. We then proceeded to the west. The Adlets turned back to giant wolves and ran toward the small forest.

Despite the rough start, I knew we stood a good chance of persuading at least this pack to join our fight, since they were willing to listen to what we had to say. Most importantly, they knew Jack. Looking at the pit wolf as he ran alongside Scarlett's horse, I noticed the similarities in his bone and muscle structure —despite his black, hairless skin and flaming red eyes, Jack had a lot more in common with the Adlets than I'd thought, prior to meeting them.

It dawned on me then that Jack could very well be an Adlet himself.

12

SCARLETT

W e entered the patch of woods less than a mile west, our horses gracefully keeping up with the six Adlets and a very excited Jack. The more I watched them run together, the more similarities I noticed between them, and the more certain I became that Jack was, somehow, related to the Adlets.

The rainy drizzle stopped by the time we reached a clearing, where two dozen other Adlets waited. The entire area was lined with mounds, all of them riddled with holes—each camouflaged with twigs, weeds, and dead leaves. In the middle, a small campfire burned. The Adlets all jumped to their feet, in humanoid form—the look of wariness on their faces unsurprisingly familiar. All Nerakians who had suffered at the hands of daemons and Exiled Maras wore it. No one was eager to welcome us, not until we made our intentions clear.

Gasps erupted from the pack when they saw Jack approach with the other six Adlets. Several males growled, moving in front of the females and children. The first Adlet that we'd met in the field shifted to humanoid form, grabbing a cloth from a pile near the fire and wrapping it around his waist. The other five followed suit, including the young Mahlon, who still had trouble taking his eyes off Jack.

"Don't be alarmed," the first Adlet said, nodding at us. "They're here to help."

One male Adlet caught my eye as I got off my horse and moved closer to Jack, who whimpered and sat on his hind legs. He was slightly taller and bulkier than the others, and wore white locks through his rich, reddish hair, along with several battle scars across his chest and arms.

"You had better have a good explanation for bringing strangers into our camp, Isom," he said, glaring at the first Adlet, who raised his hands in a defensive gesture.

"They just want to talk, Colton," Isom said. "They're fighting the same foes as we are. And look who's helping them."

Isom then pointed at Jack, who was somewhat restless, but stayed by my side. Colton, their pack leader, stilled at the sight of my pit wolf. Recognition flickered in his amber eyes, briefly followed by surprise, then grief. His chest deflated as he exhaled sharply, the tremor in his voice confirming that they all knew Jack.

"How did you get *him*?" Colton asked, his gaze fixed on Jack.

"We rescued him from the Valley of Screams," I replied. "The daemons use charmed collars to subdue creatures like him. I accidentally broke his during a fight, and he's stayed close ever since."

"State your business here, before we tear you to shreds!" A young male Adlet stepped forward. He froze when Colton growled at him, then slowly moved back, his cheeks burning red with embarrassment.

"Mind your tongue, Jahiem," Colton barked. "Leave the questioning to me. You're not the alpha here."

Jahiem's mother whispered something in his ear, prompting the young Adlet to nod slowly and stare at his feet. Colton crossed his arms, measuring each of us from head to toe, before settling his gaze back on Jack.

"Jahiem is my eldest, and a little too hot-headed for this conversation. We've been having more trouble than usual with daemons in these parts over the past few months, and we're all on edge. We don't take kindly to strangers, as there are few of us left, and, despite our stronghold here, the daemons have been getting more brazen. We sleep less, eat less, and fight more, but we still have these woods and most of the plains."

"Are you the only Adlets in the region?" I asked.

"There's another pack farther to the east, but they've been having the same troubles as us," Colton replied. "Like I said, the daemons are starting to close in on us. The frequent rains work in our favor, but they won't for much longer. We're able to spot daemons and organize the occasional raid on their camps when they least expect it. Otherwise, we would've all ended up like *him* by now."

He nodded at Jack.

"Wait, what do you mean? So, Jack *is* an Adlet, right?" I said, my gaze shifting between Colton and Isom.

Colton sighed, his shoulders dropping. "There's a reason why the daemons aren't in too much of a rush to exterminate our entire species," he said. "They very well could, if they wanted to. All it'd take would be a small army of death claws in the middle of the night, and that would be the end of us. But they need us. They source their beasts from us."

"Pit wolves are Adlets, subjected to months of torture and swamp witch magic," Isom added. "They lose their thick coats, and their eyes turn red in the process. They also lose their ability to shift back to their bipedal form. Once the daemons snap those wretched collars on, that's it. The Adlet is gone, and the obedient, bloodthirsty pit wolf is born."

"The daemons raid our camps once a year and steal our people," Colton continued. "They leave the younglings behind because they need full-grown adults to turn and use against the Imen, and anyone else who defies them, for that matter. Including us."

My heart sank as I listened to this most painful confirmation. Somewhere behind those red eyes, Jack was an Adlet. He'd once belonged to a family, a pack of his own. *Oh, dear.*

"Jack is one of your own, isn't he?" I breathed, connecting the dots as Jack looked at me.

"His name is Hundurr," Colton replied, his eyes glassy with tears. His brow furrowed. "He was once our pack leader, the alpha before me."

"Oh, Jack." I sighed, then leaned into the pit wolf and wrapped my arms around his thick, muscular neck. He nuzzled my ear, then licked it, showing his affection in a way that surprised everyone around us, including the Adlets.

"It's all in the collars," Colton said. "The worst part is that, once they're off, the pit wolf doesn't turn back to Adlet. Once you become a pit wolf, that's it. That's all you'll ever be. And, frankly, I'm surprised he's still here, with you. We've managed to free some pit wolves ourselves, but they ran off. They don't stick around. They're consumed by shame and loneliness. They just... disappear."

"The daemons use them for protection," Isom added. "They're big and can tear pretty much anyone to shreds. And Hundurr... He was our pride and beloved brother."

"When was he taken?" Patrik asked, moving closer to Hundurr/Jack and me. The look on his face broke my heart, over and over, as I remembered his experience as the slave of an evil spell.

"A couple of years back," Colton replied. "Hundurr, Isom, and I used to be inseparable. Pack leadership is passed down through the bloodline. Hundurr was... *is* our eldest brother. It's a shame our mother passed away before she could see him return, even if *this* is all that's left of him."

A few moments passed as we all adjusted to the harsh and painful reality. Hundurr had been taken from his pack, torn from his family and friends, and turned into a pit wolf. He'd been forced to do the daemons' bidding, killing innocent Imen and other creatures who dared to defy them. It was no wonder that he'd become so quickly attached to me. I'd given him something he'd never thought he'd get to experience ever again—freedom.

"He's still in there, somewhere," Patrik murmured, tears gathering in his deep blue eyes as he looked at Hundurr. "I know what it's like to be turned into something you would never allow yourself to become. He must've fought long and hard to free himself, but to no avail. I'd thought he was just a savage beast, thankful to Scarlett for having freed him of the collar. Turns out Hundurr and I have more in common than I would've thought."

I swallowed my own tears, watching as Hundurr inched closer and nuzzled Patrik's face. Even Heron was getting emotional, the memories of his own ordeal at the hands of Azazel coming back to haunt him, no doubt.

"Back in our world, there was an evil Druid named Azazel," Heron explained. "He turned to the dark side of magic, and used it to kill and destroy everything that was good and peaceful. He was greedy and cruel, and he imprisoned those of us he deemed useful. He turned other Druids into Destroyers, mindless beasts who did his bidding. Those he couldn't benefit from, he simply killed."

"I was once a Destroyer," Patrik continued. "Forced to be something awful. I can never take back what I did under his influence. I cannot change the past. And neither can Hundurr. But we are both free now. And that's all that matters."

"What happened to Azazel?" Colton asked, taking a few steps forward. Isom joined him. They both kept their eyes on Hundurr. I could no longer bring myself to call him Jack. That was a name I'd given to a creature I'd known nothing about. Hundurr had a history, a life and family, well beyond the beast I'd rescued from the Valley of Screams.

"We defeated him," Patrik said. "I broke my curse. I fought tooth and nail to regain my Druid form. I put myself through agonizing pain, just so I could look him in the eyes and watch him die. And I am telling you now, Colton, that your enemies can, and will, suffer the same fate. We'll make sure of it."

He gently patted Hundurr's neck before stepping back for Colton and Isom to get closer. Both Adlets stared at the pit wolf for a while, then hugged him. I noticed the tears streaming down their cheeks—the entire pack was crying, and I couldn't hold mine back any longer, either. Hundurr shuddered, his muscles twitching as he yelped in his brothers' arms. *A family reunited.*

They'd all missed him, and I could only imagine what a

wonderful leader he must have been. I was already fond of him, and I'd never really met him—the original Hundurr, the Adlet who led his pack through these woods and across the Plains of Lagerith, who had friends and went hunting moon-bison on rainy mornings. The Adlet who would've stopped at nothing to protect his people.

But I knew the pit wolf Hundurr. The vicious fighter. The gentle giant who tore my enemies to shreds, and did everything he could to keep me and my friends safe from daemons and Exiled Maras. And my heart swelled as I watched him rejoice at the touch of his brothers. Hundurr was home.

13

PATRIK

The Adlets welcomed us into their camp, now that they understood how much we had in common, despite our origins. We gathered around the fire while the younglings went off to prepare several holes in one of the mounds for us to sleep in.

At first, I'd been worried that Hundurr might end up hurting Scarlett. However, the more time I'd spent around him, the more I'd understood that the pit wolf was fiercely loyal to her. But there was an Adlet behind those glimmering red eyes. A creature who understood more than I'd given him credit for.

Like me, Hundurr had fallen victim to the machinations of an evil overlord. Unlike me, Hundurr was stuck in that form. But was he, really? What magic was truly permanent and irreversible in the end? I'd thought the same of my existence as a Destroyer. I'd thought I could never come back, and yet, thanks to Vita, I'd managed to break free.

"Tell us about what brought you here," Colton said, taking his seat by the fire.

Scarlett and I sat next to each other, and Hundurr settled by our side. Dion and Alles stayed close to Heron and Avril, visibly intimidated by the Adlets. Compared to them, the two Imen scouts were tiny and a little too easy to break, especially after they'd seen their full wolf forms.

"After we defeated Azazel," I said, "we aligned ourselves with GASP, an organization that spans across multiple worlds now and is dedicated to protecting creatures of all kinds, to restoring peace and balance where chaos and murder reign. We opened up a base on my home planet, Calliope, and we chose our strongest and brightest to join new teams. The purpose was to help rebuild our society and return it to its former glory. We were well into that when an Exiled Mara returned to Calliope using swamp witch magic. Rewa of House Xunn, to be precise."

"Ugh. I'd love to chew on her entrails right about now," Jahiem muttered.

"You know her?" Scarlett asked.

"We know all the so-called royals in Azure Heights," Isom replied. "We made it our business to know our enemies, and their friends. We've also had a couple of altercations with the Exiled Maras. In fact, the last time we had issues with a convoy of House Xunn Maras, Hundurr nearly ripped Darius's throat out. Rewa promised vengeance, and, well, two weeks later, Hundurr was taken by the daemons during a hunt on the far east side of the plains."

As tragic as what happened to Hundurr was, I couldn't help but think this would work in our favor now. The stronger their hatred of the daemons and the Exiled Maras, the better the chances of us counting on the Adlets' support for what came next.

"Rewa told us about Azure Heights, about how they'd resettled here on Neraka—"

"Mind you, the Maras were already kicked off one planet, thousands of years ago, for doing the same crap they're doing now," Heron interrupted me, and for good reason. It dawned on me that the Adlets might not be fully aware of the Maras' dark history.

"The Maras came from Calliope," I said. "They killed innocent creatures for blood, and were exiled as a result. Those who repented were allowed to stay and rebuild, including Heron's forefathers. We never heard from the Exiled Maras again, until just recently, when Rewa came to us asking for our help. She told us her people were vanishing, and that the Exiled Maras had turned over a new leaf here, on Neraka. That they were peaceful and kind, and so on."

"So she lied to your faces and brought you all over here for what, exactly? And how long did it take you to figure out what Rewa and her people have been up to?" Colton replied.

"Well, they put on quite the theatrical display, I'll give them credit for that," Avril chimed in. "It took us a few days, and we almost got ourselves killed in the process, but we managed to get out of Azure Heights."

"Thing is, we can't get off the planet," I added. "A powerful shield went up after we came here. It's stopping everything and everyone trying to leave. We can't communicate with our base, and they can't reach out to us, either. We know about the Druid delegation that the Maras hijacked, and we know that the swamp witch who was on it is still alive. If we find her and rescue her, she'll bring the shield down. It's the only way for us to stop all this madness and obliterate both the daemons and the Maras. We have armies of creatures far more powerful than these fiends. We have dragons and Druids, witches and jinn. All the daemon cities would be reduced to a pile of dust in a matter of hours. We just need to find the swamp witch."

Colton nodded slowly, occasionally glancing at Hundurr and smiling softly. "For bringing Hundurr back to us," he said, "you have our strength and our allegiance, Druid. But I don't know how we could possibly help, since we don't know where they're keeping the swamp witch."

"We suspect she's in Draconis, and the rest of our team is currently on their way there," I replied. "What we need from you is exactly what you offered—your strength. A time will come, and soon, when we will have to fight the daemons and the Exiled Maras. Our strength does not lie in numbers, but in our abilities, and we will have to keep these bastards at bay while the swamp witch brings down the shield. You know as well as I do that, once they lose the witch, the daemons and the Maras will stop at nothing to get her back."

"That is true. They've been using swamp witch magic for millennia now, and they won't give up their mystical motherlode so easily," Colton said. "I have to give her credit, though, for surviving until now. But what if she's sided with them? What if she's willingly helping them?"

"It's against a swamp witch's very nature to tilt the balance of the world in the favor of darkness," I said, remembering everything I'd learned about swamp witches during the months I'd spent on Calliope. "Swamp witches use the power of the word for their magic. They function with precise formulas and exact quantities. Everything is measured. Everything is balanced. They would never empower one nation against another. They don't even get involved in wars. Most importantly, they know how valuable their magic is, which is why they keep their distance from creatures who are prone to such mindless violence. Frankly, I don't think she belonged in that delegation in the first place, but what's done is done."

"We've only heard rumors of the witch still being alive, you know," Isom replied. "We've never seen her. The only thing we're certain of is the damage of her magic. Hundurr, here, is a prime example. Does that look like balance to you?"

"The collars, much like all the magic the daemons use, are a perversion of the original swamp witch spells," I said. I'd read Viola's translations of the witches' tome over and over. I knew their mindset better than most. "Swamp witch magic doesn't adhere to good or evil. Those are abstract terms. Instead, their spells focus on what is ethical. What hurts other creatures, and what doesn't. What is useful in times of war, and what is necessary in times of peace. The collars themselves would have been meant to tame violent beasts, for example. Not to enslave innocent creatures. It's not the spell that is evil; it's the person wielding it."

"Besides, I doubt that the witch gave away the most powerful of her spells," Heron added. "From what we've seen so far, the daemons' knowledge of swamp witch magic is somewhat limited."

"You know more than they do?" Colton replied, raising his eyebrows.

"We probably do, but we don't have the ingredients," I said. "Every spell that the daemons are using is adapted to Nerakian plants and crystals. We have the recipes for powerful magic, but they're based on Eritopian ingredients. So we're a bit stuck on that end. Which is one more reason as to why we need to get the swamp witch away from the daemons."

"Before they adapt the more powerful spells to our world, right?" Colton asked, and I nodded. "I understand. So you're trying to strike up some alliances with those of us who continue to resist the daemons, then?"

"Yes. We're also hoping to reach out to the Dhaxanians, provided they're still holed up on their mountain, up north," Scarlett replied, scratching Hundurr behind the ear.

"You can spend the night here," Colton said. "We'll provide you with food and shelter, and you can try your luck with the Dhaxanians tomorrow. Although I doubt they'll be much help. No one has seen or spoken to one of them in decades. Rumor is they're all dead."

"I guess you've heard different rumors," Dion smirked, "because we're told the Dhaxanians are still up there, holding their ground."

Colton shrugged. "Either way, be careful. Try not to travel at night, either. The daemons fare much better in the dark than they do during the day."

"Thank you, Colton," I replied, then offered a half smile. "I'm glad we're able to count on you and your people for this."

"Father?" The voice of a young male Adlet reduced us all to silence, and we turned our heads to the right. Hundurr sprang to his feet and whimpered softly at the sight of two children, a male and a female, cloaked in animal skins and carrying two baskets of roots and vegetables they'd picked from the forest.

They both stared at Hundurr, their amber eyes wide and glassy as they recognized him.

"Saya, Embry, you're back," Colton said, then stood up and looked at Scarlett and me. "These are Hundurr's children. They haven't seen their father in two years."

"It's him, isn't it?" Saya asked, setting her basket down with slow movements. Colton nodded, and she let out a long, most painful sigh.

They both came closer. Hundurr waited, still and quiet. "Does he know it's us?" Embry murmured, taking a couple of steps forward, until there were only a couple of feet between him and Hundurr, his father-turned-pit-wolf. My stomach churned. I could only imagine how ravaged Hundurr probably was, deep down.

He didn't react to their proximity in any way, but I could see that glimmer of recognition in his red eyes. He knew exactly who they were. I had a feeling he was playing his pit wolf role, in a way, to make them think that he wasn't truly there anymore—at least, that's what I would've done, to spare my loved ones the suffering of seeing me in such a state.

"I don't know," Colton breathed. "I don't think we'll ever see the real Hundurr again. I'm sorry. I think this creature is all that's left of him."

Saya was the first to break down and cry, while Embry did his best to keep a straight face. He reached out, and Hundurr sniffed his fingers, then licked them. Saya came to the front, weeping, and Hundurr lowered his head farther, allowing her to wrap her arms around his neck.

She held him like that for a while, whispering in his ear. Hundurr listened and kept his gaze fixed on Embry. "He's alive," Embry whispered, his lower lip trembling. "That's all that matters."

Hundurr huffed, then nuzzled Saya's red curls. Embry then

patted the top of his head and nodded slowly. They were all communicating without words, their blood connection stronger than any swamp witch magic.

I understood, right then and there, that I couldn't let Hundurr stay like that forever. He was in there, somewhere, between layers of darkness and suffering, and I knew I'd eventually find a way to bring the Adlet back to the surface.

Scarlett sniffled by my side. A sharp pain clawed at my heart when I looked at her. Her suffering was mine, and I couldn't bear to see her crying. She cared about Hundurr, and she'd become very attached to him—knowing what he'd been through was really doing a number on her. Coincidentally, I, too, was broken and dysfunctional. I understood the darkness that had turned Hundurr into a pit wolf. Except that I went on like that well after I turned back to my Druid self. I'd allowed the pain, the grief of losing Kyana, to turn me into a lifeless husk.

I'd spent a lot of time wallowing in self-pity and grief, until she came along. Scarlett was my way out, my ray of sunshine, that glimmer of hope I held on to. She was the unexpected change in my life, the one who brought *all* of me back. Judging by how Hundurr looked at her, he saw the same creature as I did. I could tell, from his eyes, that he was fond of her.

The Adlet inside him was harboring strong feelings toward her—feelings that would've made me uncomfortable, and downright jealous, in different circumstances. All the times he'd growled whenever I got close to her were starting to make sense. But maybe that was what Hundurr needed to get himself out of that state. My love for Kyana had helped me break out from my Destroyer form.

As awkward as it sounded, maybe his feelings for Scarlett

could do the same for him. I promised myself that I would do everything in my power to help Hundurr cross that threshold. One way or another, the Adlet was going to come back. I'd make sure of that.

14

SCARLETT

W e spent the next couple of hours learning more about the Adlets and how they'd been keeping the daemons at bay. While most daemons kept their distance from the pack and only came after them when orders came from the daemon city, there were still plenty of hunters who preferred stalking them, searching for their camps so they could consume their souls. Despite their apparent organization and allegiance to the king and his plans, the daemons were still savage and selfish and sought that temporary high that the soul offered.

According to Colton, these rogue daemons believed that turning the Adlets into pit wolves was a waste because their souls were "absolutely delicious". The Adlets had learned to hunt during the day, particularly when it was raining, mainly because the daemons were vulnerable without their invisibility spell—the wolves' size was double that of a daemon, and their fangs and claws could inflict deadly damage.

Saya and Embry stayed close to Hundurr throughout the evening, showering him with hugs and kisses. "Hundurr was a great father," Colton said, watching the kids with their pit wolf dad. "He used to take them out hunting every morning, then out picking fruits and vegetables from the hills nearby in the afternoon. He taught them how to survive, and how to keep a low profile while out in the plains. If anyone can spot a daemon from five hundred yards away, it's those two rascals."

"Hundurr did a good job of raising them, after the daemons killed their mother," Isom added. "She died trying to defend them from rogue daemons."

"This world wasn't always like this, was it?" Avril asked, and I was secretly thankful that she changed the subject. It was all too painful, especially as I watched Patrik gaze at Hundurr and his kids. It hurt him deeply on the inside. He clearly had some kind of post-traumatic stress disorder, and I had no idea how to help him, how to make it all better. I felt helpless, and, at the same time, I was falling deeper in love with him—Patrik was a survivor, and one of the most noble creatures I'd ever come across.

"Neraka was once a glorious, bountiful land," Colton replied with a melancholic sigh. "Or at least that's what we're told in legends passed down from our ancestors. Personally, I only know the turmoil that we have today, but, back in the old days, long before the Maras came here, this was a land that belonged to all creatures. There are stories that survive to this day of heroes and villains among us. Jada, the Manticore who defeated the first daemon king, or Lige, the only Adlet to unite all the packs against the Dhaxanians when they tried to freeze the entire north. The Imen were renowned as noble creatures who advocated peace and prosperity. They were known as the architects of this world, building cities in perfect harmony with nature—"

"Until the daemons rose to power and started hunting them for their souls," Isom added. "Then the Exiled Maras came along and joined the hunt, hungry for the Imen's blood. Everybody wanted something from those poor Imen. They were all systematically dumbed down and reduced to savages, fearful villagers, and slaves, purely because they weren't as strong or as vicious as the daemons. Neraka wasn't always this cruel, you know. Our nations used to live in relative peace. I mean, sure, you had the occasional conqueror, but there was some kind of balance."

"That, of course, stopped when the daemons learned how to eat souls. They turned from aspiring overlords to the very plague that has decimated our people and stripped us of our lands," Colton said, gritting his teeth.

"You know, there are daemons who don't follow that path anymore," I said. "They're called pacifists among their people, and, of course, they're deeply frowned upon. But still, they refuse to eat souls. They keep to themselves, but they've been spreading, lately. They want to see Neraka restored to what it once was, before this bloodbath."

Colton straightened his back, then cocked his head to the side, looking genuinely surprised. The other Adlets were equally nonplussed, judging by their collectively raised eyebrows. "That's new," Colton muttered. "We've never heard of the movement before."

"Probably because they fear discovery too much, at this point," I replied. "But they're there, deep within the daemon cities, ready to help us."

"Do you really think they'd turn on their own kind just to assist you?" Isom said, pursing his lips.

"They will do whatever it takes, as long as all the murders and soul-eating stop, for good." I sighed. "I imagine they're just as exhausted as you. Personally, I'm not surprised. They're not all evil by nature. Most of them adhere to what they know, to what they've been taught. The freethinkers are persecuted and killed. The pacifists are freethinkers who, to this day, have evaded capture, waiting for people like you, people like us, to come together and rid Neraka of its daemons once and for all. So, yes, I believe their intentions are pure."

"They're not the first or the last to be willing to rise against their leader," Patrik added. "I've seen it before. The pattern is familiar, and it transcends space and time. Good and evil may be relative terms, but most creatures follow a moral path. To some, it's no way to live if it doesn't feel right. Personally, I completely understand that."

Colton nodded slowly, then lay on his side by the fire. "I'll speak to the rest of my pack tonight. We'll send word out to the others, too, and we'll give you an alliance offer by morning. Before we agree to anything, we need to assess the risks and resources involved. We have our cubs to think of first. Surely you understand."

"Absolutely," Patrik replied. "Take as long as you need. We're grateful with whatever you can provide in terms of support. We hope our friends will find the swamp witch in Draconis, but if she's not there, we may need help to find her—wherever she may be."

"Our trackers might come in handy for that," Isom offered, looking at Colton, who nodded in response. "We'll hold a council at midnight and discuss our options. In the meantime, you should all get some rest. Your shelters are ready."

A young Adlet girl came forward and pointed at three holes

in the northern mound to her right. "We've prepared three. There are plenty of furs down there to keep you warm during the night," she said.

"Thank you," I replied, giving her a warm smile. She blushed, then settled by Isom's side. Based on the facial similarities, she was definitely his daughter—an assumption reinforced by the kiss he gently dropped on her forehead.

"It gets extremely cold after midnight," Isom said. "If you need more covers, just let either of us know."

We all got up and walked over to the shelters. Some quick math made me realize that I'd have to share a hole with one of my team members. In any other circumstance, and based solely on my upbringing, I would've thought of Avril as my "bunkmate", but Patrik took my hand and claimed the first shelter.

"We'll take this one," he said, prompting Heron to put on one of his devilish smirks. Hundurr wasn't too happy with the idea, letting out a low, guttural growl. He glared at Patrik, who was unfazed and narrowed his eyes at the pit wolf. "If you have a problem with that, I'm more than happy to talk to you about it, once you turn back to your original self. Until then, however, I'd really appreciate it if you could just stay out here and watch over us. Over Scarlett, in particular."

Hundurr shook his head, visibly displeased, but obeyed and sat down in the grass. I chuckled softly, then scratched him behind his ears. "Thank you," I whispered. The look in his eyes made me melt on the inside. It also hurt me deeply because I knew I'd be leaving him here, with his family, once morning came. It would be cruel to take him away from the pack with whom he'd just been reunited.

Patrik climbed first into the hole, and I followed, just as the others claimed their shelters in pairs—Dion with Alles, and

Heron with Avril; the latter pairing made me giggle, mainly because I knew how close they were bound to get to each other.

Speaking of close...

As soon as my feet sank into the fur with which the Adlets had lined the floor in our hole, I stilled. Patrik stood right in front of me, his warm breath warming my face as he took off his backpack and weapons. He didn't take his eyes off me while I did the same. My heart was jumping back and forth, struggling against my ribcage.

"What did you mean when you told Hundurr about his 'original self'?" I asked, trying to fill the intense silence with something that would distract me from my racing pulse. "Pit wolves can't transform back into Adlets, not even after the collar is removed."

"That's a known theory, yes, but not a fact, per se," Patrik replied. "I've looked into his eyes, Scarlett. Hundurr is still in there, deep inside the pit wolf. And he's very attached to you. I'm hoping it will help if I push his buttons a little, where you're concerned. It might help him fight his condition. Who knows, he might even revert to Adlet form, if he's strong enough. It's worth a shot."

That made me laugh lightly. "So, because he gets jealous whenever you're close to me, you're hoping to get him riled up enough to turn back to his humanoid form?"

Patrik's gaze softened, and he inched closer, lowering his head. "Scarlett, there's an Adlet inside that pit wolf, desperate to come out. As cruel as it may sound, it might be his feelings for you that will help him break free."

"How do you know he has actual feelings for me? For all we know, he's simply fond of me because I broke the collar off him," I replied, shrugging. It did make sense, and it was a little flattering, I had to admit, but I knew, deep down, that even if Hundurr were to turn back to his Adlet form, I wouldn't be able to reciprocate. My heart belonged to the Druid whose lips gently pressed against my forehead.

"I know that look in his eyes better than anyone, Scarlett," he whispered. He then took me in his arms and kissed me, deeply. Patrik tasted like summer sunshine, and it was the closest I'd ever get to feeling that light on my skin—that warmth pouring through my veins. "It was love that helped me break my own chains, Scarlett. And it could be love that sets Hundurr free, too."

"It was your love for Kyana," I replied, my voice unsteady. I didn't want to go there, and open that wound, but it had to be addressed. "That's a once-in-a-lifetime kind of thing. I'm just the vampire who released him from daemons, and I'm certainly not the one who pulled you out of your Destroyer form."

"You're giving yourself very little credit, Scarlett," Patrik said, caressing my face. "I'm still very much broken on the inside, and there are days when I can barely get myself up on my feet. Yet one thought of you is all it takes to get me moving again. You have no idea how important you are to me, and how much good you do to my very soul. I have all the faith in the world that you can have the same impact on Hundurr, if not more."

Tears came up to my eyes. I pressed my lips tight, struggling not to cry. "You're the one who gives me too much credit," I breathed, wrapping my arms around his waist.

"No, Scarlett," he replied, cupping my face, "I'm not giving you enough. Don't you see? I'm falling for you, more and more each day, at a stage in my life where I didn't think I'd ever feel this way again. And my feelings for you just keep getting stronger, to the point where I find it difficult to breathe if you're not around."

He kissed me again, this time more hungrily. I parted my lips, once again welcoming the wonderful taste of him, before he pulled himself back.

His breath was ragged, and his gaze was clouded as he looked at me. My lips tingled, and my heart thundered in my chest, watching him as he pulled some furs together into a pile resembling a makeshift bed. He took his boots off, then removed his vest and the rest of his gear. All that was left was a slightly disheveled Patrik, wearing a white shirt and dark blue pants, his curly hair framing his gorgeous face. I was hopelessly and irrevocably in love with him, and I could no longer deny it.

He sat on the furs, looking up at me with a warm smile. His blue eyes glimmered in the darkness of our shelter, and I wondered if he could see me as well as I could see him. I slipped out of my boots, then removed my protective gear and belt—the leather suit was ridiculously comfortable, once all the metal plates were off, the material soft enough to make it the perfect onesie in the absence of proper pajamas.

I sat on my knees in front of him. "You do know that I'm in love with you, right?" I asked, almost rhetorically, as I pulled the elastic band from my ponytail and let my hair loose.

His breath hitched, his pupils dilated, and his lips parted as he ran his fingers through my hair, then gripped the back of my neck. "Can you say that again? I'm not sure I heard you the first time," he replied, a smile blooming on his face.

I was almost trembling, overrun by my own emotions. We'd been through enough together, and I'd been holding these feelings in for months now. If we died tomorrow, at least he knew exactly how I felt. "I'm in love with you, Patrik," I breathed.

His eyes softened, and then he pulled me into a kiss that drew the air from my lungs, one hand holding my head, while the other slipped between my shoulder blades and pressed me against his muscular chest. His broad frame made me feel small, but safe and cherished, and butterflies erupted into a frenzy inside my stomach.

"Honestly, Scarlett, you continue to surprise me in the most incredible ways," he said between kisses. "I can see in color again, thanks to you."

"I'll never leave your side, if you'll have me," I whispered against his lips, feeling my heart open up wide, eager to receive everything he had for me. "I... I'll be there, through thick and thin. Whatever you need, I'll give you."

His lips moved to the most sensitive part of my neck, just beneath my ear, and I felt them brush against my earlobe as he whispered. "Give me you, Scarlett. Your heart, your soul, everything. I'll take it... and I won't let it go."

He dropped a tender kiss at the side of my neck, then pulled me closer, until I was almost straddling him. We ran our fingers through each other's hair—he seemed to enjoy the length of mine, while I relished his dark curls and the thousands of tiny electric sensations that the very touch of him sent through my body.

Hundurr's growl from outside reminded us that he was still there, and that he could hear us—a little too well. I giggled softly as Patrik laid us both down and wrapped us in a thick fur. He didn't stop kissing me, though. His mouth made love to mine beneath the cover, his hands exploring the length of my back.

"You're here," he whispered, "and I couldn't ask the universe for anything more."

"I didn't think you'd ever have eyes for me," I confessed, trailing a finger along his jawline, then holding his chin.

"The moment you walked into the base on Mount Zur, I was

done for, Scarlett," he replied softly. "I just didn't realize it. Not straightaway. The image of you became permanently fixed in the back of my head then, and I found myself thinking about you whenever I was left on my own. Grieving and suffering felt too comfortable at the time for me to truly look at you and see the incredible creature I'm lucky to hold in my arms tonight. But I see you now, Scarlett. And I'm not letting go."

Good. Because I can't let go, either. Not anymore.

No matter what happened, we were going to emerge victorious from all of this. There was no other option in my mind—not after we'd just found each other.

Come morning, Patrik and I would get back out there and push everything we felt for each other aside so we could focus on the mission and keep moving forward.

But for tonight, hidden in a hole somewhere in the woods of Lagerith, Patrik and I let sleep claim us, wrapped in each other's arms with our lips almost touching, dreaming of the end to this Nerakian mess, a time when we could focus on ourselves, and what we might become together.

15

AVRIL

Technically speaking, after I'd blurted out my feelings to Heron earlier, having a moment alone with him would've been a good opportunity to follow up on that—since he'd yet to respond to my declaration. However, at this precise moment, as we climbed down into our hole in the mound, the silence was awkward and weighed heavy on my shoulders.

What could I possibly say? I'd already told him how I felt about him. I had no idea whether he felt the same or not. And he wasn't saying anything, either.

Oh, man, I should've kept my mouth shut.

No, no, I did the right thing. I let it all out. Now I just have to deal with the consequences, whatever they may be.

The hole was spacious enough for the both of us to lie down comfortably, the floor covered with soft layers of fur. We didn't need any light, as our eyes functioned perfectly in its absence. I could see the frown pulling his eyebrows closer as he avoided my gaze, seemingly looking for his spot on the ground.

I was so nervous my hands were literally shaking. Figuring I'd have to make myself busy, somehow, and get my mind off our earlier, mostly one-sided conversation, I started fumbling with large pieces of fur, pulling them together into a makeshift mattress. There wasn't enough room in here for me to move without occasionally bumping into Heron, who instantly reacted with a muffled "Sorry" whenever we got too close. I just couldn't take that silence anymore.

"So, yeah, we can share this, I guess," I muttered, pointing at the "bed". "I mean, it's the size of a single, but, given the circumstances, it'll do. This isn't exactly a hotel room." I chuckled nervously.

"Avril, I—"

"Or you could make your own pile on the side, if you want. I'm okay regardless. There's plenty of fur here for the both of us." I kept droning on, comfortable with how my senseless words were filling up the emptiness between us. As long as I kept talking, I wouldn't have to bring up my feelings toward him—feelings which, by the way, were messing with my senses.

The close proximity thickened the air and made it difficult for me to breathe. My heart thudded, and my pulse was on a constant race, to the point where I was getting lightheaded. I didn't even realize that Heron was standing still, watching me as I gathered more furs in the middle.

"Can you just—"

"These are really soft furs, though," I said, once again cutting him off. In my panic to avoid silence, I'd completely tuned Heron out, as well, along with his attempts to speak. "I wonder what animals they got them from. Oh, God, they'd better not be from other Adlets, because that would be insanely creepy and—"

"Avril!" Heron raised his voice, finally snapping me out of my fidgeting frenzy. I straightened my back and looked at him, with only a couple of feet between us.

"Sorry," I mumbled, clutching a piece of fur at my chest. "You were saying?"

"Well, then, good to see you're finally still and quiet for a second, so I can gather the courage to tell you that... I like you, too, Avril," he said. My heart made its way up to my throat, dissolving into a heatwave that then spread through my entire body, leaving my toes and fingers tingling. "More than before. More than I ever thought possible. You're not the only one dealing with this, as far as *this* is concerned. I can't get you out of my head. I've tried, believe me, but the thought of you is incredibly persistent. Just wanted you to know that."

I blinked several times, while trying to get my heartrate under control. My chest burned, and my stomach tightened. It was now my turn to reply, and... *What do I say?*

"Would've been nice to hear that *hours* ago, when I first told you how I felt," I said, my cheeks catching fire.

"I was just about to say it when we spotted the Adlets," Heron replied, raising his arms to the sides in exasperation.

I couldn't help but chuckle nervously. "Better late than never, right?"

"I would've said something sooner, if I'd know that this is how you feel," Heron said, then let out a heavy sigh. "I've had a thing for you from the moment you handed my ass to me during training. I just didn't think you'd even look at me."

"Why *wouldn't* I look at you? You've got two legs, two arms,

and the ability to formulate a coherent thought, right?" I
retorted, seeking refuge in sarcasm. I didn't really know how to
handle such confessions, and my foot-in-mouth syndrome was
clearly taking over.

Heron raised a sarcastic eyebrow at me, crossing his arms.
"Really, Avril? Is that your standard, as far as guys are
concerned?"

"No. Dammit, that's not what I meant," I replied, rolling my
eyes, frustrated with myself. This was bad and getting worse, and
I had no idea how to stop it. "I feel like I'm riding a train off a cliff
right about now, Heron. How do I stop?"

"You can shut up for five minutes and formulate a coherent
thought," Heron shot back with a smirk. *Ah, there he is, the Mara I
fell for.* The biting sarcasm and using my own words against me,
infuriating and amusing me at the same time.

"This is how you get yourself kicked in the mouth, Heron."

"By being the smartass you fell in love with?"

"Yes!" I replied, then stilled, realizing what I'd just said yes
to. In all fairness, it was the truth. I loved our banter, and, ugh,
I loved him. His jade gaze softened on me, a smile tugging at
the corner of his mouth. My breath hitched. There was no
turning back now. "This isn't the right time, I know. It's what
really ticks me off. But we could die tomorrow, or the day after,
or we could get out of this mess in one piece. Either way,
there's no guarantee I'll have another chance to tell you this.
But yes, Heron. I'm in love with you. You overconfident
smartass."

Heron took a step forward, and my heart stopped for a sweet
moment. He closed the distance between us, his eyes locked on
mine. I stared into the endless jade pools beneath his black
eyelashes, and time stopped. Everything contracted, then

expanded around me, as he lowered his head, his mouth capturing mine.

I closed my eyes, relishing the explosions of bright colors as I parted my lips and allowed Heron to take me over, body and soul. His arms came around my waist, tightening. He pressed me against his hard, toned chest. Heron wasn't big, as far as muscle mass was concerned, but he was tall, and his frame enveloped mine in a way that made me feel small, even fragile, and perpetually cherished in his embrace. I ran my fingers through his short black hair, and he grunted softly against my lips. We were in so much trouble. We couldn't get enough of each other, and we'd been carrying this tension around with us for a long time.

And now, as we unraveled in each other's arms, everything we'd been holding back was gradually, but surely, coming undone. His hands traveled up and down my body, discreetly and skillfully removing my weapons and protective gear, dropping each with a muffled clang or jingle on the fur-covered floor.

Heron cupped my face, the gentle touch of his fingers on my cheeks making me shiver as he brought the kiss to a soft end. His darkened gaze found mine, and my body bucked from the intensity emanating from him. My breath was rapid and ragged, my heart struggling to keep up with this incredible moment. For a few, deliciously long seconds on this savage planet, Heron and I had only each other to deal with, and the feelings we'd been trying to ignore for days.

"Avril, I just want you to know that if we get out of this alive, I plan on taking you on a real date. Dinner, great view of a forest or a waterfall, music in the background... the works," he whispered.

"Your lady friends back home will hate me," I replied, chuckling softly.

"I'm sorry I gave you the impression of a Grade A philanderer," he said, his gaze dropping to the ground. "It's not really me. I know I've said it before, but I feel the need to say it again. Don't worry about any lady friends or whatever. Nobody sees me the way you do, and you're all that matters to me."

"I'll be honest, that's what scared me the most about this. I mean, *us*," I breathed, then offered a faint smile, watching as he took off his weapons, his belt, and the rest of his protective gear, then sat on the furs, looking up at me. "That you'd consider me one of... well, one of your lady friends."

With lightning speed, he grabbed my hand and pulled me down. The move caught me by surprise, and I landed in his lap. He kissed me with insatiable hunger, with one arm wrapped around my waist and the other taking a firm hold around the back of my neck and pulling me closer.

I could hear his heart thumping, and his natural scent threw me off balance completely. The sweet fragrance of desire and affection mingled and tickled my nostrils, and I inhaled deeply, taking it all in.

"I don't deserve a creature like you, Avril," he whispered gently in my ear, parting our lips, "but I'd be foolish to turn you away, or treat you like anything other than the goddess that you are. All I can do is worship you and all your quirks, and hope you'll take me, as I am."

"You mean the smartass I fell in love with?" I replied, then turned my head and dropped a kiss on his neck. "Yeah, I'll take you."

He laughed lightly, then rolled us over on the side so he could envelop me in his arms. I fell asleep to the rhythm of his heartbeat—frantic and irregular, mostly because of me. The pattern carried me off to dreamland, where Heron and I somehow met again, beneath a giant magnolia tree.

If only for one night, it was just the two of us, lost in streams of our subconscious, relieved that we'd fallen for each other. That we felt the same way.

16

HARPER

The darkness that cradled me felt snug and warm as I gradually regained consciousness. I kept my eyes closed, relishing the sensation, fearful that, once I opened them, reality would crash back into me, cold and unforgiving. The murmur of a heartbeat guided me through the silence. Caspian's scent, that soft mixture of musk and raging seas, filled my lungs and stretched my lips into a smile.

The memories of what had thrown me into my dormant stasis came back—snippets of my fight with the Manticore queen's daughter. The punches, our blades slashing and drawing blood. The venomous spike of Pheng-Pheng's scorpion tail that pierced my flesh. The poison.

Am I dead? Did Manticore venom actually kill me? Could it kill a vampire?

If this was death, it felt amazing. My eyes peeled open and quickly dismantled that theory. I was still very much alive, and

I'd been sleeping in Caspian's arms beneath the cover of a small tent. The animal skin blocking the sunlight was a soft, crackled brown, thick enough to protect us from the sun.

"Harper?" Caspian's voice made me turn my head, slowly, so I could see his face. His jade eyes were dark, emotions flickering in bright flames of emerald and gold as he smiled gently and caressed my cheek.

I was awake. Pheng-Pheng had not killed me. But I'd fought her for a reason. "What happened?" I murmured, stirring in Caspian's embrace. He'd covered us both with woolen blankets and a thick layer of fur, and he'd laid down beside me, probably watching over me as I recovered from the Manticore sting. My entire body hurt, but the venom burn was gone. "Pheng-Pheng... Did she win? No, wait. She yielded, didn't she? But I passed out..."

"You fought like the warrior that you are, Harper," Caspian replied, his voice rich with pride. "And yes, you got Pheng-Pheng to yield, just before her venom took its toll and rendered you unconscious. But she administered the cure and admitted her defeat. You won. *We* won."

I glanced around, breathing a sigh of relief. Judging by the brightness peeking through the tent's stitched edges, it was early morning. "How long have I been out?" I asked, unwilling to move from Caspian's hold.

"You were unconscious for most of the night," he replied, using his thumb and index to grip my chin and pull me in for a deep, sweet kiss. I loved the taste of him on my lips, especially after my near-death experience. "I thought I'd lost you when Pheng-Pheng stung you. I thought that was it. But you... You found the strength to defeat her, despite the poison working its way through you."

I blushed, brushing my fingers against his lower lip. "The thought of never seeing you again enraged me," I whispered. "I was horrified that I'd never get to be with you like this. You're the reason I'm still here, I guess."

"Good." He nodded slowly. "Good to know I'm still useful, despite my current condition."

He meant the blood oath. I knew he wanted to tell me everything that we were missing to complete the picture of the conspiracy between the Exiled Maras and the daemons. His inability to do so made him feel helpless, but judging by his warm, golden aura, that wasn't the emotion dominating him at this point. That glimmer was all for me, and I welcomed it.

"I don't know, I think we can find a couple more uses for you, still." I smirked, then bit my lower lip as I looked up at him. His gaze darkened, and the shadow of a smile flickered over his face.

"What were you thinking?" he replied.

"Oh, I imagine you already have an inkling of that."

"More than an inkling, Harper. I'm painting an endless stream of images in my mind right now," Caspian said, then captured my mouth in a hungry kiss.

I was still in my leather suit, and as his lips began to make their way along my collarbone, for the first time, as much as I loved its comfortable design, I genuinely loathed its presence on me. Caspian found the hem of my collar, and growled, equally frustrated. And yet, he didn't let it stop him.

The sound of my zipper going down made my heart somersault. Caspian was determined to discover more of me beneath my leather suit. He kissed me again as his fingers settled on my throat, then gently traveled downward, peeling away my suit so he could touch and explore my soft flesh.

As his fingers inched lower, he sucked in a breath, then

paused and looked at me, his gaze clouded, his aura brimming with bright gold. "I would love nothing more than to take this further, Harper," he murmured, "but I'm afraid it would mean we wouldn't leave this tent for a very long time."

I giggled softly, barely recognizing myself, all flushed and breathless. I stroked his cheek. "Let me guess, they're waiting for us outside."

He nodded, then smiled and dropped a brief but intense kiss on my lips. He sat up and offered me a hand. I took it and allowed him to pull me into a seated position. His gaze lingered on my torso, my pale skin and sports bra in full view. My cheeks burned delightfully as he slowly reached out and zipped my suit back up, with a disappointed groan.

"I'll bookmark this moment then, so we can pick up where we left off, later," I said, then used one of the elastic bands on my wrist to pull my hair up in a loose bun.

"Oh, no, we'll have to start all over, I'm afraid," Caspian said, grinning as he geared up, then passed my protective plates, boots, belt, and weapons over. I got up and began preparing myself for what waited outside—my team, the Manticore queen, and a lot of sunlight in the middle of the Akrep Gorge. "My memory isn't what it used to be. I forget things..."

I burst into laughter, surprised to see this brighter side of him. It was a sight I rarely saw, and I loved it. "Don't tell me you're getting old," I replied, as he moved closer and took me in his arms.

"I'm full of energy and spry like a flame, Miss Hellswan," he said, and kissed me again. "But whenever you're near, my brain and my body refuse to cooperate. Now, gear up while I go get the others. I'll meet you outside."

He smiled, then put on his goggles and pulled his hood and

mask to protect him from the sunlight. I felt my heart swell with instant longing, watching him leave the tent. Caspian certainly had a way of riling me up, in more ways than one, and being so close to him offered me previously hidden facets of who he really was—a strong, determined Mara whose soft side made me melt like a candle before a fiery blaze.

I let out a breath. *I'm going to be a puddle of wax before long.*

Five minutes later, I was ready to go, loaded with my protective plates, my weapons and backpack on, and my head and eyes covered as I stepped out into the morning sunshine. The tent had been erected on the very edge of the Manticores' bowl-shaped arena, next to three others for the rest of my team.

As soon as they saw me, they all rushed to hug me—Hansa, Jax, Caia, Blaze, Fiona, and even Vesta. I was close to tearing up as they held me close and told me how relieved and thrilled they were to see me up and walking again, while Queen Neha, Pheng-Pheng, and Kai stayed behind, quietly watching us.

"You were amazing yesterday," Fiona said, patting my shoulder. "It's a shame she stung you, but damn, you fought back!"

"And you won, too," Hansa added, pulling me into another hug. She held me tighter this time, whispering in my ear. "Be more careful next time, kid. My heart can't take another scare like this."

"I swear I tried my best not to get my ass handed to me," I chuckled, as Caspian discreetly moved to my side and snaked an arm around my waist, bringing me closer to him.

"You didn't get your ass handed to you. Well . . . kind of. Almost," Caia replied, pursing her lips. "Okay, technically speaking, you did. But you still won."

"And I have to admit, no one has ever lived to make me yield, not after I stung them." Pheng-Pheng stepped forward, hands behind her back. Her wounds had already healed, but I could tell, from the dark colors radiating from her, that her ego was still bruised. "Nevertheless, I must congratulate you. You won fair and square."

"That is my daughter's way of expressing admiration," Queen Neha interjected with a dry smile, using her own voice. "In fact, my little Manticore likes you a lot."

Pheng-Pheng rolled her eyes and scoffed in response. "Let's not get all sentimental, Mother. She won the fight. That's all."

"You fought extraordinarily well," I replied with a nod. "I do appreciate how quickly you were able to mirror my movements. No one has ever worked me over the way you did. I say this genuinely—I am floored by your fighting abilities and consider myself lucky to have survived for long enough to get you to yield. I know my life wouldn't have been spared otherwise."

Pheng-Pheng offered a brief half smile, then stepped aside for her mother to come forward. Queen Neha was a vision, once more. White silk flowed down her luscious curves, with a heavy belt made of thick, gold disks resting around her hips. More gold plates covered her neck and chest, and her auburn mane was tamed and braided with white silk thread. She carried a strange bird on her left shoulder, the size of an eagle, with a curved beak and fiery red plumage. Its tail was rich with long, crimson feathers, and its glassy blue eyes fixed on me.

"You proved yourself worthy of my support," Queen Neha said to me, then smiled at Hansa and the rest of my team. "You have an ally in me, from now on. I do want to rid this world of daemons, and the pests that are the Exiled Maras, in particular. They don't belong here, not at the expense of my people's lives and wellbeing. So, yes, I will help you. The Manticores will stand with you."

"Thank you, Your Grace," I replied, then bowed curtly. "Your support will be much appreciated. We'll need all the help we can get, when the time comes."

"And you have our word that, once our people get here and balance is restored on Neraka, the Manticores will have GASP's full support in your rebuilding efforts. I'm sure you'd all like to leave this gorge, at some point," Hansa said.

"We'd like to have that freedom, yes," the queen said, nodding, "but I doubt we would actually abandon it. We've adjusted to the climate, and we thrive in the heat. Barring a couple of exceptions, we were never a people who expanded aggressively, but we've always enjoyed free movement. We don't have that, as long as King Shaytan still rules."

"Rest assured that once we get GASP here, King Shaytan won't be a problem anymore. Neither will the Exiled Maras," Jax added. "Too many lives have been wasted for their mindless greed. We'll put an end to it."

"We're off to Draconis next, to look for the swamp witch," Hansa said. "We're due to meet back at Ragnar Peak with the rest of our team in five days, with or without her. Once we get her back, it will be over for the daemons."

"Whatever you do, I wish you the best of luck," the queen replied, then slipped her fingers under the bird's feet. She handed the bird over to me, gently stroking its feathers. "This is an Ekar. We use them to communicate across large distances. Use it when you're ready to call for our help. Just tell it to return to me, and the bird will find me, then guide me to wherever you are."

"Thank you, Your Grace," I murmured. The Ekar's claws

gripped my hand firmly. It didn't hurt or scratch me, and it seemed calm and curious as it scanned my face, its head twisting like that of an owl.

"The Ekar travels at an average of ninety miles over the span of an hour," the queen said. "So take that into consideration when you send it back to me, depending on your location. You can even fit it with a message, if you wish."

I placed the bird on my shoulder, and it seemed comfortable there, grooming its wings and occasionally glancing around at the others. "He knows to stay with you now," Pheng-Pheng added. "I've raised Ramin from the day he hatched from his egg."

"What if we encounter issues in Draconis?" Jax asked, while Caspian stared at Ramin. "Would you be able to come to our aid there?"

Queen Neha thought about it for a second, then exchanged a knowing glance with Kai. "It's not something we're eager to do, but, should you need our help to get out of there, Kai can certainly take some of our best warriors and infiltrate Draconis to rescue you. It wouldn't be the first time we snuck into that city."

"You've been there before?" I replied, suddenly curious as to her experience in the daemons' prison city. The queen looked at me and exhaled.

"I was a prisoner there for a while, until Kai got me out and brought me here," she said, resting a hand on Kai's shoulder. A warm, golden aura enveloped them both, and I understood then that their relationship went well past that of a queen and her subject.

"I suppose your nest will always know where to find you," Fiona replied, nodding slowly. I figured they'd had plenty to talk about while I was out cold and recovering from the venom.

"We are connected, for life, yes," the queen replied, then looked at me. "Our fate is in your hands now, outsiders. I trust you will put your life on the line, if that's what it takes to stop the daemons from killing more of our people, little vampire."

"Yes, Your Grace," I said, then offered another curt bow. "We're allies now. And we will bring fire and fury to those who wish to hurt us."

"Good. Because those daemons need to burn," Pheng-Pheng replied, crossing her arms.

They most certainly do. I felt as though I could breathe again, knowing that we now had the Manticores on our side. Our journey and our mission were nowhere near over, but we had allies that we could rely on. I hoped that Scarlett and the others were okay, too, getting the Adlets to join our crew against the daemons and Exiled Maras.

We needed all hands on deck. And paws. And claws. And everything in between, as long as they helped us hold our enemies back while we retrieved the last swamp witch. With Caspian by my side, and fighters like Hansa, Jax, and the others backing me up, I knew that victory was no longer a distant dream, but a palpable reality.

17

HANSA

W e readied the indigo horses, and Fiona brought Harper up to speed on what we'd learned about the Manticores, and what we'd agreed on with their queen already. Kai gave me some dried food and fresh water to carry for the non-vampires, including myself. Jax and Fiona had spent the early part of the morning hunting in a nearby ravine and had secured enough blood to sate the vampires and Maras on our team for at least a couple of days.

Harper was still guzzling her portion, while Fiona fastened the saddle on her stallion and told her about the Manticore nest. "The queen is like the mother here," Fiona said. "She protects and nurtures the females, but there are no actual couples. They mate once every full moon, and that's it. The females give birth, and the children are sorted by gender. The males raise and train the boys, while the queen raises the females, with the help of their mothers."

"That's not too far from how the daemons raise their young," Harper replied. "More or less, anyway. I know the daemon king takes wives at his leisure, but the Manticore queen is single, isn't she?"

"Yup, she flies solo, so to speak," Fiona said. "Pheng-Pheng is one of her three kids. She's got two other girls, but Pheng-Pheng is the youngest."

"What about Kai? There's definitely something going on between him and the queen." Harper smirked. She must've read their emotions—those sentry abilities of hers never ceased to amaze me.

"Maybe, but they're not displaying it in public," Fiona replied with a shrug. "But get this! The queen is telepathically connected to the entire nest, just as we thought. She speaks through them. She can't read their minds or anything, but she can communicate through them, whenever she wants. And they're eternally bonded to her, too. You heard her yourself. They'll always know where to find her."

"That reminds me of the queen bee and the hive," Harper muttered. "Makes sense. So, what about the female Manticores? Are they just baby-makers or what?"

"Oh, no," I interjected, remembering my conversations with Neha from the previous night. "Not at all. They fight if they have to. But they're precious, and cherished. The queen keeps them close, mostly for protection. You see, a female Manticore's venom is far more powerful than that of a male. It kills faster, too."

"So, they're like the royal guards," Harper concluded. "Damn, I was lucky then, to survive Pheng-Pheng."

"Of course." Pheng-Pheng joined us, followed by Queen Neha. "My venom takes less than ten minutes to kill. It usually paralyzes within the first minute, which is why I'm still very much impressed by your stamina after I stung you, Harper."

Harper chuckled softly. "I'll be thanking the stars for the rest of my days, believe me."

"Are you all ready for your journey?" Queen Neha asked.

"Pretty much, yes," I replied, patting my horse's neck. The creature nuzzled my ear in response, making me giggle.

"I've decided to have Pheng-Pheng join you," the queen said, wearing a faint, sad smile.

A couple of moments passed in silence. Jax and I looked at each other. I couldn't see much of his expression, given his mask and goggles, but I had a feeling we were both wondering the same thing. "Why?" I asked.

"I figured you could use the extra help," the queen replied, and Vesta nodded in agreement.

"A Manticore will definitely come in handy down in Draconis," the young fae said.

"Personally, I'm thrilled to welcome Pheng-Pheng on our team," I added, smiling. "Like we've already said, we need all the help we can get."

"And we're lucky to get a fighter like you on board," Harper told Pheng-Pheng, who smiled in return, her tanned cheeks taking on a vibrant shade of red as she blushed.

"I'm honored that you'll have me," Pheng-Pheng replied, then playfully nudged Harper. "I'm riding with you. We don't have any horses to spare."

"Oh, okay. Sure, not a problem," Harper said.

We then bid the Manticores farewell and got back in the saddle. Our horses were well fed and rested, their muscles twitching as they anticipated the ride. "We're looking at another strip of hot desert once we leave the gorge," Jax said. "We'll go fast."

"We've got about three hundred miles before we reach Kerentrith," Vesta replied. "I think the horses can do it seamlessly. The sand dunes fade out the closer we get to the city, and the temperatures will drop a little, too, as the lava lakes are not directly underneath it."

"That's good to hear. I definitely don't want to walk into Draconis in a medium-rare state," Fiona grumbled, then gently pulled the reins of her horse, guiding it into the ravine that would eventually lead us to the northern exit.

Vesta took the lead, and Pheng-Pheng climbed up behind Harper on her horse. We shot after Vesta, the thundering of hooves echoing throughout the gorge, its tall, red walls casting a mild shade over us.

As soon as we left the Akrep Gorge behind us, I could feel the desert heat coming down hard on us—mostly on our vampires and Maras. I was sweating myself, but the high speed of our horses did make it slightly more comfortable, given that I was warm-blooded by nature.

Several hours later, as the sun left the noon peak in the clear blue sky, I could see the white city of Kerentrith rising in the distance. The reddish sand dunes began to fade away into flat, dry dirt. It must have been a beauty to look at, in the olden days —back when the Imen thrived and lived freely between its walls.

Not much was left standing, from what I could see as we got closer. The towers pierced through the sky, their white marble bricks glistening in the sunlight. The city of Kerentrith had been built on a steep hill, most of it carved into the hard white marble, with narrow stairs and alleys snaking down from the top. In many ways, it reminded me of White City, back on Calliope.

"I can see where the Exiled Maras got their inspiration for their precious city," Harper muttered, staring at the gleaming ruins of Kerentrith.

"They most certainly did. The ancestors of some of the Imen still living in Azure Heights came from Kerentrith," Vesta replied. "They probably died building that place."

"It's beautiful, still," I said, gazing at the marvelous structure. I could see the central palace from our position, rising proudly above the dilapidated buildings around and below. "It must have been splendid in its heyday."

"Stories about it survive to this day," Vesta replied. "Kerentrith was once a hub of artists, merchants, and lawmakers, the beating heart of the Imen civilization. It was crossed by multiple trade routes, connected to other cities around the continent. The Imen royalty lived in the palace, there."

Jax grunted, then nudged his horse with his heels, prompting the animal to go even faster as we reached the solid ground and left the sand dunes behind. Harper, Fiona, and Caspian did the same, and the rest of us had no choice but to keep up.

"Sorry, but I'm kind of boiling at this point," Jax said. "I'd kill for some shade right about now."

"I have to say, it's kind of funny to see you guys so uncomfortable." Caia giggled. Blaze stifled a grin and focused on the road ahead. We still had about ten miles to Kerentrith at this point.

"The worst part is that if I see another underground pond, I would rather burn in the sunlight than get in," Harper said with a bitter chuckle.

"You must be boiling," I replied, smirking, as Jax briefly glanced at me over his shoulder. Not that I could see his face, but I had a pretty good idea as to what his expression could be. "I know, redundancy is definitely my strong point right now."

"Oh, chill out, Jax," Caia added, then burst into laughter. "Wait, that's basically impossible!"

"Yuck it up, ladies. And fire boy," Jax shot back. I could sense the slight amusement in his tone, though it was carefully hidden beneath layers of irritation.

"Don't hate on us fire folk," Blaze replied, no longer able to hold back his grin.

"Okay, okay, that's enough fun at the expense of our cold-blooded mates," I said, feeling a little sorry to see Jax in so much physical discomfort. "We'll reach the shade in no time. Besides, the temperature is dropping a little already, just like Vesta said."

"That's because we've left the underground lava lakes behind, along with the dunes," Vesta said.

"Actually, Harper, I'd gladly battle those water snakes again right about now, just for a few minutes of cool comfort." Fiona laughed lightly as we reached the base of the marble hill.

Kerentrith was massive from up close, towering over us like a silent giant. The early afternoon sun cast its white glow against the broken walls and partially crumbled stairs. Birds chirped from the many trees that had grown out of the fertile soil beneath, splitting the alleys and squares open. Nature had taken its course, growing through the Iman-made structures with no regard for the architectural craftsmanship of an era long gone.

"Remember, we need to keep a low profile," Vesta murmured. "There could be daemons patrolling the area during the day."

"Unfortunately, Blaze, that means you don't go dragon unless we really don't have another choice," Jax added, and Blaze replied with a soft nod.

Pheng-Pheng stared at him, her amber eyes wide with wonder. "You're a dragon?"

"He doesn't look like one, does he?" Harper smirked. "He's what you Nerakians call a two-spirit, like the Adlets. He turns into a dragon, but you *really* need to get out of the way when that happens."

"Yeah, I'm kind of a big fella," Blaze replied.

"A gentle giant, you might say." Caia giggled. "Unless you get him mad."

"In which case, Pheng-Pheng, you run. You don't look back, you just run, as fast as you can," Fiona chimed in, prompting me to stifle a laugh. They were virtually demonizing the poor boy, just for fun. Judging by the blush in his cheeks, however, Blaze seemed to enjoy the attention. He was adorably shy and quiet by nature, and it was nice to see him come out of his shell once in a while, despite our dire circumstances. After all, daemons and Exiled Maras were still hunting us. And King Shaytan *really* wanted Blaze for himself.

"I'd love to see you turn," Pheng-Pheng breathed, unable to take her eyes off him.

The Ekar bird joined us from its flight, settling on Harper's right shoulder. It chirped briefly, its blue eyes looking up at the city. Vesta was the first to notice. "I think the Ekar spotted some-thing. Or someone."

Harper narrowed her eyes, following the bird's gaze. "Yeah, I see the air rippling in three different spots, three levels up. Daemons are lurking around. We should get out of sight before they spot us."

"Let's go around the hill. There's a back alley few creatures know of," Vesta replied, and guided her horse to the right.

We followed her around the hill, and Harper kept her eyes on the city above, using her True Sight to spot and count poten-tial hostiles. We reached a patch of trees with thick crowns and bright yellow blossoms. The smell was delightful, reminding me of the roses we had back on Calliope. For a brief moment, the thought of home sent a painful pang through my stomach. *Soon...*

"I can't see beyond the trees," Harper muttered, frowning slightly.

"It's a meranium wall," Vesta explained, as she guided us between the flowery trees. A white wall rose before us, a marble coat for the meranium obscuring Harper's True Sight. "They built one here and at a few other access points when the daemons first started snatching Imen from Kerentrith. They thought it would keep the monsters at bay for good."

"Little did they know, huh?" I replied with a scoff.

A large door was mounted in the middle, painted gray. "Also meranium," Harper said, nodding at it.

We all went quiet as Vesta listened closely. She gave me a brief glance over the shoulder, followed by a nod. "I don't hear anything," she whispered.

She then got off her horse and checked the lock, while we constantly looked around, checking for air ripples. Vesta took out a long, thin knife and used it to unlock the door. It turned open with a loud clang, and she cursed under her breath, frozen.

After about twenty seconds of absolute silence, except for the distant chirps of birds and the wind whispering from the west, she slowly pushed the door open.

A swish made my whole body tense, my muscles twitching as I recognized the sound.

"Vesta, get down," I hissed, relieved by the speed with which she obeyed my command.

An arrow shot out from the darkness beyond the door, missing her horse's leg by less than an inch.

"Out of the way," Jax breathed.

More arrows followed, just as we pulled to the sides. The air rippled as one invisible daemon emerged from beyond the door.

I jumped off my horse and drew my broadsword.

"We have company," I muttered, gritting my teeth.

We were getting into that daemon city, and daemons certainly weren't going to stop us.

18

HARPER

J ust as the first invisible daemon came through the door,
Pheng-Pheng and I jumped off the horse, along with the
rest of my team. Vesta swiftly rolled over to the side and
out of the daemon's way.

"You take his left, I'll take his right," I said to Pheng-Pheng,
and she replied with a brief nod, then drew her sword.

With my twin blades ready, I darted over to the daemon's
right side, as Pheng-Pheng rushed to the left. I caught a glimpse
of the creature's red eyes and launched my attack. His claws
caught one of my swords, and he was forced to block the second
one, too—giving Pheng-Pheng the momentum to drive her
sword through the fiend's neck.

Vesta unscrewed the cap from her water bladder and pulled
the liquid out with graceful guidance from one hand, using her
wrist and finger movements to coax it into a fine mist spreading
through the now-open door.

I heard gurgling as the first daemon collapsed on the ground with a thud. One down, four more to go—the mist counteracted the invisibility spell worn by the other fiends coming through the door. With flashing steps and swift moves, Hansa, Caspian, and Fiona tackled three of the remaining daemons.

Pheng-Pheng and I handled the fourth, while Blaze, Caia, and Vesta kept to the side, ready to intervene if needed. Our blades cut through the beasts' throats before they could call for help or sound an alarm. One by one, the daemons fell in pools of their own crimson blood, before Blaze and Caia dragged them off to the side.

We pulled large leaves from nearby bushes over their lifeless bodies and managed to hide them all from whomever might come along—friend or foe. "Hopefully, the rest of our incursion into Draconis will be just as discreet," Hansa whispered, panting slightly.

We hid the horses in a crevice to the side, and I ordered them to wait there for us, using my sentry "persuasion".

I peeked into the darkness beyond the open door, using my True Sight. "Coast is clear, for now," I said, then looked up. "There are more hostiles up on the first floor. They're not invisible, though. I bet they didn't hear or see us, yet."

"Either way, have your red lenses ready," Jax replied, then motioned to Vesta to lead the way inside.

I fumbled through one of my pockets and pulled two lenses out—after our mission in Shaytan's palace, I'd managed to hold onto a couple, adding strings so they could be tied around the head. I handed one to Pheng-Pheng, who stared at it with eyebrows raised.

"Not into the whole monocle thing," I muttered, and put mine on.

"I have no idea what you're talking about," she replied, and tied hers around her head as well.

"This single round lens was quite the fashion in the human world, back where we come from," Fiona said, making me smile. We'd studied the human history during our high school years, and we'd often laughed at men's fashion in the late nineteenth century. Seeing how the Druids were dressing up on Calliope made us laugh even harder—we got used to it, eventually, but it still brought a grin to my face once in a while, especially where accessories were concerned.

"Okay, what next?" Hansa asked, looking at Vesta.

"We go up to the palace," the young fae replied. "There are several shorter access routes into Draconis, but the one close to the city library is the best for what we need to do."

"I'm guessing the others are heavily guarded?" I asked, sheathing my swords.

"Precisely," Vesta replied, then went through.

We followed, one at a time, as she led us deeper into the narrow tunnel. It had been carved directly into the white marble base, its walls rounded and smoothed to perfection. Those daemon guards we'd just killed had probably been stationed there on a regular basis, since it was the closest entrance to ground level.

A cool draft howled through the passageway, giving us the much-needed cooldown we'd been thinking about since the Harvaris Desert.

"Oh, yeah, that's what I'm talking about," Jax nearly purred like an oversized cat, a grin splitting his face as he took his mask and hood off.

"I concur. I no longer feel like a steamed bun." I chuckled.

"We need to be ready for whatever comes ahead." Vesta

pulled us back to the present, still brimming with threats that awaited at the end of the tunnel. Nevertheless, it was nice to relish the chill for a few minutes, especially after a boiling ride through the desert.

"I suggest we cover ourselves, just in case," Jax replied with a low grumble. "Not sure how the sunset plays out on the first level of this city."

That said, he pulled the mask, hood, and goggles back on, as did the rest of our blood-drinking team members, myself included. I'd welcomed the nippy draft against my face, too, but it was time to get back to business.

Once we reached the door at the end, we all stilled, fingers gripping our weapons, as Vesta slowly picked the lock with her long knife. This time around, she was careful to avoid another resounding clang that might give away our presence here when lifting the latch. The upside was the absence of meranium in this part of the tunnel.

I scanned the area carefully, but my True Sight didn't reveal any movements, not even air ripples. "They must've moved farther away," I murmured. "There's no one out there waiting for us."

"Perfect," Vesta replied, and slowly pulled the door open.

We were on the first level of Kerentrith, on the edge of a small square, with four alleys leading deeper into the city and one connecting it to the dry plains from which we'd come. The roads were narrow, paved with white, cubic stones, and snaked through large buildings with beautiful, ornate facades. Most of the windows were broken, but the colorful frames remained— although their intricate patterns had somewhat faded with the passage of time.

Large, brick-red flower pots had once held ornamental trees, lining the square. They were all shattered—not by violence, but rather by the growth of said trees into giants with rich, flowery crowns that stretched all over, blocking most of the sun. Using my True Sight, I noticed the natural pattern repeating itself up the roads and on higher levels, too. Nature had taken over this place, for the most part. The skeleton had been adopted from Kerentrith, beautifully crafted white marble structures that still stood, despite the overall damage. The flesh, however, was made up of thick trees, lush bushes, and an explosion of flowers in a myriad of dazzling colors—a quiet, tropical paradise nestled between the white marble walls of a city that had lost its people.

It was sad and beautiful, at the same time. Small animals scurried around—rodents and birds, mostly, but I also spotted a few deer-like creatures chewing on the bark of trees nearby.

Vesta took one of the alleys leading farther up into the city, and we followed, quietly marveling at the eerie symbiosis between artificial and natural structures. "This would be a gorgeous tourist destination," Fiona muttered. "You know how the humans back on Earth visit the ancient Greek ruins, for example? This is even better. It's lush and vibrant. Beautiful."

"And what a glorious past it holds," Vesta replied with a sigh.

"Yeah, I'd pay good money to come here," Blaze chimed in. "If I weren't a dragon, hunted by daemons so they could eat my freakin' soul."

"I see the tourism potential," I said, then chuckled softly. "Think about it this way, Blaze. When all the daemons are vanquished and the Nerakians get their lives back, surely you wouldn't mind bringing Caia here on a date, right? I can already see a candlelight dinner in the middle of one of these squares, a dude playing a slow, romantic violin..."

"I'm swooning already." Fiona giggled.

The flustered looks on Blaze and Caia's faces were hilarious, to say the least. They both glowed pink and gold—clearly crushing on each other, but embarrassed that we'd called them out on it. *That's what friends are for, anyway!*

"Don't let them get to you," Jax told Blaze, then gave Fiona and me a playful wink. "Girls can be *mean*."

Caia couldn't even look us in the eye. Either she was too focused on our hostile surroundings, or I owed her a hug and a mild apology later. But, in my defense, Caia and Blaze had been orbiting around each other for ages. It was about damn time they got together, sooner rather than later.

"I don't know, it does sound pretty cool to dine and chill here," Blaze replied with a nonchalant shrug. I had to give it to the dragon: he knew how to keep a straight face, despite his reddened cheeks. He even surprised Caia with that remark. She gawked at him for a good half minute before we reached the palace square.

"Yeah, provided we clean the daemons out first." I chuckled, then came to a stop, gazing at the magnificent structure rising ahead. "Whoa. Looks even better from up close."

The royal palace was something out of a fairytale, with hundreds of bedrooms and banquet halls. Sculptures of godlike creatures of legend adorned the façade, and pieces of stained glass were still covering some of the windows. Greenery had spread across the walls, pale yellow blossoms opening up to welcome the afternoon sun. A set of wide stairs guarded by white marble statues of warriors, heroes of times long gone, led up to the front terrace.

We covered our heads as we left the shade of nearby trees and followed Vesta to the side of the titanic building, its towers capturing a pale pink hue as the sun moved to set into the west. "There's a service entrance farther ahead. The least traveled path is usually the one lacking guards," Vesta said. "The daemons have had control of this place for a very long time, but I've studied the blueprints over and over."

"Where'd you get the blueprints from?" I replied, scanning the area.

"They keep copies in a tiny library down in Azure Heights," she said. "The Maras don't even know they have them."

"So you've been to their city," Hansa murmured.

Vesta gave her a quick, slightly amused glance over the shoulder. "Of course," she replied. "I used to sneak in through one of the many secret tunnels. Before they sealed them, that is. I like to know what the enemy is up to at all times."

"Well, that's definitely one way of keeping your enemies close, I guess," I said.

Vesta took us to a small side door covered in wild greenery. Judging by the amount of dust collected on the brass knob, no one had used it in ages. She picked the lock and went in. I followed, quietly joined by the rest of our team, while the Ekar was firmly anchored to my backpack—side note, I'd never seen a bird as discreet and as obedient as Ramin. I was impressed. I'd tried leaving the Ekar with Pheng-Pheng a couple of times, since she'd trained it, but the bird insisted on staying with me.

We went deeper into the palace, using the dark service corridors. My True Sight helped us steer clear of areas where daemons were patrolling. There weren't too many of them, only two dozen, but we really needed to keep a low profile if we were going to infiltrate Draconis completely undetected.

"There's an old passageway connecting the royal library to

the daemon city below," Vesta whispered as we crossed one of the banquet halls.

The walls were covered in gold leaf and gemstone mosaics, muffled by layers of dirt and dust. Ancient brass candelabra lay lonely on top of large marble tables, with more wild greenery stretching across the floor and working its way up the corners, toward the domed ceiling. I could only imagine the gloriously lavish balls they must've held in this place.

"Isn't it guarded?" I asked, just as we entered the enormous library.

It was home to thousands of abandoned books and scrolls, resting beneath inches of dust on wooden shelves, built into the walls. The entire library was divided into sections by floor-to-ceiling partitions, filled with more works of Nerakian literature. It was dark, with barely a few rays peeking in through several windows at the very end of the hall.

"These all look in great shape after all these years," Fiona murmured, getting closer to a shelf. "They should've been mush and dust after thousands of years."

"The Imen stole some swamp witch preservation spells a long time ago, Fiona. They had to preserve these ancient writings in case they were gone... The daemons don't know about this place, though," Vesta replied, then pointed at a set of double doors, subtly obscured by one of the partitions. "That'll be a good refuge to use, going forward. You know, to sleep in, and rest, if needed. It's a circular hall with several rooms, and we could cloak it with some swamp witch magic, once I get the spell from one of my pacifist friends below."

"That's a great idea," Hansa replied. "In case we have to hide once we get what we came for."

"This is one of the less-circulated areas of the palace. There's no known access tunnel to Draconis around here, so the guards don't usually patrol these parts," Vesta added, then pointed at the end of the library corridor. "Over there."

We reached the end of the hall and went behind one of the last wooden partitions, where vines with thick, waxy leaves had grown over the entire corner, stretching out onto the wall. Vesta took her knife out and cut some of the greenery off, clearing a section of shelves loaded with large, leather-bound books and decorative brass goblets.

She looked at me, grinning, as she pulled one of the cups toward her. It didn't come off the shelf entirely, and I understood then that it was a secret lever. It clicked once she brought it down to a horizontal position, and the entire wall section shuddered. Dust rolled out, released by the movement after scores of years.

"Secret passageway, huh?" I smirked.

Vesta nodded, then pushed the shelves forward as the secret library door moved back. The wheels at the bottom screeched and scratched against the marble floor, echoing through the library. I instantly looked around, using my True Sight to check whether any of the daemon guards out there had heard the ruckus—there weren't any hostiles on our level, and the ones on the top floor didn't seem to notice, either.

I breathed a sigh of relief. Vesta led us into the dark corridor waiting beyond the faux shelves. "This will take us down into Draconis," she said. "There was a time, long before the Imen abandoned Kerentrith, when daemons used to smuggle stuff through a series of secret tunnels. This was ages ago, before the Maras even got here. During periods of war, the Imen set some smuggling routes with the daemons. Each side had something precious that the other needed. Despite the fighting, the Imen and daemons found some common ground where certain foods and valuable goods were concerned. The daemons longed for the Imen's fine silks and jewelry, for example, while the Imen needed the red garnet and obsidian found below. This was one of those secret routes, sealed off before the arrival of the Maras, after the last peace treaty between daemons and Imen was signed."

A circular staircase unraveled before us, spiraling down into the ground. The stone walls were covered in moss, and we had to constantly tear through layers of cobwebs as we descended.

"So, daemons and Imen smuggled stuff behind the royals' backs, right inside the palace?" I concluded with a grin. "That's absolute badassery."

"It all fell apart when the Maras came here," Vesta replied. "As soon as they grounded that Druid delegation and got their claws on swamp magic, that was it. The deadly alliance formed, and the rest of us were doomed."

Thinking of all the lives ruined and lost tore me apart on the inside. I channeled my rage into sharp focus, while secretly listening to Caspian's heartbeats. He belonged to a species that had wreaked havoc in this world, and felt horribly about it. He wasn't like any of the Exiled Maras, and I knew how badly he wanted to prove that, how desperate he was to completely distance himself from the others.

I was determined to help him achieve that, and more. At the end of this staircase was the answer to many of our most burning questions and, potentially, the key to earning our freedom and *his* freedom, too. Once we managed to get the swamp witch back, it would be over for the Maras of Azure Heights.

My heart swelled with excitement at the thought of watching Darius and the others swallowing their sneers and paying for their horrendous crimes. Especially for what they'd done to

Caspian and his family. We were going to bring this back full circle, by removing the Maras from the Nerakian landscape and subduing the daemons. That seemed like the most logical and least intrusive path, since every species of Neraka had its purpose to serve, including the horned fiends.

19

CAIA

"**D**o you think there will ever be peace again between the daemons and the Imen?" I asked, using my lighter flame to guide me down the stairs, while Blaze covered my six.

"I don't know," Vesta replied with a shrug. "They might, if the daemons agree to a solid peace treaty. Assuming, of course, that they'll be too scared of GASP to try anything silly. I'm thinking that once we get your people here, it'll be game over for them and the Exiled Maras."

"Absolutely," Jax said, then scoffed. "I doubt the Exiled Maras will get another shot at a new beginning, not after all this. No one thought they would devolve into worse creatures through exile. But they definitely don't belong in this world. I will person ally make sure that their punishment fits their crime."

"And the same goes for the daemons," Hansa added. "Yes, GASP will definitely help set some clear rules. I'm sure the Daughters and the witches of The Shade will gladly work together to establish permanent portals to monitor Neraka going forward. Rest assured, Vesta, that what they've been doing up until now will stop once we get our people through."

"Maybe, once this is all over, I'll even find my parents. Who knows?" Vesta replied, exhaling deeply.

"You don't remember them at all, do you?" I asked.

"No, just mild snippets. A pair of green eyes, a soft smile, but nothing precise," she said. "I don't even know if they're still alive. They might be. The daemons wouldn't waste a good soul meal. Apparently, us fae are quite the delicacy, like the dragons."

"Yeah, don't remind me," Blaze muttered from behind me.

"On the other hand, they could very well be dead," Vesta added. "Maybe they didn't make it. I try not to get my hopes up, of course."

We kept going for about an hour, carefully, as the temperature started to rise again—a sign that we were approaching the daemon city.

"What's the plan, Vesta?" Jax asked. "I assume we have some heavy challenges ahead."

"This tunnel deadends behind a large stone, from what I've read about it," Vesta replied. "And the stone is just around the corner from one of the cloaked entrances into the city. There's a network of corridors surrounding Draconis on different levels, all cloaked and guarded. There will be a guard there, and I'll need his blood to get us through."

"That's easily doable," Harper said. "And your pacifist connections?"

"One will be there to greet and guide us."

The bottom of the tunnel was riddled with spiderwebs and dried-up weeds, and we had to claw our way out of it—in Harper and Fiona's case, literally. They hacked and slashed at the clutter until we all got out, and reached the massive stone that Vesta had mentioned. I had to admit, she kept good and accurate notes on the place.

Harper used her True Sight to look through the stone without having to reveal her presence, and confirmed Vesta's knowledge of the guard's position. "There's one daemon, visible, sitting by the wall, twenty feet straight ahead," she whispered.

"Would you like to do the honors?" Caspian breathed, giving her a soft smile.

"It would be my pleasure." Harper grinned, then went out and caught the daemon off guard. She rammed both swords through his torso, through the sides and right where his chest plate didn't provide any cover.

Pheng-Pheng shot out next and finished the job, plunging her blade deep into the daemon's throat. Blood gushed out as the life left his gleaming red eyes. We all came out from our hiding spot, and Vesta smeared some of the daemon's blood on her hand, which she then pressed against the warm limestone wall.

The surface rippled, and we followed her inside.

Another tunnel lay ahead, larger and made entirely from black stone. We drew our weapons, ready to fight, if needed, as Vesta led the way to the very end. We stopped in front of an iron door. Vesta knocked in a specific pattern—three times fast, twice slow, then three times fast again.

A loud clang made my muscles stiffen, and I flicked my lighters open out of sheer reflex.

The door opened. Vesta smiled, prompting us all to breathe a collective sigh of relief, at the sight of a tall daemon—he seemed to be well into adulthood, with fine lines forming at the corners of his red eyes. His black hair had white streaks and was combed back into a tight bun, and his leather tunic stretched over his muscular chest and thighs. He was big and burly, but the look on his face was soft and gentle.

"You made it," the daemon breathed, and offered a hand.

Vesta shook it firmly, then nodded back at us. "Yeah, we had a slight detour to make, but good news, Davo. There are still some Manticores out there," she replied.

Davo looked at our group, measuring each of us from head to toe. His eyebrows popped up at the sight of Pheng-Pheng, whose expression was stuck in a permanent frown, the kind that said "I'll kill you if you make the wrong move".

"I'm impressed," Davo said, and offered a curt bow. "Where do you come from, little Manticore?"

"The Akrep Gorge," Pheng-Pheng replied dryly.

Davo smiled. "Good. It means help is not too far away, if needed. And is that... That's an Ekar, isn't it?" He pointed at the bird still clutching to Harper's backpack, visibly amused.

"I take it you don't see them often?" Harper replied, while the bird watched Davo curiously.

"Not in these parts," Davo said, then frowned. "But, anyway, we need to get you all someplace safe. Guards patrol this part of the city quite frequently, since word of the outsiders escaping spread."

"Oh, that would be us." Hansa chuckled, sheathing her broadsword and crossing her arms. Davo gave her a brief glance before shifting his focus back to Vesta.

"Are you sure you want to do this, little fae?" he asked. "My brothers and I have risked our lives for peace. I don't want us to jump into anything unprepared and get ourselves killed. Get myself killed, to be precise."

I couldn't take my eyes off Davo. His features seemed oddly familiar, as if I'd seen him before.

"Who are your brothers?" Hansa asked, narrowing her eyes at him. Judging by her expression, she was probably on the same wavelength as me.

"Mose and Beryn. Mose lives in Infernis, and Beryn is here, on the other side of the city."

"Mose... Oh, dear," Hansa replied, pressing her lips into a tight, thin line.

Alarm quickly settled on Davo's face. "What is it? Do you know him? Is something wrong?"

"Ugh, I wish I didn't have to say this. I'm sorry, Davo," Hansa replied softly. "Mose was arrested a couple of days back, and we don't know if he's still alive or not."

A couple of moments went by as Davo crumbled through all the stages following such terrible news, shaking like a leaf. He was bigger than his brother in size, but small and squirrely in character, compared to the calm and composed Mose.

"This can't be. No, what will I do without him?" Davo said, his lower lip trembling as tears gathered in his eyes. "I knew this was going to happen. I wanted to do this, to do right by this world. We knew the risks, but still. This is all too real. It's really happening. They took my brother, and they'll probably come for me and Beryn next!"

"Davo, we need to get out of sight," Vesta replied, trying to rein him in before he caved in completely.

"No, no, no. I can't. My brother, they have my brother," Davo muttered, his gaze frantically darting around as a full-on panic attack set in. My heart tightened in my chest with both grief and fear—the former aimed at the loss of his brother, and the latter due to the fact that we were standing in front of an access point leading in and out of Draconis. "No, I can't. It's not too late for me. I can go back to my hut and mind my own business, and not get involved in any of this anymore."

Caspian took over the conversation, firmly gripping the daemon's shoulders—which meant raising his arms and tilting his head back a little, so he could look Davo in the eyes. "Snap the hell out of it, Davo! Your brother would slap you silly if he were here right now," he said. "Mose is willing to give his life to restore peace to this world. He was taken away for it, too. If you back out now, his sacrifice will have been in vain. Will you let your brother die for nothing, or will you pick up the torch and carry the fight forward, to honor him and every other pacifist out there?"

Red blotches bloomed on Caspian's face, his skin burning as he broke his blood oath to speak those words. Davo blinked several times, stunned by both Caspian's encouragement and his body's reaction. "You're under a blood oath," he murmured.

"Yes. And I will gladly burn, if it helps to put an end to this senseless massacre of innocent people and noble ideals," Caspian grunted. "I'm here, fighting for everyone's freedom. Mose did the same, and more. He's gone now, but you're still standing. And you can help us."

"We are so close, Davo," Vesta chimed in, while Harper moved closer and gently pulled Caspian back, pained by the burns already healing on the Mara's face. "So close! You see these people?" she said, pointing at us. "They've come from very far away to help us. They have powerful armies, witches and dragons that will end this horror incredibly fast. But we need to get the swamp witch out of the daemons' reach, first. We need the pacifists' help. We need *your* help!"

Davo stared at us for a little while, contemplating his options as he gradually calmed down. I couldn't see anything past the massive black wall behind him, but I had a feeling I'd see something akin to Infernis beyond it—black buildings and streets, amber flames and daemons swarming through the place.

"You have dragons?" Davo asked, wiping his tears with the back of his hand.

"Guilty as charged," Blaze replied, smiling as he raised his hand. "If we get the swamp witch back, we'll take down whatever shield the daemons have put up, and more of my people will come and put a stop to all the violence and abuse."

"And witches?" Davo added, nodding slowly.

"Powerful beings that can virtually reshape the fate of Neraka with a handful of spells," Harper said. "And Druids, and jinn, and other creatures that have been living in peace and harmony for years. We've been doing this for a long time, Davo. Our mission is to restore the balance of this world, and we don't make a habit of failing."

"Davo, Caspian is right," Jax replied. "You don't want your brother's sacrifice to be for nothing. Help us. Mose fought as best as he could for this. You're here, now, which simply tells me that you want to do the same. I understand that you're afraid, too, but that's okay. We're all afraid. And yet, we've come down to do our part."

"I promise you that, once it's all over, we'll make sure that you, Beryn, and all the other daemon pacifists are given an active role in rebuilding the daemon society," Hansa added. "We're very close, Davo. But we need heroes like you to get us through to the next stage of our mission."

Davo took a deep breath, regaining his composure. He straightened his back and turned his attention to Vesta with a look of newfound determination on his face. "What do you need me to do?" he asked. "I can offer shelter, and get you through the outer parts of the city."

"I need you to take us to Velnias," Vesta replied.

"He's smack in the middle of Draconis," Davo scoffed. "You're not making this easy at all."

"It's not meant to be easy," Vesta shot back. "Velnias has the information we need. And the clearance to get us into the upper-echelon parts of the prison."

"And I can't just waltz in there with outsiders under my coat!" Davo hissed.

"Figure something out." Vesta held her ground. "Come on, Davo. We're not leaving until we get what we came for. Either pitch in, or run off. If you do run off, however, do it after you take us to Velnias. It is literally the least you can do to honor your fallen brother."

We'd tried the soft approach, but, in the end, it seemed that Vesta's tough love was what really got Davo motivated. "Fine. I'll take you to Velnias. But you all follow my lead, and do exactly what I tell you."

"Deal!" Vesta replied with a satisfied smirk. "Okay, now that Davo has seen us, it's time to gobble up some invisibility paste and get cracking—"

Five daemons came through the door behind us, probably returning from guard duty outside. We would've used the invisibility paste sooner, but, as Vesta had advised us, we had needed to let Davo see us first, and understand who he was helping.

"Crap," Harper muttered, then drew her swords.

The daemons growled and immediately charged us, their sharp rapiers eager to slice us open. Harper and Caspian teamed up against two of them, with Pheng-Pheng dashing between them, looking for the right moment and angle to deliver her deadly sting. Jax and Hansa took on the other two, as Fiona joined in to finish the job. Blaze and I took the fifth daemon, while Vesta pulled Davo away from the scuffle.

I fashioned a sword from pure fire, thrilled to see my control over its form improve with each draw. Blaze used his sword to block the fiend's blows, and I lunged forward, then slid on my knees and drove my fire blade upward, straight through the daemon's chest and throat.

The sound of his flesh searing made my skin crawl. Blaze kicked him back. The daemon fell to the ground, then gave his last breath. Fiona rammed her sword through one daemon's back, then brought out her knife and slit his throat. He landed flat on his face, lifeless, with Fiona on top of him, while Jax and Hansa swiftly disabled the third one.

Harper and Caspian had a good handle on the other two, until Pheng-Pheng snuck up behind one and stung him with her scorpion tail. It was enough to distract the daemon, and for Harper to drive both swords through his chest. Caspian managed to take care of the last one, dodging his sword attacks before he could slice the fiend's throat open with an elegant and swift backhand.

As fearful as I'd been of daemons before, the more I fought them and vanquished them, the more confident I got. Daemons fought well, and they were insanely fast and vicious, but, with a little bit of practice and a good extra reason to stay alive, I fought better.

I straightened my back, then smiled at my extra reason, whose midnight eyes found me as he sheathed his sword. With Blaze by my side, I was perfectly okay with burning the entire city of Draconis down, if that's what it took to get our swamp witch and our freedom back.

20

HARPER

W e dragged the bodies out of sight, dumping them behind a nearby rock, then used their supply of invisibility paste, keeping ours for later. I gave some of the paste to the Ekar, as well—the bird trusted me, and gobbled it up. "Stay close to me," I whispered, using my mind control on Ramin, just to make sure he'd obey. The bird blinked several times, then pulled the zipper on my backpack and slipped inside. Caspian zipped it back up, chuckling as the Ekar settled inside.

One by one, we vanished, but we had the red lenses on us to keep track of each other—thanks to the swamp witches' magic skills, the invisibility spell was designed to protect the individual and hide everything he or she wore or touched. The moment one of us touched a red lens, for example, it also became protected by the invisibility spell, without affecting its function. This little side benefit came in handy in our situation, since we could pick up weapons and other useful objects along the way, without anyone seeing them just float around.

Davo fumbled through his tunic pockets and took out his lens, then put it on so he could see us, too. "You people are vicious," he said.

"We had some practice on our way here," I replied, smirking. "I mean, sorry if any of them were your friends, but, you know, we're pretty much at war here."

"No, no, that's fine. I completely understand," Davo replied, shaking his head. "I'm just impressed. Didn't know any of those guys, but I've never seen anyone fight them the way you people do. I thought daemons were the fiercest of warriors."

"Seriously?" Pheng-Pheng shot back, raising her eyebrows and crossing her arms.

Davo's forehead smoothed, his eyes wide as he realized what he'd just said, with a Manticore standing right in front of him. "I thought you were all extinct, little Manticore. My apologies," he said. "Now, let's take you crazy folk to Velnias. Follow me, and stay close. Watch out for other red lenses, too."

"Yeah, we know the drill, thanks," I replied, then followed him along the side of the black wall. A set of stairs led us onto the ground floor of the city.

The wall itself faded into the ground at the bottom, revealing Draconis in all its frightening glory. It was an enormous dome carved into the black stone, with a permanent orange glow from the lava lakes surrounding it, stretching for hundreds of miles.

"We managed to get in and out of Shaytan's palace, after all," Jax added.

"While I find that impressive, to say the least, you'll soon learn that Draconis is drastically different," Davo replied, walking up an alley that led deep into the heart of the city.

It *looked* different, compared to Infernis.

Thousands of obsidian boxes covered dozens of square miles, with a network of narrow streets between them. I couldn't see inside them because of the meranium panels on the inside, but they were laid out in a circular pattern, with several observation towers scattered across the city, probably for guards to keep an eye out. From what I could tell with my True Sight, there were several areas with open spaces, fenced with black stone walls and rolls of barbed meranium wire at the top—similar to prison yards.

In the middle, there was a massive square block with thousands of small windows. I couldn't see inside, most likely because it was made of meranium, despite its obsidian façade. Daemons didn't make a habit of hiding something in meranium unless they wanted it fully secured and protected from outside influences. There were symbols carved into the metal skeleton of the building, as well as the smaller boxes throughout the city, most likely swamp witch magic. I recognized some of the writing from Shaytan's palace—specifically the meranium box in which they'd kept Blaze and Caia.

Death claws flew overhead, hissing and screeching as they monitored movement on the ground. Daemon guards patrolled the streets. The closer we got to the main prison building, the more daemons we saw, as well as giant generals with collared pit wolves.

Four giant columns connected the ground to the domed ceiling, strategically built on the north, south, east, and west edges of the city, just before the lava lakeshores. They weren't just support pillars, holding the ceiling up there—stairs were carved into them, spiraling all the way up. "Those are access routes into Kerentrith, right?" I asked.

Davo nodded. "The main access routes, to be precise. The living quarters are on the outskirts of the city, mainly on the north and west sides," he then explained, keeping his voice low as we walked. I did a quick scan of the area, looking for red lenses on any of the daemons, but the ones wearing some were farther to the east, and around the main building. We were in the clear for the time being. "That big building in the middle is the main penitentiary. We keep the common folk there."

"Define 'common folk'," Jax murmured, staying close to Hansa, right behind me, followed by Caia and Blaze. Fiona, Caspian, Pheng-Pheng, and I kept to the front, with Davo and Vesta leading the way.

"It's for Imen, mostly," Davo replied. "We keep some of the lower-level daemons there, too. The ones who break the laws. Thieves and killers, mostly. It's the main feeding ground for soul consumption."

"Aside from the fact that the whole soul-eating part still creeps the hell out of me," I said, "I'm impressed to learn that daemons imprison their thieves and killers. However, for the sake of clarity, killers of what, exactly? Because I doubt it's Imen, since your people love sucking the literal life out of them."

Davo scoffed, bitterly amused. "You are well entitled to ask that question. Daemons who steal from and kill other daemons. That is against our rule of law. We do not kill our own unless we have to. Unless they were sentenced to death. Unless they attack first."

"What about the smaller boxes?" I asked. "They're all made of meranium and inscribed with swamp witch charms."

"Those are private prison cells," Davo replied. "Daemon traitors—pacifists, such as myself—get private spaces. Other creatures, too. Exiled Maras we come across, who do not adhere to the alliance. Rogue Adlets, before they go into training."

"Training?" Hansa repeated, her brow furrowed.

Davo sighed, his shoulders slumping. "Pit wolves aren't born pit wolves. They're Adlets, taken from their packs. They're put in private cells and deprived of food and light of any kind, for a long time. Then they apply a series of swamp witch spells that eventually force them to transform. Their eyes turn red, and they lose their hair and their ability to shift back to bipedal form. Eventually they lose their minds, and then they get the collars and lose their free will, too."

My stomach sank, bile threatening to work its way up, as I realized the amount of cruelty inflicted on Adlets in order to turn them into pit wolves. Sleep, light, and food deprivation. Then torture through magic, chipping away at their very essence until all that's left of them are mindless, broken beasts. Tears made my sight hazy. I wiped them away, cursing under my breath. I put my red lens back on.

"Daemons need to go through the same ordeal," I breathed. "Each and every one of them."

"It's horrible, I know," Davo replied, and I could hear the sadness in his voice. "It's one of the reasons I started passing messages around for the pacifists, and ended up supporting them."

"Oh, wow. Jack!" Caia gasped. "Scarlett's new friend. He's an Adlet, then."

"Imagine her surprise, once they find an Adlet pack in Lagerith," I scoffed. "Man, it's going to break her heart, for sure. The poor thing."

"No wonder he was so eager to help her," Caia said, and I

could see the grief glowing out of her in painful shades of soft red.

"So traitors get special treatment, then?" Jax asked, steering the conversation back to the boxes.

"Yes. Thing is, the private cells are like luxury meals for the daemon lords and royalty," Davo explained. "The rest of us feed off the souls of the common folk. Daemon traitors, Adlets, rogue Maras, and other creatures are kept in private cells."

"What other creatures?" Jax replied. "Dhaxanians? Manticores?"

"Probably. I'm not sure," Davo said, shrugging. "Technically speaking, I'm not allowed this deep into the city. I don't know who else they're holding in here. I'm only allowed in the penitentiary, and there are separate, designated corridors to access that. This is as far as I can go, I'm afraid."

He stopped, then stepped to the side. I spotted a red lens daemon coming in from the east side. "Hold that thought, Davo," I whispered. "We need to go around the corner here for a few seconds."

Caspian followed my gaze, spotting the red lens daemon, then nodded and followed me behind the nearest obsidian box, along with the rest of our team.

"What do *I* do?" Davo hissed, suddenly left on his own, out front.

"Pretend you're waiting for someone," I shot back, then hid behind the box, just as the red lens daemon reached the alley and walked up toward the penitentiary—now less than a mile away from our location.

He sized Davo up and frowned. "What are *you* doing here?" he grumbled at Davo, who instantly straightened his back.

"Nothing. Just waiting for a friend to finish his shift," Davo replied, his voice trembling slightly. He was clearly intimidated by the red lens daemon. I figured the higher-ranked daemons were feared among the others in the city.

"Don't hover around for too long. You're not supposed to be here," the daemon retorted, then continued his walk up the road. I inched forward, enough to see him turn a corner farther up the road, and out of sight. Breathing a sigh of relief, I came out of hiding and gave Davo a friendly pat on his massive back.

"Well done," I quipped. "Now, tell me more about why this is as far as you go."

"Didn't you hear that guy?" Davo shot back, genuinely worried. *He's no Mose, that's for sure.* "I'm not allowed here. I guard the penitentiary, not the private cells. They're very strict about this, and I don't want to end up on the other side of a cell door. Trust me, our prisons are not a good place to be."

"So what do we do now, then?" Vesta replied with a frown.

Davo pointed at a box sixty feet up the main road. It was only then that I noticed the small number plates mounted on the western corner of each private cell box. That one was number 132. "Go to Cell 132," he said. "You'll find Velnias in there. I hear there's a new prisoner coming in there today, and Velnias likes to greet them personally. He's in charge of this entire block."

"Wait, Velnias is a warden here?" Vesta asked, her eyebrows raised with surprise. I found her reaction somewhat alarming.

"I thought you knew whom we're supposed to meet," I said.

"I do! I just didn't know he got promoted," she replied. "Last time I spoke to him myself, he was still somewhere on the outskirts of Draconis, cleaning the pit wolf kennels for a living."

"Oh, no," Davo sighed, then pursed his lips. "Velnias moved

quickly through the ranks. Now he looks after this entire block, and, from what I hear, he's quite good at his job. Which is why I'm still finding it hard to believe that he's a pacifist. Rumor has it he's a sadist."

"Most daemons are sadists," I said.

"That being said, are you sure we can trust him, Vesta?" Jax replied, crossing his arms.

Vesta nodded firmly. "Absolutely. I personally vouch for him."

"You shouldn't vouch for anyone in this city. Not even me," Davo said bitterly, shaking his head. "Anyway, Cell 132. Good luck. I'm out, before anyone else spots me here."

"Thank you, Davo," Vesta murmured, giving him a warm smile. "Your brother would be proud."

Davo didn't wait a second longer, and rushed back to the edge of the city. Just in time, too, as more daemon guards emerged from around the corner. Luckily, none were wearing red lenses. "Stand still," I whispered.

We all froze, quietly watching as the daemons patrolled down the street, cackling and trading crude jokes as they passed us. I exhaled sharply once they turned another corner, and got out of sight.

"Okay, then," Fiona said, wearing a sarcastically bright smile. "Let's find out what's behind door number 132!"

Davo's warning to Vesta had left me with a churning stomach. What if he was right? What if Velnias couldn't be trusted after all? What if he'd been turned back on the daemons' side, seduced with "luxury" souls and riches?

There was only one way to find out. We had to check it out ourselves.

Arming myself with courage and determination, and stealing a glance from Caspian for good measure, I nodded and boldly walked up the road toward Cell 132. "Let's do this."

Fingers crossed, I guess.

21

HARPER

We made our way up to the door of Cell 132, still unseen and wearing our red lenses. I briefly checked my backpack, to find the Ekar nestled and perfectly quiet inside. Ramin was truly a phenomenon. I made a mental note to check again later.

To my relief, there wasn't much movement in the main alley, but I could hear three voices inside. The meranium box was charmed, and, since I couldn't see through its walls, I only had my hearing to rely on.

"I don't care whose arms you have to twist, just make sure he gets fresh meat every morning," Velnias barked.

The door burst wide open, prompting us to take a couple of steps back, then freeze as he gazed around the street. Velnias wore a military-style leather tunic, and he was twice the size of the two guards who followed him outside—both signs of his ranking superiority, along with the genuine fear imprinted on the other daemons' faces.

"Yes, sire," one of the guards replied.

"He may be a prisoner, but he's important," Velnias muttered, his hands behind his back. "We need to make sure he's well fed. You never know how the succession order changes these days, if Shaytan's in a horrid mood. I've seen him kill some of his sons for less. He's clearly attached to this one. If, by some miracle—or, in others' views, disaster—this one ends up being next in line for the crown, I certainly want to make sure I'm on his good side."

"Yes, sire," the second guard said, nodding firmly.

Velnias came across as abrasive and demanding, and, judging by the look on his face, cruelty was definitely one of his main traits. There was a glimmer I'd seen in creatures like him before—the spark of someone who'd inflicted great damage on others and didn't mind doing it again. It filled me with doubt as to his usefulness in our mission.

We stood there, quietly, watching and listening as he instructed the guards on how to keep the new prisoner secured *and* pleased—both equally important to him, it seemed. "If he requires a soul, speak to Mavis in the penitentiary," Velnias said. "I hear he's into eating the souls of murderers. I'm pretty sure Mavis can fix someone up for him."

"Yes, sire."

"And don't get too close to him," Velnias added. "Keep at least five feet of distance from him. He's extremely fast."

Noises up the road made him turn his head to find the source. His eyebrows arched upward at the sight of a small military convoy. A red glimmer caught my eye, and I instantly dashed over to our left, behind the meranium box. The rest of my team followed, and we hid from the two red lens daemons leading the convoy.

There were eleven of them in total—two at the front with red lenses, six carrying a massive, covered cage, and two at the back, their weapons and shields out, closing the ranks. At the very front walked Cayn, the first of King Shaytan's sons, his chin up and an insufferable smirk stretching his thin lips.

He was a handsome devil, I had to admit, but with so much evil oozing out of him, along with that irksome sneer, I couldn't look at him with anything other than disgust. He carried himself with great pride, half of his well-built frame covered in a luxurious black leather cape, gold medals around his thick neck, and a bejeweled scabbard attached to his narrow waist.

"There he is," Velnias muttered, visibly irritated. I had a feeling he wasn't too fond of Cayn—and he wasn't making an effort to hide that. At all. "Prince Cayn, I didn't think I'd see you here."

The convoy stopped in front of the open meranium box, and the daemon guards lowered the covered cage to the ground. Cayn placed his hands on his hips in a confident pose. "I had to deliver him myself." He smirked. "This is the first time I get to put a brother in jail. I couldn't deprive myself of such a pleasure."

"Ah, true. Your father prefers slitting your brothers' throats, instead," Velnias retorted, pursing his lips.

Cayn chuckled. "He's got plenty of them. I doubt they'll be missed."

"I imagine their mothers might think differently."

"And who gives a damn about what they think?" Cayn spat. "They're well dressed, well fed, and treated like queens for the rest of their lives. That's more than any other daemon female could possibly dream of, in this land. They're baby-making animals, nothing more."

My hands balled into fists. I struggled with the urge to go out there and punch his face until there was nothing left but a shapeless, bloody mass of broken bones and torn muscles. Caspian put a hand on my shoulder, then squeezed gently. We'd only just met, and yet he already knew what was bound to push my buttons. How could I not fall for the guy?

"I'd love to hear you say that to your own mother," Velnias replied with a grin, then changed the subject before Cayn could snap into an aneurism. "I trust he's well behaved, Your Grace?"

Cayn glanced over his shoulder, scoffing at the covered cage. "Like a collared pit wolf," he said. "I doubt he'll give you any trouble."

"Do you have any leverage on him? You know, in case he decides to pull a fast one on us. I hear he's quite resourceful," Velnias asked.

"Father said not to, but I made sure nonetheless to let this scoundrel know what will happen to his mother if he irks me," Cayn said, crossing his arms.

Velnias nodded firmly, then motioned for his two guards to attend to the cage. "Don't just stand there, you stooges! Uncover the box, and let's put our... *guest* into his new home!"

"Just make sure all the charms are in place," Cayn replied. "He's a cunning bastard and knows his way around the swamp witch magic."

The two guards took their positions on both sides of the cage, then pulled the cover back, revealing Zane, the Seventh Prince. I held my breath, but Fiona barely managed to stifle a gasp, and quickly covered her mouth. We all stared at the cage, our eyes nearly popping out as we peeked from behind the corner.

Zane grinned at the sight of Velnias, then casually stood up and put his hands out, while the guards removed the lock and opened the cage. "Velnias! Last time I saw you, you were cleaning up pit wolf crap in these kennels," Zane said matter-of-factly. "I see your dedication has finally paid off to a better position."

"And better benefits, too, Your Grace," Velnias replied, bowing reverently.

Cayn rolled his eyes. "Oh, please, spare me the faux pleasantries. Zane is a criminal. He's no royalty."

"I'm sorry to disappoint you, Your Grace, but, shackles or not, he is still the son of a king," Velnias said, his voice smooth and sweet as honey, the complete opposite of his acid sneer. He really didn't like Cayn and couldn't resist any opportunity to make Shaytan's firstborn feel miserable. Velnias may have been a sadist, as per Davo's words, but he seemed like *my* kind of sadist.

"You can kiss his ass all you want, Velnias," Cayn retorted. "It won't get you a general's position!"

"Now, now, Brother, we both know envy is not a good color on you." Zane chuckled. "It's not my fault that, even in a cage, I happen to be more likable than you. You know what they say about the firstborn, right?"

Cayn stilled, blinking several times. Given the confused look on his face, he didn't know.

"I smell a solid burn coming," I whispered, and heard Fiona chuckle softly, barely audible.

"Ah, yes," Velnias grinned.

"The firstborn are usually accidents, and parents keep trying to do better with more siblings," Zane said, keeping a straight face despite the twinkle of amusement in his red eyes. "So, you know, don't beat yourself up. There's only so much grandeur that my father was able to fit in you. He had to try, and, by the time he got to me, he finally got the formula right. It really isn't my fault that I'm better than you. At absolutely everything."

"And yet you're the one going to jail," Cayn shot back, seething. A vein furiously throbbed in his temple, and his eyes burned red with rage.

"And even behind bars, I'm more likable than you ever will be, brother. That says a lot," Zane replied, unforgiving and barely holding it together.

"Cuff him!" Cayn barked at the guards, and ended the conversation there. He then shifted his focus back to Velnias, gritting his teeth. "He doesn't get a single soul until he apologizes for insulting the first in line for the throne."

"Judging by your failure to capture the outsiders, Your Grace, I'm not sure who the first in line for the throne will be by the end of this week," Velnias replied with a flat smile.

It was my turn to cover my mouth to stifle a cackle. As much as I wanted to drive my swords through all the daemons who were after us, I had to admit that Velnias was slowly but surely becoming one of my favorites of his species. His takedowns of Cayn, the first freaking prince of daemons, were deliciously brutal, and, judging by how influential Velnias seemed to be at this point, it didn't seem like Cayn could do much about it. Even the other guards were glancing to the side, struggling to hide their smiles.

As a private prison warden, Velnias was surely slathered in useful and influential connections in the kingdom, that probably extended well beyond the city of Draconis.

One of Velnias's guards slapped a pair of engraved cuffs on

Zane, then politely escorted him out of the cage and inside Cell 132. Zane continued smiling, as if he were being checked into a hotel, rather than a prison cell. Somehow, he didn't seem all that affected—on the contrary, he was more delighted by the jabs he could still launch at his obnoxious elder brother.

"Rest assured, the outsiders will end up in Draconis sooner or later," Cayn hissed at Velnias. "I'm the future king, and I don't do anything by half measure."

"Technically speaking, we're already here," I whispered, then glanced over my shoulder and noticed the smirks.

"The key here is to not end up in one of these *boxes*, that's all," Hansa replied.

"Easy breezy," I said, then gave her a wink before shifting my focus back to Velnias, who watched Zane go into the box, then turned his head to look at Cayn once more. The guards came back outside, carrying the charmed cuffs they'd slapped on him for the short walk from his cage to his new "residence". I figured they were an additional security measure.

"Your Grace, the prisoner has been delivered." Velnias smirked. "I imagine you have more business to attend to back in Infernis?"

"What are you implying?" Cayn replied, narrowing his eyes at the warden. The rest of the daemon guards took their positions in the middle of the road, ready to head back with the empty cage.

"Not implying anything, Your Grace," Velnias said, shrugging. "I just figured there are some outsiders you are probably eager to capture. After all, the entire kingdom knows about how they escaped, and the many casualties they left you with. Not to mention the humiliation. Surely that must sting. I can only imagine what King Shaytan is thinking right now."

"You need to mind your own business, warden!" Cayn barked, losing his composure. "Before I have you jailed for disrespecting my authority!"

"Your Grace, being frank with a member of the royal family is not prohibited, nor frowned upon in any way, especially since I have been nothing but courteous and respectful," Velnias replied. "You could order my imprisonment right now, and my guards would, of course, obey. But I would be walking out by midnight, once the king heard of your very thin skin."

I had to admit, I was impressed with Velnias. Whereas most lower-level daemons seemed frightened of the king and his sons, Velnias was the exact opposite. He had enough knowledge of the laws and the royals' weaknesses that he could dance circles around them without getting himself arrested. I doubted that Cayn would have Velnias killed, either. The warden didn't strike me as a suicidal maniac—he obviously knew his limits, and most likely had great connections throughout the kingdom.

Like Zane had said, it took one hell of a dedicated worker to move up from pit wolf kennel-cleaner to private prison warden. At this point, my only hope was that this was all a façade, and that Velnias was still very much on our side as an undercover pacifist. Otherwise, it would be an absolute shame to have to kill him in order for us to get to the swamp witch.

22

FIONA

There was something about watching Zane go into his meranium cell that didn't sit well with me—at all. In fact, it made me sick to my stomach, and anger coursed through my veins. Then again, he kind of had it coming for helping us the way he did. It was a miracle he was still alive, based on what I knew about his father.

"Just keep an eye on Zane, Velnias," Cayn scoffed, then walked over to the front of the convoy. "He's surely a conspirator, working with... GASP, or whatever those outsiders call themselves. He's plotting against my father and our great kingdom, and he's incredibly lucky to still be alive. My guess is that my father wants to snack on his soul sometime in the near future."

"At least he'd want to consume my soul," Zane shot back from the box. "He'd toss your corpse into the pit wolf kennels, if given a choice."

"The day will come when you will die, Zane, and I'll be

taking my front row seat to watch you give your last breath!" Cayn hissed.

"Whatever helps you sleep at night, Brother," Zane didn't let go, either, and that made me smile. "I can only imagine what it's like to sleep with so many inadequacies."

Cayn muttered a curse under his breath, then waved Velnias away and motioned for the ten guards to follow him. Velnias stood there for a while, watching until Cayn and his guards disappeared behind a corner, farther up the road.

With no red lenses present, we were able to leave our hiding spot and return to the front. Caspian, Fiona and I quietly followed Velnias and his two guards inside the box, where Zane had already made himself comfortable in the double bed. I motioned for the others to wait outside and keep a look out. The box wasn't big enough to hold all of us without Velnias or his guards noticing or bumping into one of us—even in invisible form, the air still rippled. The seasoned eye could spot us. There wasn't much furniture for him to work with, but it seemed spacious and comfortable enough not to drive him crazy in his isolation—provided he'd be there for a long time.

I'd already decided that Zane wouldn't die in this meranium box, and that I'd be the one to get him out. He'd saved me more than once, and, despite his arrogance and daemon origins, I owed him a very big favor. *Let this be it.*

"Boy, you've really pissed the king off this time," Velnias said, clicking his teeth as he sat in one of the chairs. The two guards stood firmly in a corner, while Harper and I snuck in.

"At least my head didn't come off," Zane replied with a shrug, then put his hands behind his head and leaned back against the wooden headboard. My eyes wandered up and down his body— he was truly massive, his bare chest and the ropes of muscle on his abs making my cheeks catch fire. He wore a pair of tight leather pants and combat-style boots, and he'd caught his long black hair in a tight bun on top of his head. Despite his circumstances, Zane was still bold and defiant, and that made my heart skip a few beats. My gaze settled on his face.

"That being said, you'll be here with us for a while, Your Grace," Velnias said, crossing his arms, then looked at the guards. "You two can resume your posts on Cell 67. He's not going anywhere, and I've got the keys."

The guards nodded, then walked out, prompting both Harper and me to quickly step to the side so they wouldn't bump into us. Zane seemed to notice us—he'd probably caught some movement ripples in the air—but didn't say anything. I wondered if he'd figured out it was us. The thought actually warmed me up on the inside.

A few moments went by in silence. Velnias and Zane stared at each other.

"So, for how long have you been a pacifist, Velnias?" Zane asked.

I almost heard Velnias's stomach drop. His eyes grew wide, then narrowed into angry slits. "What are you talking about?" he hissed.

Zane chuckled, shaking his head slowly. "I thought I was pretty clear earlier, when I said that the firstborn are usually dumber. You must think I'm blind, or something."

"What makes you think I'm a pacifist, Your Grace? I'm one of the High Wardens of Draconis, not an Iman-hugger."

Harper and I looked at each other, while the rest of our team quietly sneaked inside the cell box. They were all watching the exchange between Velnias and Zane with renewed interest, now that the guards were gone.

"Oh, come on, Velnias," Zane scoffed. "No loyalist takes as much pleasure in jerking my brother around as you do. Besides, I have my sources."

Velnias didn't say anything for a while, carefully contemplating his next move. He took a deep breath, his shoulders dropping in the process. "How did you know?"

Yes! Thank the stars, we still have a daemon on the inside.

"Like I said, I have my sources," Zane replied with a smirk.

"You see, that's the kind of attitude that gets you imprisoned in the first place. And I'll be damned if I'm going to end up in a meranium box like you. So, please, Your Grace, how did you know?"

"No one told me, Velnias. Relax. I move around the kingdom a lot, most of the time unseen. I've been secretly listening to pacifists whispering to one another behind corners for a few days now," Zane explained. "And, like I said, your disdain of Cayn kind of sealed the deal for me."

"And I was holding back, believe me." Velnias chuckled. "I'd love to slice his head off just for being such a pompous piece of trash."

"I'm right there with you on that one, my friend. So, tell me, Velnias, for how long have you felt that this kingdom wasn't headed in the right direction?"

Velnias let a sigh roll out of his chest. "Years, Your Grace. Many years. It's been going horribly wrong from the moment the Maras set foot in this world."

Zane nodded slowly, processing the information.

"Are there others in Draconis? Specifically, are there others who have yet to be discovered?" Zane asked.

"I'm not sure I can tell you, Your Grace," Velnias replied. "Why do you want to know? I certainly hope you don't wish to use any of this knowledge as leverage against me. I am literally the only one who can make your stay here more pleasurable. Surely you're not hoping to score some points with the king over me."

"Do you think I'd actually do that?"

"To be honest, no. Especially not after the way you helped the outsiders escape," Velnias said, smiling. "I'm simply curious as to what your end game really is, regarding the pacifist movement. I doubt it's to get back on the king's good side. You knew exactly what you were doing when you aided those people."

"I most certainly did." Zane grinned.

"I heard you went all the way to Azure Heights to get the others out of the Maras' reach, too."

Zane looked incredibly satisfied with that account, his broad smile making it difficult for me to keep a straight face. "Yup. And it paid off, too."

"How so, Your Grace? You're in prison."

"Not for long."

Velnias was once again confused. I walked over to the cell door and closed it. The clang from the automatic lock made him jump to his feet and spin around, with one hand on his sheathed rapier.

"Relax, Velnias," Zane added, not moving from his laidback pose. "I imagine they're here to talk to you. Which is exactly what I would've done, by the way, Fiona."

My heart leapt into my throat as I turned to face him. It was time for us to reveal ourselves, so I took out a water bladder from my backpack and passed it around for each of us to counteract the invisibility spell. One by one, we became visible. Velnias held his breath, surprised to see us all here.

"Vesta! I didn't expect you'd come all the way here!" he

exclaimed, then gave Vesta a warm smile. Zane didn't take his piercing eyes off me. I suddenly felt naked and vulnerable, given that he could finally see me.

"Well, where did you expect me to be? I told you I'd be bringing the outsiders in for help, and that I'd find you, wherever you are," Vesta replied, raising an eyebrow.

"You crazy girl, I figured you'd at least wait for me at my private quarters!" Velnias shot back.

"I didn't even know they made you warden." Vesta scoffed. "We would've wasted hours looking for you in the pit wolf kennels."

"Ah, yes. That's true. I forgot to send word to you about my... promotion."

"How did you know I was here?" I asked Zane, crossing my arms in the hopes I'd feel less like a deer in headlights before him.

"I caught a glimpse of your eyes during movement," Zane replied. "I'd recognize those amber beauties anywhere."

Lord, the charming smile he put on made my knees melt. The amount of self-confidence in him was enough to disarm an entire kingdom. I was helpless on my own.

"Well, then, good to see you're still in perfect working order," I muttered, desperately trying to hide my blush—I could feel my cheeks almost melting under his persistent and fascinatingly intense gaze, which softened in response.

"I have to admit, I have been worried about you, little vampire," he replied, his voice lower than usual.

I paused, not sure what to say to that. He felt genuine, and that further chipped away at my defenses. Each of our encounters had been riddled with dangers and unanswered questions, and, for the first time, we were facing each other with nothing but relief and faint smiles. In the absence of dark secrets and mysteries, I could feel that little string connecting us—an invisible bond that I didn't even know had come to be. *This feels too intense to be Stockholm Syndrome, for sure.*

"No need," I said slowly. "I thought I told you I can take care of myself."

"I can see that." He laughed lightly, positively beaming. I felt my lips stretch into a smile.

"Velnias, we've come for your help." Hansa then joined the conversation, with Jax standing right behind her. "As you know, we've made it out of Infernis and Azure Heights in one piece, but there isn't much we can do right now. We need to get to the swamp witch."

Velnias scoffed, visibly amused. "Wow, you people don't play around."

No, we do not.

The stakes were too high. Our lives, and the lives of many others, depended on our ability to get the swamp witch away from the daemons and the Exiled Maras.

We'd come too far to back down, and, as I'd repeatedly said to myself, the only reason I ever would've stayed on Neraka would've been because I wanted to, not because there were bloodthirsty fiends out there who wished to eat my soul. Besides, now I had an extra reason to fight back harder than ever, and he was looking at me with his fiery crimson eyes.

23

HARPER

"I'm afraid we can't afford to play around at this point in time," Hansa said. Velnias measured each of us from head to toe, occasionally narrowing his eyes—as if assessing us on an individual basis, and trying to figure out our strengths and weaknesses.

"I have to say, I'm already impressed," Velnias replied, turning his chair around to face us and resuming his seat in a casual pose. There was something about him that I truly appreciated—this quiet, but equally blaring way of asserting his position. One could tell, just from his uniform and confident half smile, that he was pretty much in charge of this place. Aligning him with the pacifists was nearly impossible, unless he personally confirmed it. Everything about him said "budding authoritarian sociopath," not "Iman-hugging pacifist".

He played his part with thespian dexterity, and that was probably what I liked most about him—his ability to seamlessly blend into a society that thrived on spilling the blood of innocent creatures, just to secretly help and free said innocent creatures.

"I'm with Velnias on this one," Zane added with a smirk. "It's not every day that you see outsiders infiltrating a daemon city not once, but twice, even after they were discovered and nearly neutralized."

"Agreed. You people are either brilliant or downright suicidal," Velnias said, his appreciation perfectly noticeable.

"We had no choice," Hansa replied with a shrug. "We were brought here as part of a sick farce. We thought we were helping the Maras defend themselves from your kind when, in fact, we were just being tested and skillfully prepped for dinner."

"The Exiled Maras sorely underestimated us," Jax muttered. "Unfortunately, there isn't much we can do until we get the swamp witch back. She doesn't belong here. Her magic has already caused irreparable damage to the current ecosystem of Neraka, and we need her to bring down the shield that's blocking our communication with the outside world. Once we get the whole of GASP down here, this whole daemon and Exiled Mara alliance will come to a very abrupt and painful end."

"I take it you have an army or something, eager to come over and spank us unruly daemons?" Velnias shot back, crossing his arms with a grin.

"A handful of dragons alone will do the trick," Hansa replied. "Our core mission is to restore peace and balance in this world. That means subduing the daemons into a less corrosive position and facilitating a peace treaty between your species and the others inhabiting Neraka. A treaty that we would closely monitor, once everything is said and done."

"A treaty that will not include the Exiled Maras," I added.

Velnias nodded with keen interest, then smiled at Caspian, who stood by my side, his hand discreetly resting on the small of my back. "And is that something you're amenable to, Lord Kifo?"

"Absolutely," Caspian said firmly.

"The Exiled Maras were given the chance of a new, better life on Neraka, and they chose to do worse than the carnage they were nearly wiped out for back on Calliope," Hansa replied. "They've willfully renounced any chance that they had at redemption."

Zane raised an eyebrow, wearing an incredulous half smile. "So, what, you'll just wipe them all off the face of Neraka?"

"Obviously not all of them. Judgment will be made on each individual, and those who tried to live a peaceful, non-murderous life will be granted amnesty and allowed to try again, under careful monitoring, this time around," Hansa said.

"The same will happen to the daemons," Jax replied. "Those who continue to resist and assault the innocent will be jailed, or executed, in extreme cases. Neraka needs to be a tolerant society in order for it to rebuild itself and find its balance."

"You sound quite intolerant for a bunch of people advocating tolerance." Velnias grinned.

"Unfortunately, it's a paradox we have to enforce. We must be intolerant of those who are intolerant, in order to create a tolerant society," Jax said. "Otherwise, this will continue, like a vicious and bloody circle. It all needs to stop. Too many innocent creatures have died. Too many lives have been ruined. We do not like having to resort to such extreme measures, but we have no other choice."

"I get it," Velnias replied, stretching his arms out. "And, as much as it pains me, it's true. It's time for a good old-fashioned cleansing in this place. I just need a guarantee that the pacifists, and the daemons who align with us, will be spared. Then I'll help you."

"I think everyone will be subject to a review, but those who want peace will have nothing to fear," Hansa declared. "However, I recommend resuming this part of the conversation once we bring the shield over Neraka down. Until then, our promises are useless, with daemons and Exiled Maras hunting us down."

Velnias stood, scratching the back of his head. Zane continued to watch us with slight amusement—and a hefty amount of interest, particularly in Fiona. That daemon had the hots for her, and, judging by the way Fiona was trying not to steal glances at him, the feeling was mutual. I smiled inwardly, then gently nudged her toward him.

She gave me a brief frown, and pursed her lips when she noticed my mischievous half smile. We didn't need words between us. We'd basically grown up together, and Fiona was perfectly capable of reading my expressions. She exhaled, shaking her head as if to express some kind of faux disappointment in me, then moved slowly, almost unnoticeably, toward Zane, while the rest of our group focused on Velnias. I figured she needed a few minutes closer to the guy, given our current circumstances. Who knew when she'd see him again—or if she'd see him again. *Maybe we should get Zane out, to join us.*

"Fair enough," Velnias replied. "However, I don't know where they're keeping the swamp witch."

Disappointment kicked me hard in the stomach, but I'd yet to lose hope. "I thought you were well connected in these parts," I said.

"Oh, I am. Just not well connected enough to know where they're keeping the still-living-and-breathing grand prize," Velnias sighed. "She is, by far, our kingdom's most prized possession, and that's shared with the Exiled Maras, who are particularly protective about her. Only the higher-ups know where she's being held, but the rest of the Druid delegation might have a clue, too. I can take you to them."

"So the delegation members are still alive," Vesta breathed. I could see the hope blossoming in her heart. The longing to find out what happened to her parents burned deep red around her.

"Most of them, yes. It's been a long time for them in these private cells, though," Velnias replied. "They're not what they used to be. Heck, I wasn't even born when they crash-landed on Neraka. All I know are the tales. They were fearsome. They fought back hard against the Exiled Maras and their devious plans. But, once the daemons figured out how much they stood to benefit from an alliance, and from the swamp witch magic, they were done for."

"If we manage to at least free some of them, we'll get more of an upper hand until we do find the witch," Hansa mused, pressing a finger against her lips, then smiled at Velnias. "Yes. Take us to them. I'm sure that, regardless of the state they're in, they'll be pleased to see us. They'll have some hope, at least. I can only imagine what it must have been like for them. What's it been, ten thousand years?"

Velnias nodded slowly.

"Sheesh," I murmured. "Long freaking time to spend stuck in a meranium box. Speaking of which, we should take Zane with us. Assuming he's not interested in hiding behind his daddy's skirt."

I gave him a sideways smirk, which he playfully returned. *Yeah, I can see why Fiona likes you.*

"I'd love to, but I can't let him loose until Cayn goes back to Infernis," Velnias muttered, gritting his teeth, visibly displeased.

"Once we get him out of here, no one will be able to track him down," Fiona insisted, then looked down at Zane in his bed. "Surely you're capable of keeping a low profile."

"Oh, I absolutely am, as you already know," Zane replied with a soft smile. The daemon was smitten with Fiona, and I found that oddly refreshing. "But Velnias is right. If I get out now, Cayn will get word of my escape. Velnias won't be able to keep it under wraps for more than a few hours without getting himself in hot water. And that'll just open another can of worms, given his side gig with the pacifists."

"It's best if Cayn gets out of Draconis first. It'll be easier to orchestrate an escape then," Velnias added. "If we do it now, Cayn won't leave the city until he finds Zane, and you've all seen and heard the moron. He's a persistent, frustrated oversized worm."

"You really dislike him." I couldn't help but chuckle.

"You have no idea," Velnias breathed. "Now, do you people have a safe meeting spot outside Draconis?"

"We do," Vesta said, and I remembered the library in the Imen city above.

"Don't tell me. Tell Zane," Velnias replied. "That way, once he gets out, he'll know where to find you or track you. I can't know. I'm afraid that if I am captured, they might force it out of me. I'm not susceptible to Maras' mind-bending, but there are some excruciating swamp witch spells that the likes of Cayn wouldn't hesitate to use on me to get to you all, and Zane."

"Fair enough," Fiona agreed, then whispered into Zane's ear. His gaze darkened as she got close to him, and he took a deep breath, as if to memorize her natural scent. Judging by the clouds gathering in his red eyes, Fiona had quite the physical impact on him, and he didn't bother to hide it at all. I wasn't sure if Fiona was aware of it, but I made a mental note to ask her later —preferably when we were no longer infiltrating the enemy's lair.

"Good. Everyone ready?" Velnias asked, looking at us.

We all took out our batches of invisibility paste and swallowed enough to last us for about six hours. "We should definitely stock up along the way," Jax said, checking his pouch with a slight frown. "Just in case. I think we have enough for another six-hour session."

Velnias then glanced at Zane. "Your Grace, I'll be back for you once that pest of a brother of yours is out of Draconis. I hope that will be sooner rather than later. In the meantime, however, you'll be locked here, and guards will be at your door. I've arranged for a shift to come in soon enough."

"That's fine, Velnias, thank you," Zane replied, then gave Fiona a most mischievous smile. "I'll kill some time thinking about the little vampire while I wait."

Oh, wow, he does not beat around the bush.

Fiona lit up like a stoplight, her cheeks unnaturally crimson. She gave him a weak nod, gradually vanishing due to the invisibility spell. Once we were all under the radar, Velnias fumbled through his tunic pocket and took out his red lens. "I don't like wearing this often—it hurts my eye—but I'd hate to lose track of you crazy kids," he said, fitting it over his right eye.

He then walked over to the door and opened it wide for us. Carefully checking both ways for other red lens daemons, we got out into the main street, while Velnias locked the door behind him.

"I'll take you to Cells 5 and 6, where some Druid delegation members are being kept, as they're part of my daily route as the High Warden for this block," he said, then walked up the road.

We quietly followed. "Provided the conditions are convenient, you may be able to get at least one of them out of here without anyone noticing until the morning. Either way, I'll give you all the cell numbers for the entire delegation, just in case. Assuming your safe spot is actually safe, you could very well do multiple extractions and get them all out."

"Can you help us get some more invisibility paste, while we're here?" I whispered.

"Sure. I'll write down the recipe for you, too. You can fetch the ingredients yourselves," he replied, giving me a sideways smile.

Whatever came next, we were fortunate to have someone like Velnias on our side. Mose, bless his heart, was old and retired, forced to the outskirts of Infernis because he'd outlived his usefulness in the daemon society. But Velnias was strong, and very much engaged. His position as a High Warden was an unexpected surprise, and a tremendous advantage.

For the first time, as I walked with Caspian by my side and the rest of our team behind us, Velnias leading the way, I had more than just a flicker of hope. I had the conviction that we were definitely going to achieve our objectives in this place, and that the daemons were significantly closer to the end of their era as the dominant species of Neraka.

Most importantly, I knew for sure that we were certainly closer to kicking some serious Exiled Mara ass—they more than had it coming, at this point.

24

AVRIL

O nce more, I slept incredibly well in Heron's arms. I lost track of time, his embrace keeping me warm, and his breath further heating me up as it spread over the back of my neck.

My dreams were all connected to him—vivid and filled with color, as if we'd somehow met, deep in our subconscious, to continue what we'd started back in the real world. My own moans of dreamy pleasure woke me up, and I held my breath for a few seconds, wondering if he'd heard me. I listened to the heavy silence around us. We were still submerged in the darkness of our hole in the ground.

The furs beneath us were soft, and had done an excellent job of keeping the cold at bay—though I had Heron to thank, too, for refusing to leave my side. His arms were still tightly wrapped around my waist, his frame spooning mine, and his face was buried in my hair.

I could've stayed there forever. For a brief moment in time, all my worries and fears had evaporated, and all I could focus on was the sound of his heartbeat. It was soft and steady, as he was still dreaming. I wondered if I'd left him alone in there, looking for me.

No matter what lay ahead, Heron and I were certainly no longer the same. The version of us that had first landed on Neraka was gone, swiftly replaced by a pair still trying to figure each other out. After our first kiss, however, the dynamic between us was undeniable. After everything he'd said to me, and after what I'd first said to him, there was simply no point in hiding anything anymore. I'd fallen for Heron Dorchadas—deep enough for me to choke up at the thought of losing him in any way.

It scared the hell out of me, but, at the same time, it filled me with unexpected energy and courage, the latter to do things I'd never done before. Frankly, I was used to asking all the questions and keeping most of myself neatly wrapped beneath snappy comebacks and dry jokes. Yet, with Heron, I had this uncontrollable urge to reveal myself to him—my dreams, my thoughts, and, most importantly, my feelings toward him.

He stirred, then exhaled slowly. His heartbeat picked up the pace a little. He was waking up and readjusting to our new reality. His natural scent filled my lungs, and I couldn't help but smile as I recognized the strong, masculine hints of musk and ocean breeze. Heron was naturally a pleasure to be around for someone like me—and that was before he stood in defiance of all the odds, and before he opened his mouth to make me laugh.

"Avril."

His voice was low and raspy, gently pouring into my ear. *I could get used to this, for sure.*

"Yes?" I replied softly.

With one, sudden move, he rolled me around so I could face him, and I found myself locked under the hypnotic intensity of his jade eyes—his gaze clouded, prompting my heart to perform a very athletic series of backflips in my chest.

"I dreamed about you," he whispered.

"Was I chasing you down a sketchy corridor with a bloody axe?" I giggled, eager to see him smile.

The hint of one flickered across his face. "No, you were doing... other things. Less murderous things."

"Care to elaborate?"

"I can show you." He smirked, then pulled me closer, nearly crushing me against his chest.

He kissed me deeply, and with the hunger of a lover long lost who'd only now just found me again. The longing filled me to the brim, and I relaxed in his embrace. The taste of him was exquisite, better than blood and infinitely better than the morning coffee I used to look forward to, during my human days.

I rested my palms on his chest, relishing the feel of his toned muscles against my fingertips, even through the layer of his leather suit. Heron paused, then pulled his head back for a moment—enough to look me in the eyes.

"You are downright addictive, you thorny vampire," he murmured, the corner of his mouth twitching. His eyes glimmered with raw desire.

"And you're an excellent kisser, you loudmouthed Mara," I shot back with a giggle.

He chuckled softly, then descended once more upon me, capturing my mouth. He gently bit my lower lip, and my breath hitched in response. To my surprise, he then brought his wrist up and sank his fangs into the tender inner part, drawing a few drops of blood. *Pyrope.* He raised his wrist over my mouth, his gaze so intense that I felt close to catching fire. I parted my lips and welcomed the taste of his blood on the tip of my tongue. He watched me quietly as I slowly closed my eyes, my senses overwhelmed by him.

"I'll never get tired of this vision of you," Heron whispered in my ear, then nibbled at the lobe. His lips then trailed warm kisses down the side of my neck, before his sharp fangs grazed the skin, and he suckled gently. He tasted my blood and grunted, shifting his weight on top of me.

"Heron..." I breathed, my back arching as he continued kissing my neck. The sound of a zipper coming down made me smile. Heron peeled the leather back and gently kissed the meeting point of my collarbones, his simmering breath spreading softly over my chest.

His hand slipped down to my hip as he lifted his head and claimed my mouth in another kiss. I didn't want this to end. If anything, with how quickly this fire was spreading through me, it felt as though we were just getting started and reality was still very far away.

"So, in my dream, we were like this," he said, then rolled us over until I was straddling him.

"You know, you look devastatingly handsome down there," I replied, basking in his undivided attention as he lay on his back, looking up at me with a boyish grin.

"I'm certainly enjoying my view from down here," he said, then used his index finger to trail a lazy line up my partially bare torso, the leather still covering my upper chest.

He then caught my hands and pulled me back down, wrapping his arms around me and pressing me against his chest. He dropped kisses all over my face, and I felt soft and mellow, cherished and worshipped in his hold.

Despite the whirlwind of passion that was brewing between us, Heron found the strength to stop himself from taking our relationship to another, much more intense stage. Part of me wanted to pout because I wanted every atom of him to bond with mine. But, deep down, I knew he'd made the right choice.

It didn't stop that long sigh from rolling out of my chest, though, as he smothered me with fluttering kisses. "Avril, as much as I would love to simply peel you out of that suit and turn my every dream about you into reality, I have every intention of doing this the old-fashioned way," he said, his voice low, making me purr softly in his arms.

"Every inch of me is screaming no," I whispered in his ear, "but you're right. This isn't the time or the place."

I lifted my head so I could look him in the eyes. His lips were as tender and reddish as mine felt. We didn't do half measures when it came to kissing, so I could only imagine what everything else felt like with Heron. He tucked a lock of hair behind my ear and gently cupped my cheek.

"I've never been in a serious bond before," he said. "I only have tales from books and some half-assed advice from my equally dysfunctional brother." I couldn't help but chuckle. "But I would like to court you, with the entire ritual. Dates, dinner, long walks on the beach. And a thousand Pyropes, if that's what it takes to make you understand how important you've become to me."

I didn't know when or how he'd managed to burrow into my heart and settle there with such determination, but I was finding myself even more enamored with Heron. Just lying there, in his arms, listening to him telling me about his plans for proper dates with me—it was enough to flip a switch inside me. He could do whatever he wanted at this point. I was already his. Body and soul.

"Boy, you sure know how to woo a girl." I smiled, then dropped a single, loving kiss at the corner of his mouth.

"You're different from everyone I've ever met, Avril. I'm serious. I can't treat you like my other... lady friends, as you so elegantly described them. You're... you. And, once we get out of here, I would like to formally ask you out, so we can get to know each other better, in every possible way. We can try the sandy shores, north of White City, or I could come to The Shade. Whatever you want, I'll do it."

I loved the sound of that. The idea of us. Of him in my life. *Yes.* And then reality reared its ugly head, reminding me of our somewhat precarious circumstances. I kissed him again, then sat up and gently pulled the zipper back up on his combat suit, while he slowly did the same to mine. "I look forward to everything you've just described, and more," I said. "But, I have to admit, I'm a little worried that we might not get out of this place. It's a possibility, and, although I know it's a small possibility, it's there nonetheless. And I'd hate to—"

He didn't let me finish. He sat up and kissed me, tightening his arms around my waist—his breath ragged and downright volcanic. "Yes," he smiled, "it's a possibility. I know. I've thought about it, too. But we will fight this, Avril, and we'll do our best to get out. I'll be with you every step of the way. In many ways, you make me stronger, and I'll burn this whole place down if that's what it takes for us to gain our freedom and be together, undisturbed. However, should we fail... should we find ourselves stuck here on Neraka, somehow..."

He paused for a moment so he could trail his fingers down

my cheek and simply contemplate every inch of my flushed face. His gaze then found mine again, and the determination gleaming in his jade eyes filled me with newfound energy. "Should that come to pass, Avril, this hole in the ground is definitely not where I intend to make love to you for the first time."

Oh, wow.

I didn't see that coming. And I had no idea what to say. *What the hell can I say, other than "Take me, I'm yours!", anyway? I mean, if this doesn't score him the title of "soulmate", nothing will.*

A sigh left my chest. A breath I'd been holding in for a while, judging by how it felt as I let it out. I put my arms around him, pulled him close enough for our hearts to echo against one another, and kissed him, ever so softly. I put every single thought I had into it—my lips tender against his, saying things I couldn't even formulate into words anymore.

With cheeks burning and hearts fluttering, we stayed like that for a while, simply kissing and getting used to one another, while the morning slowly settled outside. "What can I say, Dorchadas? I look forward to a candlelight dinner with you." I chuckled between kisses on both his cheeks, making him smile in that rare and dazzling way of his. "Just make sure you don't make it excruciatingly long, with five different types of blood and whatever. I doubt I'll have that much patience left in me by then."

"Well, I was thinking just the main course, and Pyrope with you for dessert," he replied, unable to take his eyes off me.

Someone please throw me a rope, or something. Or don't. I'm falling too deep and too fast to catch it, anyway.

It took us some time to find the strength to stand apart for long enough to gear up and go outside. To face the world that awaited, with its unforgiving wilderness, its bloodthirsty fiends, and its soul-eating overlords. We were strong, though. And we stood tall and proud, with the fresh memory of our sizzling morning, when we'd promised each other that, no matter what came next, we would face it together.

As the Adlets came out of their sleeping spots to greet us, along with the rest of our team, I knew for a fact that, yes—whatever happened next, Heron and I were going to make it, one way or another. We'd only just found each other, after all. We had plenty of dates to go on, and not a single daemon or Exiled Mara would ruin that for us.

"Well, someone had a good night's sleep." Scarlett's insinuating tone and brazen grin were the cold shower I'd desperately needed, though. She made me groan, then laugh, as she quickly figured out that Heron and I were certainly at a different stage in our relationship.

"Oh, it's going to be a long freaking ride into the northern mountains," I scoffed, rolling my eyes, then leaned into Heron's side, as if to further cement our new status. He didn't seem to mind it one bit. On the contrary, he beamed with adorable pride.

"I don't know, Avril." Heron smirked, measuring Patrik and Scarlett from head to toe. "I think we've got a classic case of pot meets kettle here, because I'm more than happy to sing about the Druid and the vampire sitting in a tree, all the way to the Dhaxanians."

And that unraveled me completely. I doubled over with laughter. Scarlett was flushed and Patrik was the color of a ruby, and so were Heron and I, in the end. Four creatures who'd never thought they'd find love in a world like Neraka, and yet here we were.

25

SCARLETT

"So, you two are an item now?" I asked Avril, while we readied our horses for the long journey ahead. Some of the young Adlets had prepped some dried herbs and water bladders for us to have, in case we ran low on supplies for swamp witch spells.

They'd even given us enough dried food and mushrooms to last our non-vampire team members a couple of days, at least. Avril looked at me, smiling. Her pale cheeks took on a pinkish hue—a rare sight on her.

"Well, yes," she replied, then stole a glance at Heron, who was busy loading his horse with a few extra furs. The mountains were going to be exceptionally cold, according to Colton. "Neither of us expected it, to be honest. Maybe, if we hadn't come to Neraka, it wouldn't have happened at all. Maybe it would've remained one of those many missed opportunities that life is sometimes about."

"I guess the tension, the high stakes and all, brought you two closer together," I said, still buzzing from the night I'd spent submerged in dreams and wrapped in Patrik's strong arms. "I get it. I think it's the same with Patrik and me, in a way."

"Honestly, I'm surprised you managed to crack *that* shell." Avril chuckled. "The poor guy's been through quite a lot, and when I first met him, I didn't think he'd even consider rebuilding his life like this, not where relationships are concerned, anyway."

"I wouldn't have blamed him, really," I replied with a shrug. "Imagine putting up with a monster like Azazel for all those years, tortured in what probably felt like someone else's body, just so you'd spare the life of your lover, to end up losing her, right at the very end. I, too, am surprised that he noticed me."

Avril scoffed, shaking her head slowly. "What's not to notice? Are you nuts? Scarlett, he'd have to be an absolute moron not to fall head over heels for you, and, judging by that dopey look on his face," she muttered, giving Patrik a brief sideways glance, "he's past the point of no return."

I followed her gaze and found Patrik's eyes fixed on me, the steely blue softened by the change in the dynamic between us. He'd fallen for me, as deep and as hard as I'd fallen for him, and it felt perfect. "I guess we lift each other up, and, given our circumstances, it makes all the difference ahead of what's coming," I murmured.

"I know. Heron and I have this incredible synergy," Avril replied. "He's exceptionally good at anticipating my moves. Less than a week working together, and he can already tell what I'm about to do next, especially in combat situations. That, somehow, also transpires in our personal interactions. And he is *nothing* like the guy he tries to portray. At all."

"Oh, that I can believe, for sure." I giggled. "Mr. High And Mighty has a massive soft spot, doesn't he?"

"He's fixated on being all traditional and old school about us dating. Like, candlelit dinner, walk on the beach, the works, before we get more serious," Avril said, blushing to a more pronounced shade of pink.

"Aw. I will, of course, use this for any potential comeback if he tries another joke about Patrik and me, you know that, right?" I replied, raising an eyebrow.

Avril laughed, then pulled her hood over her head. We were all ready to leave the cover of the trees. "I wouldn't blame you. He often has it coming. Besides, we're pretty much family, all of us together. You know he won't hesitate to poke you, now that you and Patrik have pretty much confirmed that you're an item, too."

"Let him try." I grinned. "Worst case scenario is that I can always slap him, really fast, *my* kind of fast, before he even manages to think of a reaction."

We both doubled over, our cheeks flushed and our eyes glimmering with newfound joy. Given our current climate, all this was much needed, especially for morale. Both Avril and I had that extra kick in our heels, that added reason to fight back even harder against creatures that wanted us miserable and, eventually, dead.

"Everyone ready to go?" Patrik asked, bringing his indigo horse closer to mine.

"Pretty much," I replied with a nod and a soft smile. He looked at me as if I was the most important thing in his life, and that alone filled me with incredible amounts of energy. *Bring on an army of daemons. I can take them all on right about now.*

Hundurr sat quietly to the side, watching us, his red eyes glimmering with—I wasn't sure what, exactly. Curiosity, maybe longing. But longing for what?

"I've spoken to our pack members," Colton said, approaching us. "We won't come with you up north. The bigger the group, the easier it will be for daemons to notice. And you don't want to bring daemons up to the Dhaxanians' mountain. But take these."

He handed me three sticks of what looked like dark red wax with golden and white striations, and a string fuse. "What are they?" I asked, turning the sticks over a few times.

"Flares. Each is a burning signal," Colton replied. "Light one and toss it up. It'll take off and explode into a visible flare. We'll come running then, wherever you are. We're fast in wolf form, and we can cover two hundred miles, easily, in one day. Even more, if we feed first. Once lit, the signal will burn for a long time, you'll see."

"We've been using these flares for centuries, to keep track of our packs," Isom added. "The wax is a proprietary blend we use, from hives deep in the orchards on the western hills. They're highly flammable, too, so you might want to keep them away from fire. They really expand and burn like crazy. Once they're lit, you can't put them out, and you certainly can't control them."

"Use them wisely," Colton said. "If you're farther away, give us some time to reach you. Nevertheless, you have my word: once you light one up in the sky, we will come, and we will always find you. In the meantime, we'll rally the other packs. Whether you need to get to the swamp witch, or you need to protect her, you'll need as many creatures to help you as possible. Count on us."

"Thank you, Colton. Thank you all," I replied, and bowed curtly before them.

Colton smiled, then shifted his focus to Hundurr. "My friend, what will you do? Do you want to stay with us? Your children would love to have you around."

Hundurr seemed to think about it, looking at Saya and Embry, who'd flanked Isom on the edge of the Adlet pack gathering. He got up, trotted over to them, and lovingly licked their faces. The young Adlets hugged and stroked him as he rubbed his massive head against theirs. He then came over and settled by my side. I was surprised by his decision, and even felt bad for the kids.

"Are you sure?" I asked him, but he didn't even yelp or nod. "They're your children, Hundurr."

"I'm not sure that matters," Colton replied, wearing a sad smile. "You see, you saved his life. He's bound by very old traditions here, to keep you safe until you no longer need him. I think that, given the mission you're on, Hundurr thinks he'll be of more use to you than to us."

Saya let out an audible sigh. "And we've learned to live without him. The pack keeps us safe. We'd love to have him back, but I think you need our father more than we do, right now."

"Just make sure you do your best to bring him back to us," Embry added.

They weren't happy, of course, but they showed exceptional maturity for their age. They did have a point, too. We needed Hundurr more than ever, especially for what awaited ahead. These were dark and treacherous times, and, if Hundurr wanted to stay by my side, it would be foolish to refuse.

I smiled at the pit wolf, then reached out and scratched the back of his ear. "Thank you, Hundurr," I murmured. "I can't express how thankful I am to have you join us."

"Okay, cool, so the pit wolf stays," Heron chimed in, more jovial than usual. I blamed Avril for that, and stifled a smirk. "Now, let's go. I want to see what the Dhaxanians are all about.

They've been described as such icy badasses, I really hope I won't be disappointed."

"Oh, don't you worry, young Mara," Colton scoffed, "you'll find out what the Dhaxanians are made of soon enough."

"Once again, thank you all," Patrik then said, and shook Colton and Isom's hands. We waved goodbye to the others, then got on our indigo horses.

Dion and Alles were still quite groggy, prompting Heron to trot his horse over and smack them both on the shoulder. "You two! You're our guides. Snap out of it!" He chuckled as the young Imen scowled at him.

"Just because you're one of the good Maras doesn't mean we will hesitate to make your trip miserable, if you provoke us," Dion replied, and, judging by the smirk on his face, he was only half joking.

"I'd love to see you try," Heron shot back, wiggling his eyebrows at them. "You won't be sleeping for days if you do, though."

"Oh, puh-lease!" Avril interjected, rolling her eyes as she brought her horse closer to the Imen. "Why don't you pick on someone your own size, if you intend to act like a bully?"

Patrik and I tried hard not to laugh, watching the exchange, while Hundurr's gaze darted between Heron and Avril, as if trying to figure out if they were serious or just playing. The Adlets didn't bother to hide their amusement, as we bid them farewell, and Dion and Alles led us out of the patch of woods.

"Who's here for me to pick on, who's my size?" Heron replied, grinning, as we headed north and left the Adlet pack behind.

"Are you sure you want to open that can of worms, this early in the morning?" Avril asked, pursing her lips and narrowing her eyes at him.

Heron thought about it for a couple of seconds, then guided his indigo horse closer to hers, enough so he could reach out and pull her in for a short kiss. "No."

As soon as we passed the last trees of that forest patch, we pulled our masks and goggles on, as the sun kept going in and out of the thick, rain-riddled clouds.

We had a long way ahead of us, but we could all see our destination already. The Athelathan Mountains rose proudly in the north, and we had at least three hundred miles' worth of Lagerith Plains sill left to cross in order to get there. The snowy peaks of Athelathan were hidden in heavy, charcoal-colored clouds—the sign of one hell of a blizzard forming at the top.

Whatever waited for us there, we could handle it. I stole a glance at Patrik and beckoned my horse to go faster. One by one, we picked up speed and dashed across the plains, our indigo horses relishing the race through the tall grass.

Soon enough, a heavy rain set in, and I breathed a sigh of relief, knowing that the chances of us running into rogue daemons had just dropped substantially. With a little bit of luck, we had a smooth ride ahead.

We certainly need the break.

26

AVRIL

We headed northeast, toward the Athelathan Mountains —two giants flanked by sharp ridges made of white marble and gray limestone, riddled with wide plateaus of pine forests. Our horses went fast, but the closer we got to the mountains, the lower the temperatures became, making it more difficult for the animals to keep up their natural speed.

The tall grass of the Lagerith Plains scattered away, revealing the hard, nearly frozen ground beneath. The land surrounding the mountains was cold and unforgiving, home to dark green shrubs and stumpy trees that thrived only in such harsh climates.

The sun was out early, hidden behind thick layers of snow clouds. Thunder rumbled above. We were already soaked by the earlier rain, and we were now looking at a curtain of icy sleet coming down from the mountains.

The peaks were covered in snow and ice, setting off the occasional avalanche as the masses of frozen water collapsed onto the trees below. This was a cold and unforgiving land, its weather so extreme that it wasn't hard to imagine daemons keeping their distance from it. The cold was sneaking deep into my bones, locking my joints and making my teeth clatter—and I had a naturally low body temperature to begin with.

"This is a lot colder than I'd expected," Scarlett said, then looked up at the mountaintops, pointing at a pair of glimmering lights—so far away and well-hidden above the top forest plateau that I almost didn't see them. "Does that look like a city to you?"

I narrowed my eyes, trying to get a better look, but that specific area was under heavy snowfall. Barely anything could be seen from this distance, and we didn't have Harper's sentry eyes to help us. "It might. I can't really tell, with the blizzards unfolding up there."

"Yeah, we're looking at very hostile conditions here," Patrik replied, then took some of the furs he'd packed and passed a couple over to Scarlett. Heron gave me some of his, while Dion and Alles handled their own.

I looked down at my horse—the poor creature was already shivering. "What do we do?" I asked. "I'm not sure the horses can take the trip."

Scarlett and Patrik looked at each other, then at the Imen, and back to me, offering me their conclusion in the form of a nod. "We could continue up on foot," Scarlett said, "and the Imen can stay here with the horses."

"What? No, we can help!" Dion objected. "We're not staying down here. We're not kids!"

"This isn't about us treating you like children," I replied. "The truth is, the weather up this mountain is extreme, and I doubt you or the horses would survive. Whatever swamp witch magic we have, we can split in two. You guys can hold on to half, and keep yourselves and the horses safe and warm down here."

"And we'll take the other half up the mountain with us, in case we need it," Heron added. "Besides, you're better off staying down here. Who knows what the Dhaxanians are up to? They could very well look at you and say 'Oh, how sweet, you brought us dinner'."

I stifled a chuckle and got off my horse.

"Our swamp witch magic resources should be used in moderation, and taking the horses up the mountain would deplete them sooner rather than later," Patrik said, as he got off and moved half of the supplies into his and Scarlett's backpack, while Dion and Alles held on to the rest.

We wrapped ourselves in furs, which we then tied around our waists for mobility, keeping the weapons within reach. We put the shields we'd gotten from the Imen camp on our backs and left our horses with Dion and Alles, who still weren't happy with our decision.

"We could help you up there, you know," Alles muttered, stroking his horse's neck.

"We don't yet know what's up there," I replied gently, then squeezed his shoulder in an attempt to reassure him that we weren't dumping them behind. "We need someone to look after the horses down here. Besides, we'll be back before you know it."

Dion's eyes grew wide, and he didn't bother to hide his concern. "What if you don't?"

Heron, Scarlett, Patrik, and I looked at each other for a brief moment, before I shifted my focus back to Dion and Alles. "If we're not back in two days, you head back to the Adlets," I said, then gave him one of the three flares. Scarlett had kept one, handing the other two over to Heron and me, in case we split up for whatever reason. "Only use this if you have to. Otherwise, go back to Ragnar Peak, and meet the rest of our team there. Finding the swamp witch is the most important thing on our to-do list right now, so don't waste time coming right back for us."

"Either way, that's your worst-case scenario," Heron replied. "Which won't happen, anyway, because we're trained professionals. We've got tricks up our sleeves, two badass vampires, a Druid, a pit wolf, and, well, me."

I couldn't help but chuckle at that last one. "Way to blow your own horn there, Dorchadas."

"I thought it was what you liked most about me." Heron smirked, and I bit my lower lip in order to stop myself from laughing.

"Point is, Dion, Alles, stay here," I said to the young Imen. "Take care of our horses for us, and be ready to shoot out of here as fast as you can, if needed. Like I said, we don't know what's up there, Dhaxanians or worse."

The Imen nodded and pulled the horses away to a small cluster of trees, just fifty feet away. "We'll be here," Dion said, pointing at the natural refuge.

I used the last of the furs to cover Hundurr's back. He was huge, but there was enough material to keep his spine and shoulders warm. Patrik handed me his reserve of leather strings —I used them to tie the fur around Hundurr's body, making sure he stayed snug for the journey ahead. He eventually stopped shaking, unable to take his weary red eyes off me. I stroked his neck and smiled.

"We'll be fine, Hundurr," I said gently. "Just watch our backs. Hopefully, the Dhaxanians won't be too hard to find."

We left Dion, Alles, and the horses behind and trekked up the mountain, following one of the smoother western ridges.

The higher the altitude, the lower the temperatures dropped. We toughed it out, moving as fast as we could against the growing, biting winds.

Hundurr was more resilient than I'd given him credit for, but even he was starting to slow down, about halfway through. I briefly checked the others, and noticed that Patrik was starting to fall behind, too, and Heron was always a couple of steps behind me.

We stopped on one of the forest plateaus for a few minutes, during which time Patrik dropped to his knee and tried to dig a small hole in the frosted ground. Hundurr noticed his efforts and decided to help, clawing away at the hard dirt until the hole was deep enough for Patrik to fill with twigs and a handful of herbs and minerals from his supplies.

"What's that?" I asked, raising my voice as the wind howled around us.

"A little bit of magic to keep us going," Patrik replied, and muttered a Druid spell under his breath, then lit the bundle up and motioned for us to gather around the small fire. To my surprise, it burned bright and blue, despite the strong gusts of icy winds. "Warm yourselves up. It'll raise our body temperatures and keep them high for longer. It should be enough to get us to the top."

He was right. As soon as I put my hands above the flames, warmth poured through me, lighting my senses on fire, too. It was as if my focus had been amped up a few times over. "Oh, wow," I gasped. "Anyone else feeling this?"

"Lord, who needs coffee when you've got Druid fire, right?" Scarlett grinned, relishing the new sensations as she, too, warmed up by the fire.

Patrik smiled, then nodded at the citadel on top of the mountain. It was easier to spot now, with tall, white marble columns that seemed to go on forever, and sharp corners on the somewhat battered walls. "It looks like it's been up there a long time," he said. "But I don't see the lights anymore."

"Maybe they were just reflections on some patch of snow or ice, or something," Heron suggested.

"Either way, it's huge," I muttered.

Hundurr quietly made his way closer to the fire, too, warming his face. He seemed to enjoy it the most, and his eyes closed momentarily, before he snapped back to reality and looked up, sniffing the cold air. It was well below zero at this altitude. The ground was covered in snow, the layer thicker toward the edges of the plateau.

"Is that normal?" I asked, pointing at the thin crust of ice covering the pine trees. It hugged the trunks with beautiful, crystallized patterns, like nothing I'd ever seen before.

"It's frost, I guess," Patrik replied, squinting at the trees. He then got up and walked over to the nearest one, running his fingers over the frozen bark. "I've never seen ice formations such as this."

"It could mean that we're getting close," I suggested. "The Dhaxanians do like to freeze stuff, don't they?"

"With a single touch, too," Heron replied, then carefully looked around, his gaze settling on Hundurr, who was growing a little restless. "He doesn't look too happy."

"I think he smells something. Or someone," Scarlett said. "Hundurr, would you like to lead the way and track whatever scent you caught?"

The pit wolf didn't wait to be asked twice. He shot back up onto the ridge, just as another wave of heavy snowfall came down, with clusters of flakes almost as big as our fists. "Try to keep up," Scarlett gasped as she followed him.

One by one, we made our way farther up the mountain, covering another mile through the rising snow. The freezing winds continued to push back. We had our masks, hoods, and goggles on, just to protect our faces from the blizzard, while the sky darkened above us.

The citadel we'd seen was just a few yards away, at the very top of the mountain. I'd lost track of time during our climb, but we must've spent at least four to five hours just working our way up to the top plateau alone.

"Finally," Scarlett breathed, as we all made it to the city. It had been carved directly into the white marble core of the mountain peak, with narrow stairs and tall, slender columns. It reminded me of ancient Greek temples, given its rather simple architecture, but I was willing to bet it was incredibly spacious inside.

"Okay, everybody stay close," Patrik said, then motioned for Hundurr to come. "That means you too, big boy."

The pit wolf huffed, then trotted back to Scarlett's side as we walked into the ginormous cave posing as a city on top of a frozen mountain. *Add this to the stories you'll tell your kids later.*

About five minutes in, as I looked at the walls and tall ceiling that domed above us, I realized something. This wasn't white marble. Sure, there was some at the very core of the entire structure, but this was all ice, thick layers enveloping every pillar and every sheet of stone around us. "Guys, this is an ice palace," I murmured, my breath steaming before me.

It wasn't dark, either, but I couldn't identify the light sources. A cool, bluish sheen reflected off every icy surface, mingled with the pure white of the marble underlayers. The deeper we went into the city, the more beautiful it became—the walls and columns were adorned with swirling ice sculptures, while a frosted pattern developed on the floor. There was a thin layer of snow powder on top, enough to stop our feet from slipping at every second step forward.

Despite the magnitude of this construction, however, there was no sign of life.

I couldn't help but feel a little disappointed. "What if it's abandoned?" I asked, my voice low as I looked around. "What if no one's been here in eons?"

"Or maybe they're just shy," Heron replied, the corner of his mouth twitching as he looked around. Hundurr seemed restless, huffing and whimpering as he sniffed the frozen floor.

Farther ahead, the hallway opened into what looked like a massive throne room. It was shaped like a dome, with ice columns linking the ceiling to the ground—with at least a hundred feet between them. "This is huge," I breathed, looking up.

There were rectangular holes carved into the walls all around us, displayed on even rows, one above the other, all the way up to the ceiling frame beneath the dome. There still wasn't a clear source of light in sight, and yet the hall was well-lit in a white hue.

The throne itself had been carved from a giant block of ice. The level of detail was simply astonishing, consisting mostly of snowflake patterns repeated in elegant rows along the sides. It, too, was covered in powdery snow, like dust that had settled with the passage of time. And nothing but silence.

"It stands to reason that none of this would melt," Scarlett said, taking a couple of steps toward the throne. "I mean, there's a perpetual winter going on here."

"Hundurr doesn't seem to think it's abandoned," Patrik replied, nodding at the pit wolf. Hundurr started growling, his gaze darting around, most likely seeing something we couldn't just yet. My muscles jerked, and my senses flared. I scanned the entire hall from top to bottom—still, no sign of movement. Not even a passing shadow.

"Where are they?" I muttered, frowning, as Heron moved closer to my side. He, too, was on edge. Something didn't feel right. So I decided to do the natural thing. I shouted. "We come in peace!"

Silence, as Patrik, Scarlett, and Heron gawked at me, their eyes nearly popping out of their orbits. I replied with a shrug. "Worth a shot," I added, slowly.

Hundurr's warning growl was briefly followed by the whistle of something shooting through the air. I saw the source—a sharp arrow, flying right toward us from the right side. I pulled Heron back on pure instinct. The arrow missed him by a few inches and got lodged into the ice floor. That thing was fast enough to break through several inches of ice, easily.

My blood froze as I heard that whizzing sound again—but this time more than once.

"Stay close!" Patrik barked, then quickly muttered a spell and put his hands out. Bright blue pulses shot out from his palms, forming a protective bubble around us. It shimmered blue, but it was transparent enough for us to see the rain of arrows coming at us.

Thousands of them, shot at once from the rectangular holes carved into the dome-shaped throne room, flew in fast. None could penetrate the shield, though, and they all fell onto the frozen floor.

"I guess it's not abandoned after all," I gasped, as another wave of arrows came in.

The swarm of steel-tipped projectiles rained down on us, but Patrik held his own. "I drew energy from the ice around us," he grunted, holding his glowing hands up to sustain the shield against the second wave. "Otherwise we would've been riddled with holes by now."

I couldn't see anyone, but someone was clearly shooting those arrows at us. And judging by the number of them coming in, there weren't just a handful of hostiles surrounding us.

"I know it's redundant to say this now, but I think Hundurr smelled something, for sure," Heron replied sarcastically.

"Good boy," Patrik said, gritting his teeth, "but I don't know how much longer I can keep this up. I feel each arrow hitting the shield like a punch in the gut."

A third round of arrows came in, and I could see the beads of sweat forming on Patrik's forehead as he struggled to keep the protective bubble up. A couple of arrows made it through, but we managed to dodge them, while the others joined the rest on the floor.

We were in trouble.

27

AVRIL

Whether they'd come out of hiding because they'd seen us come in, or because I'd called out to them, I wasn't sure. But I sure as hell wasn't ready to die on top of a frozen mountain in the middle of freaking nowhere.

These were definitely Dhaxanians—no one else could've pulled this kind of weather, or frozen architecture. No one thrived in these conditions like the Dhaxanians. Patrik held his own for a total of five arrow waves before his bubble started to crack, and he dropped to one knee, drained by the effort.

I had no choice but to try to initiate a dialogue, despite the incoming sixth wave of steel-tipped arrows. I raised my hands beneath the shimmering blue bubble and dodged several arrows that had made it through, in the process. "We come in peace! We mean you no harm! We just want to talk!"

"Pretty sure they heard you the first time," Heron replied bluntly. "Not sure they care."

"Any other ideas?" I shot back, both eyebrows raised.

"Shields up and we make a run for it," he offered.

I looked around, and only saw two possible ways out—one back into the freezing blizzard, and one seemingly leading east, and deeper into the mountain. We pulled our shields onto our arms and drew our swords, ready to make a run either way.

"What'll it be? Back out or through there?" I nodded at the eastward doorway.

Patrik and Scarlett looked at both options, while Hundurr sneered at our unseen enemies, who were most likely loading up a seventh round of arrows on their bows. Patrik's protective bubble wasn't going to survive another wave, for sure.

"The sensible thing would be to get the hell out of here as fast as we can," Scarlett muttered.

"But we need to talk to the Dhaxanians," I replied.

"It doesn't look like they're interested in a chat right now," Scarlett groaned, shaking her head with dismay.

"Okay, let's go outside, then, and try another approach. Like, now." Heron tried to mediate the conversation, and steer it toward some kind of action before the next wave of arrows came down.

"You're not going anywhere." A low, yet delicate voice emerged from the icy dome.

We stilled and looked around once more. A figure emerged from the eastern doorway. Just then, Patrik's protective bubble popped, and my heart sank. *Oh, crap.*

"Hold fire," the creature said, raising one long, slender arm as he advanced through the throne room.

The closer he got, the better I could see him. Based on Vesta's description, we were looking at our first Dhaxanian. He was tall and wiry, clad in layers of bluish silk. His hair was long and white, flowing down his back like a snowfall, and his eyes were big and icy blue. His pointy ears and delicate features were further softened by his pale skin and almost airy walk. If he was any indication of what the Dhaxanians looked like, overall, I had to admit—this was, by far, one of the most beautiful species I'd ever come across.

He looked ethereal, his skin carrying a pearly shimmer, accentuated by the plethora of diamonds and silver used to weave the elegant crown on his head, and his decorative chest piece.

"You look like you're in charge here," Heron muttered, keeping his sword out and ready to strike, if needed.

The Dhaxanian nearly hovered over the ice, measuring each of us from head to toe, his blue eyes twinkling with chilling curiosity—the kind a scientist might wear when he discovers a new species to dissect, not the kind a kid has when he's given a new toy. My blood was already crystallized, my spine tingling from the thought of how many arrows they probably still had and were most likely pointing at us.

"Whatever gave me away?" the Dhaxanian replied with a smirk.

Oh, boy, icy all the way, then.

"Can you please stop shooting arrows at us?" I asked, unable to control my frustration. "We just want to talk."

The Dhaxanian's gaze found mine, and, for no apparent reason, my heart skipped a beat. He seemed to be well aware of the impact that he could have on people, and wasn't shy about using it, either. Heron noticed, too, and moved a few inches closer to my side—whether to protect me or to assert himself as my mate in front of the Dhaxanian, I wasn't too sure at this point.

"By all means. I'm listening," the Dhaxanian said, his hands resting behind his back.

He was tall and slender, but there was this certain noblesse about him, a masculine grace I'd only seen portrayed in ancient Greek sculptures before. And the self-confidence he exuded further lowered my temperature, mainly because it made me all the more aware of how screwed we were if we didn't take this conversation into friendlier territory.

I started with the introductions, because I was dying to know *his* name. "I'm Avril Novak. And these are my colleagues, Heron Dorchadas, Scarlett Novak, and Patrik Raymer. We belong to GASP, a now-intergalactic organization dedicated to promoting objectives of peace and balance throughout the supernatural world. We're not from Neraka."

He didn't say anything, but he didn't take his eyes off me either. Hundurr kept growling, until Scarlett sheathed her sword and patted his back in an attempt to calm him down and avoid a tragedy—whether it would be a tragedy for the Dhaxanians or for us was something I didn't want to find out.

"Go on," the Dhaxanian replied.

"Well, we've introduced ourselves. Who are *you*?" I asked.

"Oh, we're doing the whole I-am-you-are thing." The Dhaxanian chuckled. "I am the ruler of this icy kingdom, Avril Novak of GASP. I am Nevis, son of Bairn, and prince of the Dhaxanians. Satisfied?"

"Big kahuna, then," I muttered, mostly to myself, then plastered a dry smile on my face. "Thank you. As I was saying, we're here to talk. We mean you and your people no harm, I assure you."

"You're repeating yourself. Tell me something new," Nevis replied.

Wow, he does not make it easy.

"We were brought here by the Exiled Maras under false pretenses, and—" Patrik tried to speak, but Nevis raised his hand to silence him, following it up with a freezing glare.

"Let her speak. Whatever story you wish to tell me, it sounds better coming from her," Nevis said, then smiled at me. It got awkward, fast, but there was no turning back. If he wanted me to do the talking, that was fine by me, as long as it bought us some time.

Patrik nodded briefly, while Heron's glare darkened on Nevis.

"Okay," I murmured, then straightened my back and raised my chin at the prince of Dhaxanians. "We operate across galaxies, helping those who cannot help themselves. We've restored peace across many kingdoms, over many years. Most recently, some of our members toppled a dark Druid of Eritopia, a galaxy far from here. We settled a base there and helped them rebuild. We were called out here, to Neraka, by the Exiled Maras, but it turned out to be a ruse, a big fat lie. We've discovered the current state of this world, and we want to bring this alliance between daemons and Exiled Maras to an end."

Nevis nodded slowly and motioned for me to continue.

"What's happening on Neraka is not natural," I said. "Innocent creatures have been suffering and dying for thousands of years, and it needs to stop. With GASP and Eritopia on our side, we have the power to rein the daemons in, and to remove the Exiled Maras from this world altogether. They've done enough damage, and they're past the point of any redemption. Neraka needs peace."

"And you're in my palace now... why, exactly?" Nevis raised an eyebrow.

"We'd like to discuss an alliance with you," I replied, somewhat frustrated that I had to state the obvious. "The Dhaxanians have lost plenty over the years, too, right? You guys are practically extinct. Reduced to this mountain. Missing from the pages of history altogether, while the daemons and Exiled Maras wreak havoc on the world. Are you okay with that?"

Nevis crossed his arms, pursing his lips as he mulled over my words for a while. "What do you need us for, if you have your GASP and Eritopia whatever?"

"Yeah, here's our problem." I sighed. "The daemons and Exiled Maras are keeping our last swamp witch hostage. They have been keeping her here for thousands of years, using her against you and the others. Most recently, they had her put up a shield to cut off all communications with the outside world. We can't reach out to our people, and our people can't get to us, either. We're currently looking for her, and, once we find out where she is, we'll need help to get her out. Most importantly, once we have her back and she brings down the shield, we'll need support to keep the daemons and Exiled Maras at bay— long enough for us to reach out and bring our armies to Neraka to end this nonsense."

Nevis seemed genuinely amused, but equally interested. "So you need assistance. Allies," he concluded, and I replied with a nod. "You want the Dhaxanians to help you get your swamp witch back and keep you all safe until your armies come down here."

"Yes," I said. "Rest assured, we will broker peace on Neraka and help all of its people get their lives back, in a fair and democratic fashion. The Exiled Maras' influence is unnatural. It needs to stop."

"That we can both agree on." Nevis smirked. "How many of you are there? I doubt it's only you four and the mutt."

Hundurr growled, not liking the label, but Nevis didn't care.

"The rest of our team is most likely infiltrating Draconis as we speak," I replied. "They're looking for the swamp witch. We have plenty of firepower together, especially now that another fae has joined our ranks. We have a dragon, too. But we need support from the locals, for once the Exiled Maras and the daemons lose the swamp witch, they will stop at nothing to get her back. The Dhaxanians are powerful. We've heard great things about your kind, and, most importantly, you can bring frost and slow the daemons down. We've made friends with the Adlets and the Imen, and our friends are getting the Manticores involved, too, if there are any left. We need you. Your world needs you."

"I doubt there are any Manticores left, but hey, I must applaud you kids for trying. There's no trophy for trying, but you've made it this far," Nevis said, smiling. "But it's a good thing you've come here to tell me all about it."

Relief tickled my throat, and I could almost feel myself light up as I took a deep breath. "So you'll help us?" I asked.

Nevis gazed at me for what felt like an eternity, then chuckled softly, as if he'd heard a pretty decent joke. "No, darling, I'll put an end to this nonsense."

"Wait, what?" I gasped, then froze—literally.

The same frost we'd seen spreading through the plateau forest expanded from beneath Nevis. It reached our feet and swallowed us whole in a matter of seconds. We were glazed in ice, all the way up to our chins. Patrik tried chanting a spell to counteract the effect, but Nevis shook his head, and the frost covered the Druid's mouth, leaving his nose clear, in order for him to breathe.

My heart nearly stopped, as the truth sank in. The Dhaxanians had absolutely no interest in helping us. If anything, Nevis had simply prolonged what to him was probably the inevitable. As the icy cold seeped through my layers of fur and leather, I understood that our predicament had quickly shifted from hopeful to dark, and potentially deadly.

28

SCARLETT

"Y ou've got to be kidding me!" Avril cried out, struggling to move against the ice, but with no success whatsoever. "Don't tell me you're siding with those horned bastards!"

We couldn't move, our bodies encased in glassy ice. Dhaxanians quietly emerged from the rectangular holes all around us —at least a thousand of them, all dressed in soft white silks, with silver protection plates covering their chests, shoulders, forearms, and calves. They were all diaphanously beautiful, with white hair and bluish eyes, their skin pearlescent and their features delicate. They carried their bows and quivers on their backs as they slid down the ice walls of the dome and surrounded us, while Nevis sat on his frozen throne.

"I made an agreement with King Shaytan a long time ago," the prince of Dhaxanians said, though he didn't seem too happy about it. "I keep the mountains for my people, and the daemons can do whatever they want with the rest. We don't interfere in each other's business. We've kept a low profile and stayed out of sight, and we've managed to replenish our population, after millennia spent burying our loved ones. We've reached a certain balance, and I would hate to see it go up in literal flames simply because you people were gullible enough to get yourselves trapped here by the Exiled Maras."

The enthusiasm I'd come out with this morning fizzled away, and I was left with a burning mixture of anger and the will to survive. It flared through me, despite the sheet of ice keeping me in place.

"You're making a big mistake, Nevis," I replied, gritting my teeth.

Hundurr yelped as he struggled against the ice, but to no avail. Patrik tried to speak, but his lips were turning blue under the frost. My heart thumped inside my ribcage.

"I think the ones who made a big mistake are you." Nevis smirked. "Although, in your defense, you couldn't have known. We've been keeping our presence hidden from most, and the Athelathan weather is so ferocious that no Iman has dared to venture through these parts. Not that they would've lived to tell the tale, anyway."

"This is wrong, on so many levels!" Avril shouted. "We're trying to help this world, and even you!"

"Listen, as much as I'd like to sit here and listen to that sweet voice of yours, Avril, I can't. I'm afraid I cannot break the peace treaty I worked so hard to put together with King Shaytan," Nevis replied, with a tinge of disappointment.

He then snapped his fingers, and the floor beneath us started to shake. The Dhaxanians took a couple of steps back as the ice began to crackle around us. "What's happening?" I breathed, staring at the cracks spreading in a circular pattern, singling us out from the rest of the Dhaxanian crowd.

"You'll be going downstairs for a while," Nevis said. "It's warmer than up here, if you're looking for a bright side to your otherwise unfortunate predicament."

"And what's the downside?" Heron shot back.

"None for me," Nevis chuckled. "But quite the conundrum for you. I'll be sending word out to Infernis. They'll come and fetch you, and my people and I will have nothing to do with any of this."

The floor broke into a disc beneath our frozen feet, then slowly descended into a cylindrical tunnel. Nevis and the Dhaxanians watched us go down, deep into the bowels of the Athelathan Mountains.

"Nevis, don't!" I called out as the darkness of stone enveloped us. "You can still make things right! Don't do something you'll regret later!"

"I'm afraid that ship has already sailed," Nevis's voice came down from above.

The Dhaxanians gathered around the hole at the top, just so they could get a better view of us sinking deeper into the mountain.

It didn't look good for us. I couldn't free myself from the ice, and, slowly but surely, it was starting to bring my temperature down to dangerous levels—the kind that slowed my metabolism and stripped me of my supersonic speed.

Patrik and Heron were already pale, their lips blue and their teeth clattering, while Hundurr continued to whimper against his icy restraints. Avril didn't look too good either, but she, like me, was mostly distraught, and mentally preparing for a very uncomfortable freeze.

The frost wasn't going to kill us. The Dhaxanians surely knew that the daemons wanted us alive. If they had an alliance going, they most likely knew how precious we were to the soul-eaters, anyway.

Ugh. I was dangerously close to getting my soul eaten again.

No way. No way in hell. "No freaking way," I muttered, shaking my head and convincing myself that this was not over. That it was not going to end like this—not for me, not for Patrik, and certainly not for everyone else in our group, Hundurr included.

"How much time do you think we have until the daemons get here?" Avril asked, her voice low and calm. Judging by the look on her face, she was on the same page as me.

"I don't know, but—hold that thought," I breathed, as our ice disk reached the very bottom of the tunnel with a loud thud.

The underground opened up around us, beyond a cylindrical cage with what looked like meranium bars, each carved with swamp witch symbols. We were caged and restrained with ice, in the lowest part of the Athelathan Mountains.

Four large tunnels lead in four different directions. My guess was that they were all linked to a daemon city. "Oh, crap," I muttered. "They're connected. The daemons will probably just come through and pick us off, one by one."

"And the cage is charmed." Avril frowned as she noticed the symbols.

There was no way out for us. Not from where we stood, anyway. And we'd instructed Dion and Alles to run back to the Adlets, then Ragnar Peak, if we failed to return. *At least we didn't tell Nevis about Ragnar Peak.* At least Harper and the others had a chance, provided they didn't run into much trouble in Draconis.

I would've worried more about them, but, given *our* circumstances, I could only hope that they were doing better.

Chills ran down my spine, and I exhaled sharply.

"We are royally screwed," I managed.

It was cold and dark in here, and, despite being so close to Patrik, Avril, Heron, and even Hundurr, I felt incredibly lonely in this moment. The Dhaxanians had been so quick to betray us.

29

HARPER

Velnias took us deeper through the private prison block, farther to the east, where the prisoners in his care were being held. We kept a low profile, invisible and hiding whenever red lens daemons came out. Ramin, my eerily quiet feathered friend, didn't move an inch inside my backpack. I occasionally checked to see if it was still alive, only to be greeted by its curious, bright eyes. It had the patience of a saint... I used my True Sight to spot them in advance, giving our team the precious extra seconds we needed to go behind one of the many meranium boxes lining the main alley.

We turned a corner to the left, following Velnias, but his arm shot out and he pushed me back. I kept the rest of my team from stumbling forward. Velnias then cursed under his breath. "Crap, they've added more guards tonight," he said.

I craned my neck to the side and counted four daemons guarding one of the cells, with four more farther ahead. From what I could tell, Cells 5 and 6 had extra detail, while the rest of the smaller, shorter alley was empty. "Why?"

"Word is probably out that you and your people are looking for the Druid delegation," Velnias replied. "This is a new measure, and no one told me about it. And that, young lady, is something I find extremely insulting. Stay here, out of sight, and don't move until I signal you to come out."

He stalked up to the four guards, visibly infuriated. "What are you stooges doing here?" he barked, his hands behind his back.

The daemons looked somewhat confused. "We were told to be here, sir."

"You're absolutely useless here! The outsiders are just back there," Velnias shot back, pointing our way. I froze in my boots. *Oh, crap.* "I just saw them! Put your red lenses on and go get them!" he said, then motioned for the guards outside Cell 6. "You too! Go!"

"What the hell is happening here?" I croaked, pulling my twin swords out. My heart pounded as the daemons rushed toward us, fumbling through their tunic pockets for their red lenses.

"Don't let them put on their lenses," Hansa breathed, and shot out with her broadsword already drawn.

She was right: we had a good upper hand. The daemons were in such a panic to come after us that they had trouble finding their lenses—had we not been in such trouble, I would've laughed at them.

We came out and flanked all eight, two of whom had managed to put the lenses on. Caia and Blaze set them both on fire, then ran their swords through them. I tackled a third one, introducing him to both my blades, while Pheng-Pheng stung a fourth, then slit his throat.

Caspian, Fiona, and Jax took care of two more, then Pheng-Pheng and I took on the last two. We rushed around them, slashing our swords at them—enough to keep them distracted and with no time to reach for their red lenses.

I then caught a glimpse of Velnias leaning against the door of Cell 5, watching us with his arms crossed and a grin on his face. *I will punch him. I will.* Judging by his pose, however, Velnias hadn't exactly betrayed us. This was probably some kind of test. I figured he wanted to make sure, just like the Manticore queen, that we were worth all the trouble and the risk.

Pheng-Pheng and I managed to kill the last of the daemon guards, then made our way to Velnias. My fists were itching to meet his face, still, but Hansa beat me to it. She punched Velnias hard, throwing his head to the side. Velnias grunted from the pain, then chuckled, holding his reddened jaw.

"Good grief, that is a mean left hook!" he exclaimed, then took his charmed keys out—each engraved with what looked like swamp witch symbols.

"What the hell was that for?" Hansa growled, still furious, as she put her sword away.

"It was easier to have you folks take care of them than to come up with some stupid excuse to send them away," Velnias replied, then nodded at Blaze and Jax. "You two strapping young fellas, you should hide those bodies, unless you want a full red alert to go off as soon as someone comes by."

Hansa groaned, rolling her eyes, then joined Blaze and Jax in the cleanup mission. Two minutes later, with the daemon corpses stashed behind Cell 9 farther down the road, they came back to Cell 5, just as Velnias twisted one of the keys in the lock and opened the door.

Inside were two fae—a couple, judging by how they held each other close, pale as sheets of paper and huddled in a corner. The meranium box was spacious enough for the two of them to live comfortably, but, in the long run, and especially after thousands of years, it still wasn't enough.

The fae couple didn't say anything, but the weary looks on their faces told me everything I needed to know—as did their faded, dark red auras, and the circles around their bluish eyes. Their bodies were weak, and they were both literally worn out. In fact, they were barely standing, and appeared to be in a tremendous amount of pain. Worst of all, they were scared of Velnias, who let a heavy sigh roll out of his chest as he closed the door behind us.

"Idris, Rayna, I see you two are still alive," he said calmly. "I know this will come as a shock to you, but I'm not here to hurt you." He handed them two spare red lenses and motioned for them to put them over their eyes. "You're going to want to see this..."

The male fae, whom I identified as Idris, scoffed, his arms wrapped around Rayna's petite torso. "That's a new line, coming from the likes of you!"

"Idris, Rayna, he's telling the truth," Hansa said, stepping forward. "We're here to help."

The fae both stilled, then scrambled to put the lenses over their eyes. They gasped, staring at Hansa with surprise. "You're... You're a succubus," Rayna breathed.

"That I am, yes," Hansa replied with a nod and a soft smile. "I take it you haven't seen one of us in a long time."

"Thousands of years," Idris said. "What are you doing here? How did you end up on Neraka?"

"Long story short, the Exiled Maras brought us here under false pretenses, and now we can't get out until we find the swamp witch," Hansa explained as briefly as possible, given the little time we had in this place.

They looked at us, measuring each member of our team from head to toe, their gazes settling on Vesta. A thought occurred to me as I compared their features to hers, and Rayna's trembling lower lip and broken gasp confirmed my suspicions.

"Idris," Rayna managed, pointing at Vesta. "It's her... Our little Zara!"

"Whoa," Vesta replied, her jaw dropping. "Wh-What's happening? Who's Zara?"

My gaze darted between them several times, just to make sure. Pale blue drowned out the dark red in the fae's auras—a soft shade of genuine hope. After all the years they'd spent apart, their daughter had made her way back to them. Rayna was the first to burst into tears, swiftly followed by Idris.

"Vesta, they're... I think we just found your parents," I murmured.

30

HARPER

Vesta was stunned, her eyes wide and her heartbeat erratic, as she tried to process what was going on. Looking at her and her parents, I saw plenty of common features: Idris and Rayna both had pale blond hair; Rayna had sky-blue eyes, while Idris's were a wild, crude green, and Vesta had somehow gotten something in between, like the best of both.

"Zara. You... I thought we'd lost you," Rayna sobbed, unable to take her eyes off Vesta.

"You don't remember us?" Idris frowned, visibly confused.

Vesta shook her head slowly. "I don't remember anything from before five years ago, when my tribe fished me out of the ocean," she replied with a shrug. I couldn't help but analyze her emotions, enticed by the aura of deep red discreetly glowing around her. "And my name is Vesta."

"Oh, darling, it's not. We named you Zara," Rayna said, then put her arms out.

Vesta looked at me and Hansa for a few seconds, as if looking for guidance. She'd known a very different life for the past five years, and, given her amnesia, it had been the only life for her. I could only imagine what was going through her head at this point—the longing for truth, the confusion, and the revelation. Up until we'd met in the gorge, Vesta hadn't even known what she was. Of course, she'd been well aware of the fact that she wasn't an ordinary Iman, but with no other fae around to tell her, Vesta had spent years feeling different.

"Can I please hold you?" Rayna asked, her hands shaking with raw emotion.

Vesta nodded, and both Idris and Rayna came around and flanked her in a long embrace. Both fae parents cried, murmuring words of love in her hair, as Vesta gradually adjusted to the feeling of... her parents.

"So how does a fae get lost on Neraka?" Velnias asked, his arms crossed. He watched the entire scene with a mixture of amusement and curiosity.

"We escaped here once," Idris explained, "about twenty years ago. We caught a pattern in the changing of the guards. There was a small window of opportunity with a weaker daemon, and we took it. We managed to get out, and we went far to the southeast, about two hundred miles from the Valley of Screams."

"Once we realized there was no way out for us, we decided that having a baby wasn't a good option, even after we escaped Draconis. But Zara happened, and our lives were never the same again." Rayna smiled at Vesta. "We lived well for a while," she added, stroking her daughter's hair. "But the daemons caught up with us eventually. They ambushed us one night, and Zara got hurt. She fell off the cliff where we'd settled, and we were captured."

"We didn't think she'd made it," Idris said, glowing with love and relief.

"The Imen called me Vesta," the young fae replied.

"It's a beautiful name," Rayna said softly, and kissed her forehead. "I'll call you Vesta, if you want, if it makes you feel more comfortable. I'm sorry, darling, I can only imagine how confused you must be."

Vesta thought about it for a second, then nodded. "I like Vesta. It's who I've been since I woke up in the Imen's camp."

It felt so good to see a family reunited like this. With everything that we'd been through, with all the obstacles laid out before us, watching Vesta as she got her life, her identity back, was like a beacon of hope. It fueled my own motivations about this place. Just a little over a week in, and we were already tearing down the farce that the daemons and Exiled Maras had put together.

Vesta was lucky to have been raised by the Imen—she knew the land and its people well enough to help us. Unknowingly reuniting her with her parents was the least we could do.

"How did you manage to sneak into Draconis?" Idris then asked, checking us all out. "It's virtually impenetrable and inescapable."

"Well, we're persistent," Hansa replied, then pressed her lips into a thin line. "And we had no other choice, given our current circumstances..."

"I am so sorry that you got dragged into this," Idris sighed, while Rayna kept hugging Vesta. With every minute that went by, I could see Vesta warming up more and more to the mother she hadn't thought she still had.

"Nothing to be sorry about," I replied. "We're sorry we didn't bring more firepower with us. But we actually believed the

Exiled Maras to be reformed and living in peace, not... all of this," I muttered, motioning to everything around me.

"You two have been here for how long, exactly?" Hansa asked, her gaze wandering across the meranium walls, which were loaded with a flurry of swamp witch symbols.

"We've lost track, but I think we're close to eight thousand years. Maybe more," Rayna said.

Holy crap. "That is a very long time," I breathed.

It broke my heart. Rayna and Idris were visibly weakened, weighing probably half as much as most other fae I'd met, or less. Their skin was pale beyond the acceptable health limits, their beautiful eyes sunken into the dark abyss of their orbits.

Bluish veins rushed along their bruised wrists, and the shadows beneath their cheeks were dismally dark. But what really caught my eye were the small, reddish bruises on the sides of their necks. A single perforated wound persisted on each, as if systematically reopened over a set period of time.

Remembering what I'd learned from the daemon customs I'd seen so far, and Fiona's account from the Azure Heights prison invasion, those neck wounds were daemon bite marks—specifically made for soul consumption.

The daemons had been feeding on this fae couple for thousands of years. With the daemon and Exiled Mara populations increasing, the demand for "soul food" had gone up. My team and I were the first batch of an experimental replenishment of their "soul food" supply. If they succeeded in keeping us here, and feeding off us the same way they did with Idris, Rayna, and the other surviving delegation members, we weren't the only ones screwed.

The longer we allowed this feeding pattern to continue, the

worse it was for everyone involved—including the still-free Imen, the nearly extinct Manticores, the Adlets, the Dhaxanians, and every other living creature that still called Neraka home.

This has to stop.

31

FIONA

"I don't remember the dates during which the Druid delegation was on Neraka," Caia muttered, frowning as she tried to go over what she'd read in the Druid archives the night before our deployment.

"But it's something between eight and ten thousand years, for sure," Harper replied. "The Exiled Maras came here well over ten millennia ago. And the delegation itself crash-landed not long after that."

"Either way, as fae, we have very long lives ahead, still," Idris said.

"Provided we get you guys out of here," Harper said. "You two look like you can barely stand, at this point."

"They've been feeding off our souls for as long as we've been here," Rayna replied, tearing up again. "Once a month, one of the Seven Princes comes in here and leisurely consumes our very beings."

"You're much stronger supernaturals, by nature," Harper said. "You have a higher resistance to this practice, but I doubt you'll last another century if they keep draining you like this."

"It's why they came to us, after all," I sighed. "Their current so-called food supply is withering away. They need more of the fae and Mara caliber, and other strong species, as well, to continue this feeding frenzy."

Vesta exhaled, with one arm still wrapped around her mother's shoulder. "We need to get them out of here," she said.

"Not today, I'm afraid," Velnias replied, shaking his head.

"What do you mean? They're dying here!" Vesta retorted, getting angrier with every second that went by. It didn't faze the daemon, though. Velnias's cruel realism hit us all in the gut.

"Not while Cayn is in Draconis," he said. "No one gets out until Cayn leaves. He should be out in a day or two, tops. In the meantime, all I can do is help you people explore the prison, speak to delegation members, and help you find out where they're keeping the witch. If we break anyone out now, the entire city will be in an uproar, and the last thing you want is King Shaytan's undivided attention."

A few moments went by in an almost deafening silence. As much as we all hated to admit it, Velnias was right. Making a move now was counterproductive, given how eager the First Prince was to please his father. With Cayn still in town, our options were limited. Technically speaking, we could try to be cowboys and bust everyone out, but the effort would amount to nothing without the swamp witch's location.

Most importantly, if we did help the others escape right away, it could severely diminish our chances of finding the swamp witch in the first place. "Velnias has a point," I muttered, not bothering to hide my displeasure at having to say it out loud. "If we try breaking anyone out right now, the daemons might get extra paranoid and move the swamp witch elsewhere. I think, for the next couple of days, at least, that we need to be careful and discreet, while we explore this place and work out a feasible plan to get everybody to freedom and safety."

I felt just as miserable knowing I'd left Zane behind for the same reason. He'd helped me, despite our somewhat rocky introduction. He'd helped us all, and I had to leave him behind, for the time being. But, like I'd told Vesta, too, I knew where to find him. And I was definitely coming back for him—preferably sooner, not later. There was something brewing between us, the kind of magnetism I'd never experienced before, and I wanted to see where it could take me. I basically had the hots for a daemon, but, given my current circumstances, that really wasn't the craziest thing in my life.

"But I've only just found my parents," Vesta said, her voice trembling. I felt sorry for her, but it was in her best interests, too.

"At least you know where they are," I offered. "And, provided no one else knows you're related, the daemons won't try to use your parents against us. Against you, specifically. Let's focus on the main task right now. Let's keep our eyes on the grand prize. We need to find out where the swamp witch is being held. Once we know that, we can plan accordingly and get everyone out safely, not just the witch."

Vesta nodded slowly, then gave her parents an apologetic look. They both hugged her, and Idris gently squeezed her shoulder in a reassuring manner. "Don't worry, honey," he said. "They're right, actually. We are safer here, for the time being, than out there. And now that we know you're alive and fighting so hard, we'll hold out and wait for you to come back for us. We have all the faith in you."

"We don't know where they're holding the swamp witch, though," Rayna sighed. "We know she's still alive, but after our first escape, the daemons have been pretty careful about their conversations in our presence."

"They figured out that, if we could escape once, we could do it again. So they didn't want us to have access to any sensitive information, not even rumors," Idris added.

"That is true," Velnias confirmed. "We have protocols in place for creatures like Idris and Rayna. My guards are instructed to keep their mouths shut at all times. I know Rayna here loves to engage in... meaningful conversation."

Velnias chuckled, and Rayna shook her head in response. "I still can't believe you're a pacifist. You deserve to be drawn and quartered for the way you've tormented us until now."

We all looked at Velnias, our frowns making him visibly uncomfortable. He shrugged. "Don't look at me," he replied. "I'm only playing my part. I'm one of the very few pacifists that are higher up on the daemon food chain. It's thanks to creatures like me that the resistance has grown over the past few years. Unfortunately, yes, I've had to do some terrible things to maintain my image, but it's precisely this authenticity that has kept the suspicions at bay. It's why I was able to bring these people here, today."

As cruel as that sounded, Velnias was right. Despite his somewhat sociopathic behavior, his motivations as a pacifist were deeply rooted in his being—otherwise we would've found ourselves inside charmed meranium boxes, as well.

"So, what now, then?" Vesta asked. "We keep touring the prison?"

"The Druids from the delegation might have a better idea as to where they could be holding the swamp witch," Idris replied.

"I haven't seen a Druid in ages, but they're strong creatures, like us. At least two of them should still be alive, as they were still young and fresh out of the Grand Temple on Persea at the time."

"Oh, they're definitely still alive. I'm in charge of one, actually." Velnias smirked. "I suggest you bid your farewells now, so we can go see what he's up to. Once you get the information you need, you can draw up a plan to get everyone out of here. And, of course, I'll help you implement it."

"I can't believe I'm saying this, but thank you, Velnias," Rayna replied.

Vesta hugged and kissed her parents one last time as the rest of us made our way back to the door.

"I'll see you again soon, I promise," Vesta said to Idris and Rayna.

"I know you will, honey," Idris replied, smiling softly.

I checked my invisibility spell supply, concluding that I had enough for two more uses. Velnias followed my gaze, then smirked at the sight of the shimmering paste in its belt satchel. "I hope you've got enough to last you till you get out."

"We obviously came prepared," I replied, raising an eyebrow.

"Velnias, then you go out first, and make sure the coast is clear," Hansa said, scowling at him.

"Absolutely." Velnias chuckled, then opened the door and checked the dead-end alley before he confirmed it was clear. "Let's go."

One by one, we got out, with Vesta last. She once again promised her parents that she would see them again soon enough.

"Just be careful," I heard Rayna say, just as we stepped outside, and Velnias locked the cell door with his charmed keys.

"Now, let's go find ourselves a Druid." Velnias grinned, then guided us to the next meranium box.

As much as I tried to keep a clear head, I couldn't help but let hope blossom in the back of my head—the hope that the Druid in Cell 6 had all the answers we needed. It felt as though the more time we spent on Neraka, the more difficult and complicated everything got.

We needed a break, and I wholeheartedly wanted it to be in the form of the Druid next door.

32

HARPER

With no guards left on that block, we had easy access to Cell 6.

"The next guard change is in two hours," Velnias said, looking for the right key on the chain. Once he found it, he unlocked the door and motioned us to go in. "We should be fine until then. Just be ready to hide, no matter what."

As soon as we set foot inside the meranium box, I was hit by a faint feeling of hopelessness. The walls were all scribbled in swamp witch symbols, but I could see some had been scraped off in the lower corners—not easy to notice at first glance.

A Druid sat at the foot of the bed. Velnias gave him a red lens, then motioned for him to put it on. The Druid frowned but looked up through the lens. He stilled, gazing at us with a mixture of fear and confusion.

He'd arrived to Neraka as a young explorer—and the thousands of years he'd spent here had certainly left a mark. His long hair had streaks of white, and his salt-and-pepper beard further outlined the signs of aging: thin expression lines, dark rings around his wary, sad brown eyes, and sucked-in cheeks.

He did look slightly better than the fae couple, considering that he, too, was a "soul snack" for daemon royalty.

"Laughlan, my friend, you're looking better," Velnias said, closing the door behind him.

"What are you doing here? And who are they?" Laughlan replied, nodding at us. Despite his apparent abrasiveness, he was extremely curious about us. For someone who'd spent thousands of years in a box, Laughlan didn't immediately come across as hopeless, just physically drained.

"We're here to help," Hansa said. "Velnias is assisting us."

"We're from Calliope," Jax added. "We're part of an interstellar effort to restore peace and balance throughout the galaxies. We didn't expect to be here, but, well, here we are."

Laughlan's forehead smoothed. He seemed incredulous. "You've come to rescue me? Us?"

"Sort of. Just not yet." Jax sighed. "We were lured here by the Exiled Maras, but we managed to escape. However, we can't get off the planet, and we can't get help, either. Not until we find the swamp witch. We were hoping you could help us with that."

It hit me then that Laughlan's flat and doubtful reaction wasn't a defense mechanism, but rather the result of genuine hopelessness. He teared up as he carefully looked us over. A faint gasp escaped his throat when he realized that we were, in fact, standing here.

"I haven't seen Eritopians in thousands of years. I didn't think I would ever see one again," Laughlan breathed, coming to terms with the reality of our presence. He then scowled at Velnias. "And you! After all the torture and torment, you're a pacifist?"

Velnias replied with a shrug. "Hey, man, just playing my part. Sorry."

"You could've gone easier on me and the other prisoners," Laughlan muttered, crossing his arms. Despite his flannel tunic, it was still obvious he was underweight, and, judging by the wound on his neck, he'd been recently fed on. The blood was dry around the cut. That could further explain his somewhat lethargic reaction.

"Who fed on you?" I asked, frowning.

"One of the generals," Laughlan replied, prompting Velnias to scoff.

"That's it, I'm blacklisting those greedy brutes," Velnias said, crossing his arms. "Only the king and his sons are allowed to feed on the Druid. Wait till they hear about this. Who let the general in? I thought I left clear instructions with the guards!"

Laughlan sighed. "The guards let him in. He let them feed off me, as well."

"How are you still alive?" I asked. "With all due respect, you look terrible, but not as bad as the fae couple we just saw."

"Idris and Rayna? They're still alive?" Laughlan replied, his eyebrows raised with surprise. I nodded my response, and he smiled. "Thank the Daughters. I haven't seen them in... I've lost track, actually."

As much as I understood the wonder and sudden rush of hope surging through him, I knew we didn't have much time on our hands. The more questions he answered, the closer we got to our objective.

"Laughlan, what's your secret?" I asked, then nodded at the scratched symbols in the corner. He followed my gaze, then chuckled.

"You're quick," he said. "I figured out what some of these

charms do. Lumi taught me a few tricks during our trip, before we crash-landed in this hellhole. It's not enough to get myself out of here, but I was able to override some of the charms. They're meant to keep me docile and obedient, but now they help replenish my energy levels, drawing directly from the earth beneath and around us. The meranium actually works as a filter. It's the only way I've been able to keep myself in a functioning state."

"Consider me impressed," Velnias replied, then scoffed.

Laughlan rolled his eyes. "Relax, you fiend! I haven't figured out how to get myself out of here yet, if that's what you're worried about!"

"You mentioned Lumi," I said. "Who's that?"

"The swamp witch," Laughlan replied. "She heralded the expedition. It was part of an Eritopian effort to explore our universe, to see what life lay beyond our stars. It started out as a great idea, until she got sick." He sighed. "She convulsed and somehow affected the interplanetary spell. It wasn't her intention, of course, but she nudged it off course and it collided with the asteroid belt over Neraka. That's what made us crash. Those stupid, purple rocks."

"So what happened exactly, after you crash-landed here?" Hansa asked.

Laughlan took a deep breath, then scratched his beard, narrowing his eyes as he tried to remember what I assumed was the correct sequence of events. After all these years, I couldn't fault him for having a weakened memory.

"We found the Exiled Maras here. Well, up on the surface, in Azure Heights," he said. "They seemed like they were getting their act together. Until one of them stabbed my brother, Ronas, in the neck, and consumed his soul. It happened so fast, and it was so unexpected. We really didn't see it coming. They'd been so kind and hospitable, but they turned on us, fast. The first to fall was actually Lumi. When they attacked Ronas, Lumi was already bound and gagged, unable to use her magic to get us out of there. I guess that's the downside of swamp witch magic. It's useless if you can't speak."

"You know, Laughlan, a lot has happened since you left Eritopia," Jax said. "Lumi is, in fact, the last of her kind now."

"No," Laughlan breathed, his eyes wide with shock. "How... How did that happen? They were powerful creatures, stronger than all of my kind put together!"

"A Druid happened, actually," Jax replied. "But that's a story for another time. Tell us, where is she? How is she?"

"Oh, boy." Laughlan sighed, then shook his head. "It's a miracle she's still alive, but if anyone can outlive us all, it will probably be Lumi. I'm one of the few who knows where she is, and that's purely because I scrambled one of the charms in here to eavesdrop on the conversations taking place outside—"

"You sly little Druid!" Velnias chuckled, genuinely impressed.

"Yes, well, I had to keep myself entertained somehow," Laughlan shot back. "This place is incredibly boring. I haven't felt the sun on my face in thousands of years!"

"Laughlan, focus," I interjected, feeling him slip away again. His state of mind wasn't in the best shape, but, with a little guidance, he could still function, from what I could tell. "What happened to Lumi?"

"They tortured her. They've been torturing her from the beginning," Laughlan replied, his voice trembling, as his shoulders dropped. "But Lumi is strong, stronger than all of us put together. She holds out for as much as she can. Sometimes, she caves in and gives them a spell, but boy, does she string them along!" He chuckled, the bitterness in his voice punching me in the gut. Laughlan had feelings for her, judging by the golden tendrils coming out of him whenever he mentioned her name. "I think it's why they haven't killed her yet. Because she gives them spells once every few years. She started out with the minor stuff, then moved on to stronger magic. They still have to work out the ingredients, then experiment until they have a functioning spell. In the meantime, Lumi's still bound, blindfolded, and gagged, somewhere in Azure Heights—"

"Wait, what?!" I croaked.

The revelation knocked the air out of my lungs. Based on the expressions in the room, however, I wasn't the only one baffled by a most gut-wrenching truth. The swamp witch had been in Azure Heights this whole time!

"The daemons and Exiled Maras argued over this many times," Laughlan replied with a shrug. "They eventually agreed for the Maras to keep Lumi, and for the daemons to hold on to the rest of us, as long as Shaytan had continued access to swamp witch magic."

"So you're telling me that the Exiled Maras have been torturing Lumi, the last of the swamp witches, for thousands of years?" Hansa breathed, still wrapping her head around this.

I felt queasy. I couldn't even begin to imagine what it must've been like to be deprived of everything, repeatedly tortured for centuries on end. If Laughlan's hopelessness felt toxic just from being in the same room with him, what could it be like for someone like Lumi?

Laughlan shuddered, then rubbed his eyes. He was in so much pain I could almost feel it. "They feed on her, too, I hear. The daemons aren't too happy about that. They insisted that Lumi be left with her soul intact, since she had so much valuable information, but the Exiled Maras aren't exactly known for their restraint. I understand that, over the past couple of years, Shaytan has had daemon guards stationed in Azure Heights, out of sight, to keep an eye on her, and to make sure that they weren't draining her to the point where she could no longer provide them with spells."

"Oh, wow. That's just sick," Fiona murmured.

Caspian was pale as a sheet of paper. The look on his face and the tortured glimmer in his eyes told me everything I needed to know. He knew. He'd known all along, but, because of his blood oath, he couldn't say anything about it.

"I'm guessing Laughlan is quite accurate, huh?" I asked him, and he nodded slowly.

A few red spots blossomed on his cheeks, a reaction of his blood oath against the truth being exposed. "I'm sorry," he whispered.

"It's okay, Caspian," I replied, moving closer to him. "Just blink once for yes, and twice for no. Remember that worked before?"

He gave me a weak smile, then blinked once.

"Do you know exactly where they're keeping her in Azure Heights?" Jax asked Laughlan, who shook his head.

"No. I've tried to listen in on generals nearby, but the 'hearing' radius of my reversed charms is quite limited. But I do know they're keeping her mostly unconscious. They wake her up to feed her, then put her back to sleep. She's always gagged, so they force her to write the spells, whenever she finally gives in from all the pain."

"Is that true, Caspian?" Hansa asked, and Caspian blinked once.

My stomach churned, and my throat closed up. The more I

learned about Lumi's condition, the more urgent our mission became. All the days we'd spent worried about ourselves and the Imen suddenly paled in comparison to what Lumi was going through.

"Listen, Laughlan," I said slowly, "I promise you we'll get her out of there. And we'll come back for you and the others, too. This ends soon."

Hansa then nudged Velnias's shoulder. "How many Druid delegation members are still alive, and held here, in Draconis?" she asked. "We need to get them all out, and soon. Now that we know where the swamp witch is kept, we'll need all hands on deck, including the delegation's."

Velnias nodded in agreement, scratching the back of his head. "There are six left in total. Idris, Rayna, and Laughlan here are on my block. There are two other Maras, and a Druid, too, over in the western block. Cells 120, 121, and 123, to be precise. I'll help you get there once you get a plan together."

"Good," I replied, then walked over to Laughlan and placed a hand on his shoulder. "Laughlan, I need you to hang in there. We're coming back for you, and we're getting Lumi out, too. Eritopia lost plenty of Druids during Azazel's occupation, and I'll be damned if I'll let a single Druid die in this place."

"Thank you," Laughlan replied, giving me a weak smile. "Just make sure Lumi's okay. I don't really care what happens to me, as long as she lives."

"Laughlan, provided you don't get yourself in trouble with all these little reversed charms, you'll still be here when they come back for you." Velnias chuckled.

"Okay, what's the plan, then?" I asked, looking at Jax and Hansa.

"We should retreat upstairs, in that little safe space that Vesta showed us," Jax suggested. "We'll put our heads together and work out the best way to get everyone out, including Lumi."

Laughlan then got up and went over to the side of his bed. He got down on his knees and pulled a small box from underneath. He flipped it open and handed over a bunch of scrolls. I unraveled them, and couldn't help but smirk. "Velnias was right," I muttered, "you *are* a sly Druid."

I gave the scrolls to Jax and Hansa, both of them smiling as they read through the contents. Laughlan sat back on the edge of the bed and shrugged.

"Swamp witch magic," Hansa murmured, reading through the ingredient lists. "With Nerakian herbs and crystals. How did you get these?"

"I overheard some of the daemons over the years," Laughlan replied. "I have no access to the ingredients, but I kept the spells, just in case the day came that I would actually get to use them. Thanks to you all, that day is now upon us."

"It's a good thing I allowed the guards to give you charcoal sticks and paper to write on, then," Velnias chuckled. "I thought it would help maintain your sanity."

"I don't know how much the writing helped with *that*, but at least I got to record some of these little beauties," Laughlan replied, nodding at the scrolls in Hansa's hands.

"Thank you for that," I said to Laughlan. "You have no idea how much it helps us right now."

The Druid gave me one more smile, but it faded with the sound of an opening door. By the time I turned around, a familiar and blood-curdling voice came through.

"You outsiders are getting really sloppy, you know," Cayn said, standing in the doorway.

My heart stopped.

The First Prince was backed by at least a dozen daemon guards, from what I could glimpse over his shoulder. We all drew our swords, on instinct. Pheng-Pheng's scorpion tail rattled discreetly, and the sideways glance that she gave me told me everything I needed to know: we were in trouble up to our necks this time, but we *were* going to fight this, tooth and nail.

My blood quickly defrosted, and the clench in my stomach dissolved as my instincts went into overdrive. With both my swords out, I looked Cayn in the eyes, and, with no time left to wonder how he'd caught up with us, I only focused on ways of removing his head from his neck.

33

JAX

It was one thing to be on edge, perfectly aware of your surroundings while infiltrating a daemon city. But it was something else entirely to have one of the higher daemons standing in front of you, with a smug grin that basically screamed "I've got you now!", and guards behind him.

We were suddenly stuck in a meranium box, faced by the very creatures that wanted us locked up. Velnias's cover was blown, at this point. He had no way of backing himself out of this, mainly because Cayn had probably eavesdropped on the conversation from the outside—I certainly would've done that, if I were him.

My gaze briefly met Hansa's as I went over options in my head. I needed her safe and out of here. Most importantly, I could *not* let Cayn close that door on us.

"You're all probably wondering how I knew you were all gathered here," Cayn sneered, with one hand resting on the hilt of his still-sheathed, bejeweled broadsword. He didn't seem threatened by all our blades.

"Personally, I'm wondering how long it will take for you to die, from the moment I slit your throat," Harper replied dryly.

"Little vampire, I'll enjoy eating your soul the most. You've got spunk. It's refreshing. And downright hot." Cayn chuckled, then let out a playful growl. "But, still, do let me tell you about how I, the First Prince on King Shaytan's Council, outsmarted you all."

"Ugh, desperate to blow his own horn here, obviously," Fiona retorted, rolling her eyes.

"Oh, I don't need to do that. My actions are already testimony to my sheer genius. You see, I've had you tracked since you escaped from Infernis," Cayn said. "Two daemons with red lenses have been tailing you this whole time, with specific orders to not intervene until you were in a location where I could easily grab you and bring you back to my father. However, don't beat yourselves up for not spotting them. They've kept a reasonable distance this whole time."

It didn't come as much of a shock, but it was still a sore disappointment. It wasn't as if Harper could use her True Sight at all times, and, if the trackers were good enough, they could quite easily escape a sentry's detection—which, unfortunately, they had.

We couldn't have predicted this, either. After the mess we'd left the daemons with, back in Infernis, I didn't think either of them would have the skill to track us from the moment we escaped from the gorges. The odds had seemed in our favor at the time. *Chalk it up to experience, and pray you get out of this, now.*

"I didn't know about Velnias, though," Cayn added, narrowing his red eyes at the High Warden, whose expression gave nothing away. "My trackers spotted you going into my brother's cell, but I didn't think Velnias was involved until you scoundrels walked out of there with him. Velnias, my friend, you are in so much trouble. You have no idea."

"Oh, I might have a clue," Velnias scoffed, his sword screeching as he pulled it out from the scabbard.

"I knew you'd come to Draconis sooner or later," Cayn said, sneering at me. "It was only a matter of time before you self-righteous meat-bags made your way here. So I made sure to deliver Zane myself. Imagine my delight when I ran into one of my trackers on my way out. Oh, the joy! Anyway, settle in, my little ones. I added extra charms on the outside while you were catching up with your Druid. Your magic and dragon fire are useless in here. My guards will come fetch you once your transport cages are ready. My father will be very pleased."

Cayn then took a couple of steps back, ready to lock the door. In that instant, I realized how lucky we were that he was such an arrogant bastard—he couldn't resist coming in to gloat, instead of simply locking us in here.

I only had two seconds, tops, to do something, before we were really stuck in here.

"It's fine, we don't need any magic," I muttered, then shot forward, my blades thirsty for daemon blood. I went straight for the kill, and my determination caught Cayn by surprise, judging by the speed with which the color drained from his face.

He had no choice but to put his sword up to block my attack. I came at him hard, each blow pushing him farther back, until we were outside.

The rest of my team followed, spilling out into the narrow street. Cayn's plan had already backfired, prompting me to question his intelligence. I had a feeling that Shaytan was going to be king for a long time, still, given the intellectual quality of his offspring—especially since the only son I'd seen capable of great things, Zane, had turned against him by helping us.

There were two dozen daemon guards outside. One of them blew an alarm horn, and it gave us merely a handful of minutes to work with before more of them came in. Pheng-Pheng, Harper, and Caspian went first on the offensive, slashing and hacking left and right, while Fiona came from behind to deliver the fatal blows.

One by one, the daemons fell.

Hansa, Blaze, and Caia held their own, slightly over to the left, while Vesta helped Laughlan out. Velnias was nowhere to be found, and that pissed me off—a feeling which I welcomed, since I was still squaring off with Cayn at this point.

The daemon prince came back with heavy blows, but a sudden gust of wind knocked him right in the solar plexus and threw him backward. I glanced over my shoulder and saw the Druid smirking with his hands out. "Hey, I may be half dead, but I can still help," Laughlan said.

"And that is much appreciated," I replied, then frowned at Vesta. "Where's Velnias?"

"I have no idea, but we need to get out of here, fast!" she shot back, then blocked a sword hit from an incoming daemon, while Laughlan found another ounce of energy to use for a second gust of wind—enough to knock over six of the guards.

"I can't turn here!" Blaze grunted, then rammed his sword through a daemon's throat. "The meranium boxes are too close together. There's not enough room!"

I glanced around and saw that we weren't too far from one of the pillars leading back up to Kerentrith. The brain-scratching shriek of death claws drawing near sent shivers down my spine.

Not long after that, the growls of pit wolves followed, along with the thundering of more daemon boots on the ground.

Just as Hansa cut off the head of the last of Cayn's daemon guards, I pointed at the pillar. "Over there!" I shouted, then threw Cayn a brief glance. He'd been knocked out, but he was starting to move again. Soon enough, he'd come to.

Harper led the way back to the main street, but came to a screeching halt when three dozen more daemons came in from both sides, assisted by several pit wolves. This was far from over.

34

HARPER

This second wave of daemons wasn't going to be the last, either. That meant we had to strike hard and fast, and not give them the opportunity to corner us in any way. Somehow, knowing where the swamp witch was being kept had given me some much-needed clarity.

My instincts were sharp, and my brain was functioning at incredible speed, as I mentally drafted the exit strategy.

"The pillar is five prison blocks away," I said. "Blaze, Caia, fire it up, guys, we need to move fast!"

I didn't wait for a reply. Instead, I jumped right in, pushing a strong barrier into the row of daemons that were hoping to capture us alive. The pit wolves snarled as they were let off their leashes.

"Crack the collars," I shouted. "They're Adlets. They won't fight us if we free them!"

Vesta stayed back, protecting Laughlan as the Druid

employed minor defensive spells with some of the herbs and crystals that the fae was carrying. Caspian and Pheng-Pheng stayed close—the young Manticore chose to handle the pit wolves, and handle them she did, while the rest of my team slashed left and right through the horde.

Caia and Blaze split up, then came around from the sides, spraying fire at the daemons. The inferno swallowed some of them whole, while Hansa and Jax covered their heads and faces and dove in, beheading the fiends still standing.

The screams of death claws were getting louder. It was only a matter of a minute, maybe two, before they could reach us.

We needed to move before that happened.

A daemon came at me, and I managed to dodge his furious blows. He was trying to maim me, but I held my own, until another cut me from behind. Burning pain spread through my side, and I cried out, prompting Caspian to quickly kill off one of his opponents and dart over to my side. I felt the Ekar jump inside my backpack, only to settle on the left side, away from where the blade had left a cut through the material. Ramin was okay, if just a little startled.

Pheng-Pheng managed to break the charmed collar off one of the pit wolves, while Fiona and Hansa fought two others. The freed pit wolf shook its head, visibly confused, until Pheng-Pheng pointed at his brothers in suffering. "Break the collars, mutt! And you'll be free!"

That seemed to hit the pit wolf hard. It growled and did exactly that, sinking its massive fangs into another pit wolf's collar. Fiona managed to free the third, while Caspian got rid of my attackers. It gave me the window of opportunity I needed to whistle and get the pit wolves' attention.

As soon as they turned their sights on me, I employed my

mind control. "Kill all the daemons you can get your claws on, then get out and go back to your packs!" I shouted.

Their eyes glimmered gold for a brief moment, just before they turned on their daemon captors. The wolves were our best chance to get out of here, and they tore into the remaining daemons. Hansa and the others followed me as I led the way down the street.

We ran as fast as we could, headed straight for the pillar.

"Time to go invisible," I said, then fumbled through my satchel for my shimmering paste.

By the time we all ingested our spell ration, the pillar was just a block away. I could hear the pit wolves shredding daemons behind us. The ones we'd dealt with were already dead, and the wolves were now taking on the new arrivals.

A brief glance over my shoulder told me everything I needed to know—all daemon eyes were on us, and it was about to get incredibly messy. With all the prisoners stuck in meranium boxes, and very little room for Blaze to go full dragon, we had our work cut out for us.

Nevertheless, we kept running, as more daemons spilled onto the main street from the sides, while the pit wolves worked their way up through the swelling crowd. Whenever the guards released more collared pit wolves, the beasts simply tackled them to the ground and tore the charmed bands off, releasing more of their tormented kind.

I had to admit, that added an extra kick in my heels.

"You're not getting away this time!" Cayn's voice bellowed from behind.

"Then you've gone blind, because that's exactly what we're doing!" Jax shot back. Two seconds later, the invisibility paste kicked in, and we vanished. Some of the daemons had red lenses, and they could still see us, but that wouldn't matter much once we got back up to the Imen city, with its many walls, nooks, and crannies.

Just then, Blaze and Caia stopped for a couple of seconds to shoot out a thick curtain of fire at the incoming and increasing mass of daemons. They screamed and writhed as the flames ate them alive, while Cayn was forced to pull back, cursing under his breath.

The column was about a third of a mile in diameter, with stairs spiraling all the way up to what looked like an access hatch into Kerentrith. "Almost there," I shouted, and we kept going.

We were so close, I could almost feel the surface air brushing against my cheeks. I wiped the sweat off my brows, thankful to be already healing. We reached the column, then made our way up the carved stairs. I went up first, followed closely by Caspian and Pheng-Pheng. Hansa and Jax were in the middle, with Fiona between them. Vesta helped Laughlan up the stairs, while Blaze and Caia closed the line with plenty of fire against the daemons pursuing us.

I could hear pit wolves roaring below—some were killed, but others continued trashing the daemon crowd gathering at the base of the column before they fled to freedom. The daemons were focused on getting to us, and I had the feeling that capturing pit wolves was literally the last of their concerns.

Good. One free pit wolf is an extra ally in the days to come.

As expected, six death claws reached us, circling around the column. They were as gruesome and as frightening as I remembered them, with their huge black wings and leathery skin. There were also several daemons coming down the stairs from Kerentrith, but, with my speed and eagerness to get the heck out of Draconis, they didn't really stand a chance.

I bulldozed through them, slashing my swords and kicking them off the stairs. They fell over and met their deaths once they hit the ground below. We were halfway up at this point, and it was us or them. A fall wouldn't have killed us, but it would've definitely disabled us. With freedom just minutes away, it just wasn't an option.

The death claws started snapping their jaws at us, coming in like angry wasps. But they had no target precision, since they couldn't see us. They could only smell us, and that was their only indicative of our position at any time. I pushed one away with a barrier. Pheng-Pheng dodged another's claws, then pricked its neck with her poisoned spike. It was enough to send the creature plummeting into the broiling daemon crowd below.

Caia kept shooting fireballs at the daemons chasing us up the stairs, and Jax muttered a spell under his breath, tapping into the swamp witch arsenal that Patrik had left us with. It had taken considerable effort for the Mara to pull it off while running up a seemingly endless flight of stairs. He threw five small leather pouches over his shoulder.

"Watch out!" he shouted at Caia, who ducked.

Each pouch exploded into a puff of purple dust when it hit the daemons, who inhaled the powdered concoction and instantly collapsed. Some tumbled down the stairs, and others fell to their deaths. The gathering piles of unconscious daemons made it difficult for the ones farther back to advance, but they persevered.

We'd managed to put some distance between us and them, but we had the death claws to worry about, at this point. Three were still flying, with more coming in from the distant edge of the city. I pushed out another barrier, but my energy levels were starting to run low after everything I'd put into the fight.

"They can't see us," I said to the others. "They're trying to follow air ripples and signs of movement."

The access hatch was a clear fifty-yard sprint up the stairs away. Blaze used his fire breath to further confuse the three remaining death claws, prompting them to circle around the pillar again as they tried to figure out where we were.

Daemons shouted from below, roaring with anger and the eagerness to put us in meranium boxes.

Unfortunately for them, I had the last laugh. I pushed my way up through the escape hatch. One by one, we all made it into the cool darkness of one of the tunnels leading into Kerentrith.

It was far from over, though.

35

CAIA

I was the last to go through the hatch, right after I threw more flaming balls at the daemons below. I then pushed the hatch door closed and sealed it with my fire. It would take considerable effort for them to break through.

"This gives us a couple of minutes, at least," I said, following my team through the ascending tunnel. It was narrow, cool, and dark, providing me with much-needed freshness after hours spent simmering in Draconis.

"There's the cloaking spell." Vesta pointed at a shimmering wall ahead. "We can go through, but we won't be able to get back in without daemon blood."

"That's cool. There will be plenty of them looking for us on the surface," Jax breathed.

"The upside is that we now have a cloaking spell of our own, thanks to Laughlan," Hansa added.

Harper was the first to disappear through the wall, and the

rest of us followed. There were two guards stationed outside, but, by the time I made it through, they were already dead—courtesy of Pheng-Pheng, who pulled her sword out of the second daemon and kept running by my side.

Vesta moved ahead, leaving Laughlan with Blaze. "I'll take us back to the library. We can put the cloaking spell up there, and have a space to ourselves," she said. "The daemons won't think to look for us there, at this point."

"Yeah, they'll expect us to get the hell out of dodge, not go back," Harper replied.

"Do we have what we need for the cloaking spell?" Hansa asked, pulling one of the scrolls out and handing it over to Vesta.

"Yeah, minus a couple of herbs, but I can get those from anywhere here," Vesta said, briefly glancing at the list. "The city is riddled with plants."

We ran through the abandoned city of Kerentrith, invisible under the moonlight, until we reached the palace once more. We darted up the stairs and found the library, gathering in the farthest corner, close to the secret tunnel we'd used to get into Draconis in the first place.

Harper scanned the area with her True Sight, while the rest of us took a moment to catch our breaths. We'd made it.

"Yeah, daemons are coming out from all over the city, but I don't see them coming around here just yet," Harper murmured, then leaned into Caspian, who put an arm around her shoulders and held her tight.

I sat next to Laughlan on a small wooden bench, looking at Blaze through my red lens. He looked exhausted, but still very much on edge. This wasn't over. Not yet. Dammit, not by a longshot.

"I'll be right back. I know where to get the rest of the plants we need for the cloaking spell," Vesta whispered. "You guys decide the perimeter while I'm out. We need a clear path to the tunnel, but we also need to be out of the way, in case daemons start patrolling this area."

I could hear daemons barking orders in the distance, beyond the palace walls. They were frantic, scrambling to get us before we left Kerentrith. Nevertheless, Cayn had already surprised us once. Nothing stopped me from thinking he might do it again.

"What if they know we're still here, and with no intention to leave?" I asked, looking at Jax and Hansa.

"Right now, it's fifty-fifty for all of us," Jax replied. "We need a plan before we get out, and, most importantly, we need the rest of the Druid delegation."

"Hence the cloaking spell. It's like a gift from the Daughters," Hansa muttered, checking the entire library area with a soft frown. "I say we stick to this corner. It's secluded and out of the way, with the tunnel just over there." She pointed at the hidden door in the corner.

Vesta returned with a handful of leaves and green stems, smirking with satisfaction. "They're going nuts out there, but they're headed for the edges of the city. My guess is they think we're trying to run as far away as we can," she said.

"They might still track us here," I said, voicing a thought I'd been carrying with me since Cayn had first shown himself in Laughlan's cell.

"I doubt it," Vesta replied, handing the herbs over to Jax and Hansa, who were already getting all the ingredients together in a pile on the floor. "I used some bellaris to throw the pit wolves off our scent. It grows heavily around here, so I squeezed as many leaves and blossoms as I could, while moving around to get those herbs. Once touched, the bellaris lets out a faint smell. We can barely catch it, but for those with sensitive noses, like the pit wolves, it's extremely powerful and confusing. We'll be okay. Nobody will track us here."

"Smart fae." Fiona chuckled.

Jax used one of my lighters to set the entire mixture on fire. It burned fast and hot, leaving behind a mound of dark blue ashes —and still wasn't the strangest thing I'd seen all day. He then scooped the ashes into his hands and traced a line around the perimeter, which covered an area of roughly fifty square feet. It was enough for all of us to sit and sleep comfortably, flanked also by the tall wooden bookshelves.

"It needs blood from all of us," Hansa said, then took out a small knife and punctured her thumb, dripping silvery blood into the remaining pile of dark blue ashes on the floor.

We all repeated the move, dropping our own blood on top. Jax was the last, following up with the chant from the spell—the power of the word needed to seal the space and activate the swamp witch magic. The air glimmered blue around us, as the faux white marble wall rose up to the ceiling.

"Now, let's see if it works," I said, then walked over to the wall and touched it. It felt hard and cold, and very much real.

I nicked my thumb again and pressed it against the white marble. The entire surface rippled, and I walked through it. From the outside, it looked as though the library ended there, fifty feet before the original corners on the west side of the hall.

Perfect. At least we have a safe space.

thousands of years. I'd almost forgotten what a library looked like. I even caught a glimpse of the night sky on our way in here. My heart nearly stopped. So beautiful."

"Laughlan, focus," Harper said, then let the Ekar out of her backpack and fed it a handful of seeds from one of her belt satchels. "Why do you say they won't move her?"

"Oh, sorry. It's been a while since I've been this social." Laughlan chuckled. "They're not going to risk moving Lumi elsewhere. That will mean getting her out of Azure Heights, and the Exiled Maras have spent centuries fortifying that place."

"Do you know *where* they're keeping her, exactly?" I asked.

"No. But we can find out, don't worry," Laughlan replied.

"At least we know she's somewhere." Harper sighed.

"Yeah, though I was hoping it wouldn't be that wretched hellhole," I grumbled, my stomach tied up in painful knots.

I'd just escaped from that place, and the Mara Lords were definitely itching for revenge. I could only imagine how Vincent was pacing his palace, cooking up ways to avenge the mind-numbing beating I'd given him.

"We need a solid plan," Harper said. "We know they're keeping Lumi in Azure Heights. We know where they're keeping Zane, Idris, and Rayna. Velnias also gave us the location of the other three remaining members of the delegation. And we're due to meet the rest of the gang at Ragnar Peak in, what, five days?"

"By morning, it will be four," Jax replied with a nod.

"I'd call this progress," Hansa chimed in.

"You've done more than we ever could in the thousands of years we've been here." Laughlan scoffed, his bitter smile reminding him of his misery. My heart broke for him. I tried to imagine what it must've been like to try to maintain some form of sanity while locked in a meranium box for so many years.

"Worst-case scenario is we'll all go back into a meranium box. Best case is I'll finally get off this damn planet. I miss the deep, tranquil woods of Persea."

I let out a deep sigh, rubbing my face. There was dried daemon blood all over me—and the rest of my team, for that matter—and I longed for a hot shower and a soft bed. I wasn't going to get them anytime soon, but the quicker we got our fighters together, the better.

"We need to destabilize Draconis from the inside out, like we did with Infernis," Jax said, gazing at the fire. Hansa slowly relaxed, leaning against him. He put his arm around her waist and pulled her closer, while Caia and Blaze awkwardly huddled closer to one another.

Harper was virtually drained, and I knew she'd need to replenish soon. Not just where blood was concerned, but also to boost back her sentry abilities. Caspian held her tight, discreetly kissing her temple, as they both stared at the flames, while the Ekar settled on a ledge.

I couldn't help but think about Zane, worrying about him still down there—a prisoner to his brother's whims. Fortunately, he was still a daemon royal, and there was only so much that Cayn could do without stirring his father's wrath. Traitor or not, I had a feeling that Shaytan would want to deliver the punishment himself.

"We have to get Zane out of there," I murmured, "before something worse happens to him."

"I agree," Jax replied. "Zane is our ally, and we must help our own. Provided all ends with a toppled daemon kingdom, we'll need someone to take over from Shaytan. The king is too addicted to souls and power. I doubt he'll be willing to agree to a truce."

"No, no, Shaytan is mine," Harper said through gritted teeth. "For everything he's done, and for everything else he intends to do, rest assured, he won't live to see a free Neraka. And neither will the Lords of Azure Heights."

"Velnias is gone," Vesta said. "Though that might not be necessarily a bad thing. If we can find him down there, we could still count on him. He's gone into hiding, for sure, to avoid prison."

"We could, I suppose," Hansa mused, her head resting on Jax's shoulder. "We have a lot to do. Most importantly, we need an entry strategy. The spells that Laughlan gave us will certainly help. We'll need to gather the ingredients."

"We've made it this far, right?" Harper smirked, her eyes drooping.

"Besides, Patrik and the others are hard at work in the northeast," Jax added. "They'll come back with allies, too."

"Yeah, I'm positive about the Adlets," Vesta replied with a nod, then frowned slightly. "Though I'm not sure they'll find any Dhaxanians. Then again, who knows? You people have already exceeded my expectations."

"And you'll see your parents again, soon enough." Hansa gave her a reassuring smile.

Pheng-Pheng cleared her throat, then huddled closer to Harper. Her wide-eyed expression reminded me of a little girl looking up to her older sister. "The Manticores are with you, too," Pheng-Pheng said, and Harper replied with a smirk.

"Yeah, a handful of warriors against an army of daemons and a heavily guarded city that's surrounded by deadly gorges and an unfriendly ocean," Harper replied. "What could possibly go wrong?"

Technically speaking, everything.

But we'd come too far. We'd lived through too much already. Our families were waiting for us back home, most likely unable to get through to Neraka. The likes of Laughlan and the rest of his delegation had spent thousands of years locked inside meranium boxes. The Imen were constantly terrorized for their blood and their souls, as were other Nerakians.

Yeah, everything could go wrong.

But it couldn't be worse than what was already happening. I wasn't ready to let the daemons and Exiled Maras win just yet. Not while I was still alive and kicking.

With so much kicking left to do.

37

DRAVEN

I summoned Derek to a brief one-on-one meeting on the third evening since we'd deployed a team to Neraka. The inconsistencies regarding the Druid delegation didn't sit well with me, and, shortly after I came back from The Shade, I started looking into the galaxy itself.

Serena was busy with Field and the rest of the Calliope GASP team, managing the second team's deployment to Tenebris. The rebels had surprised us with an ambush, but they'd all made it out alive. I trusted her and the Hawk with handling this, just like I trusted them with my life.

Ruling an entire galaxy like Eritopia was not easy—far from it. Some days, it bordered on insane. Fortunately, I'd bonded with Serena on a sentry level, and it was finally starting to show. I didn't have any of her abilities, but my energy levels were through the roof, and that came in handy while rebuilding an empire. With twenty planets in my care, I had my work cut out

36

FIONA

Caia came back inside, and we all breathed yet another collective sigh of relief. We sat down in a circle, and Caia and Blaze prepared a small fire using a couple of broken chairs and an armful of books.

"I don't feel right burning all this literature," Caia muttered, but lit the pile. The amber flames engulfed the books, the pieces of wood crackling as the fire burned bright and warm.

"Don't worry." Vesta sighed. "Provided we succeed with everything, the Imen will have plenty of stories to tell after this."

"And if we don't, it won't matter," I replied with a soft chuckle. "Don't get me wrong, I'm doing my best to stay positive here, but Lumi is back in Azure Heights. And by tomorrow, the Exiled Maras will know that *we* know."

"They won't move her, if that's what you're worried about," Laughlan said, scooting closer to the fire and gazing around with genuine fascination. "You know, I haven't been out of that box in for me. The Shade, GASP, and all the Eritopians I'd allied with during our war against Azazel gave me their full support, though. I was lucky.

Which was why I was taking this whole Neraka business more than seriously. Our people were out there trying to restore balance to a world we knew nothing about. Others had taken a leap of faith for me when I'd needed them, several months back —it seemed only fair for me to give the Exiled Maras the same benefit of the doubt, despite their turbulent history.

And yet, something just didn't feel right. Viola and Phoenix were busy studying the galaxy to which Neraka belonged. Hopefully, I was going to get more information about it by morning. Although Derek had suggested that we discuss a course of action in a couple more days, it didn't do anything to ease my suspicions that something was, in fact, wrong with Neraka. I just couldn't put my finger on it. If anything, it got worse with every hour that passed, to the point where I could no longer hide it from Serena.

With Harper out there on Neraka, the last thing I wanted was to give her cause for concern. After all, it could turn out to be nothing—or something unrelated to the Exiled Maras.

I reached out to Jax via the Telluris spell, just as Derek came in and closed the door behind him. He greeted me with a brief nod and took a seat next to me.

"Telluris Jax!" I called out.

I'd done this spell many times before, and yet only with the Neraka team did it take so long to get a response. I still had trouble accepting distance as a factor in a spell designed to connect two souls, transcending time and space altogether.

"Telluris Jax!" I tried again, slightly frustrated.

A light frown settled between Derek's eyebrows. Looking at

him, I wondered what it must have been like for him, in the early days. Six hundred years ago, Derek was a wide-eyed vampire first making his way to a remote island that would soon become home to a plethora of supernatural species—a sanctuary that spawned an incredible organization, which I was humbled and proud to be a part of. I couldn't help but see an inkling of myself in him.

I, too, had a sanctuary to build.

"Hey, Draven," Jax's voice finally came through. "Sorry about taking so long to respond. I don't know what the hell the asteroid belt is doing. How is everything over there?"

Derek watched me quietly, analyzing my every expression as I listened to Jax.

"We're good over here, just waiting for Viola and Phoenix to gather some data on Neraka's galaxy," I replied. "The Tenebris operation had a bit of a hiccup, but they're all okay, and moving ahead. We should be seeing results by the end of the week. Apparently, the locals are getting tired of the incubus rebels. The factions have proposed nothing of value to rebuild the kingdom after Azazel, so there's a chance they'll be ousted soon, with a little help from GASP. How is everything going over there?"

"It's getting complicated, but still manageable," Jax said. "There are signs of another species living here, besides the Imen, but we've yet to see them. Upside is that no one's gone missing since we got here, though I'm not holding my breath at this point."

"Another species on Neraka?" I repeated, for Derek to hear. "That's interesting. Plus, it might explain the disappearances. But the Exiled Maras have been living there for almost ten thousand years. Surely they must've noticed something."

"They seem as baffled as we are, but we're still in the early days," Jax replied. "We're planning an expedition farther to the south tomorrow, to corroborate some of the Imen's accounts of suspicious activity. One thing I have to admit, Draven. The Exiled Maras have really done well for themselves here. Azure Heights is a beautiful place, and peaceful, too. It's a shame to see it plagued with abductions."

"It's strange to hear this coming from you," I said. "I remember you were the one most opposed to anything regarding the Exiled Maras."

"Consider me impressed, then. They've really turned their lives around here. The culture they've developed is interesting, too. A bit too artsy for my taste, but the girls are loving it." Jax chuckled.

"Good. That's good to hear," I replied, then decided to shift the conversation back to where it poked my instincts. "Jax, I need you to do something for me, as soon as you can."

"Shoot."

"I need you to talk to the Five Lords about the Druid delegation," I said. "According to the Druid archives, they never made it back to Calliope. I know Rewa said they bid the delegation farewell and never saw them again, but can you just double check with the Lords? Try to get some details regarding their departure. If they saw them actually leave Neraka's atmosphere, if they noticed any strange phenomena in the sky, that kind of stuff. Try to get a feel for the room, too. Just to make sure they're truthful. Avril could sniff out something, if needed. She's a living, breathing lie detector."

A long pause followed. It gnawed at my stomach.

Derek's eyes were on me, and, as soon as my gaze found his, it was as if he could read my mind. He shook his head slowly, and mouthed his question: "No answer?"

I replied with a shrug, quietly waiting. "Jax? Did you hear me?"

"Yes! Yes, I heard you," Jax said—but it didn't sound like Jax. The voice was lower, scratchier than the Mara Lord's timbre. I closed my eyes for a second and took a deep breath. "Sorry, got cut off for a bit. It went quiet all of a sudden," Jax continued, and this time I recognized his voice. "I'm intrigued. I'll definitely speak to the Lords about this, leave it with me."

"Thank you, Jax," I murmured, a vein throbbing in my temple. Everything about this conversation felt wrong, but I didn't want to raise the issue—not yet, anyway. Not until I figured out what was going on with Telluris and that asteroid belt. I had a feeling that Viola and Phoenix's findings might help.

"I'll be extra diplomatic when I talk to the Lords about this, too," Jax replied. "We didn't exactly hit it off from day one, but I'm starting to grow on them. Anything else?"

"Are the others with you?" I asked.

"They're down on the second level, in the infirmary. Patrik is preparing supplies for the southern expedition. I'll be joining them soon," Jax replied, once again not sounding like himself.

I couldn't resist this time. "Jax, there's something weird here. You don't sound right. Are you sure everything is okay there?"

Another pause, before Jax's husky voice came back. "Yes. I don't know, Draven, it has got to be the asteroid belt. You're not sounding much like yourself, either. Maybe the belt is distorting communications. We've floated that theory before."

I nodded slowly, and decided to quit asking Jax about it. "That's true," I murmured. "That's probably it. Thank you, Jax, and we'll talk again in six hours."

"Sure. I'll summon the Lords tonight and see what they can tell me about the Druid delegation in the meantime."

With heavy silence filling my head once more, I exhaled, then looked at Derek.

"Let me guess, something didn't feel right?" he asked.

"Yes. And, for the life of me, I can't figure out what. Jax just didn't sound like himself, but he said it must be the asteroid belt."

"What are you thinking, exactly?" Derek replied, frowning. "Give me your wildest theory, the one that's shaping up in your head, and that you're wary of sharing with anyone else. As crazy as it may sound."

I stilled, surprised by his intuition. The thoughts I'd been struggling with didn't exactly fall into a believable theory. They were wild ideas, impossible to even fathom in the absence of more information. But Derek was still able to sense them.

"Your intuition continues to amaze me," I muttered, leaning back into my chair.

He smiled, gazing at the hand-drawn map of Calliope beneath the glass surface of the meeting table. "I've been around for a long time, Draven. I've seen the craziest things come true, things I'd never dared to think could ever happen. Just say it out loud. It might not make sense, but it might at least make you feel better."

"I don't have a specific theory in my mind right now, but I'm thinking that maybe our Telluris communication was somehow compromised," I managed, scratching the back of my head.

Derek paused, his eyes widened and his eyebrows raised. "Wow. Yes, that sounds a little extreme, but still." Worry filled his eyes. "Do you think it's possible?"

"I have read about Telluris in every single Druid manuscript I could find. No one has ever experienced such issues with it before. They've used it with Druid delegations in previous expeditions, mostly around the same period of time as the one that crash-landed on Neraka. No one ever mentioned anything about Telluris glitching like this. Technically speaking, the asteroid belt around Neraka really shouldn't affect the spell itself."

Derek thought about it for a while, then let out a deep sigh. "So we have two massive unknowns, on top of the Nerakian mission's objective. Firstly, the Druid delegation that never made it back. Regarding that, you've got Viola and Phoenix digging into the archives, looking for information on the entire galaxy, and I've also asked Corinne to put together a special telescope to peek into the area. At this point, one can say that it's being taken care of, right?"

I nodded, suddenly eager to see what Corinne would come up with. We had the data, but a witch as gifted as Corinne could easily help us get a good look into the galaxy itself.

"Second, you've got a glitching Telluris spell, and team members who don't quite sound like themselves, right?" Derek continued, and I replied with another nod. "Without knowing more about this, all you have are shots in the dark, so why not take them?"

"What do you mean?" I frowned, not sure I was following his line of reasoning.

"Take all the theories about this, even the craziest ones, and start working to eliminate them, one by one."

That did make sense. A lot of sense, actually.

"Well, the first one, and the craziest, off the top of my head, is that Telluris is compromised," I said.

"Would the Nerakian team be aware of that?"

"They would certainly say something, if they were. Unless..." My voice trailed off, my mind boggled by a concept that sounded too crazy, even for this conversation. But Derek didn't let it go.

"Come on, Draven. Say it. What are you thinking?"

"Jax didn't sound like himself. Maybe it's not Jax I've been talking to?" I said it out loud, and I couldn't believe it. I shook my head, eager to let it go. The implications were downright terrifying. "No, that's insane. Other than transmission issues, and Jax's abrupt change in voice, there's nothing else to point to such an insanity."

"Nevertheless, we'll both sleep better if you cross that one off the list."

A minute passed as I mulled over it. "You're right. But how do I cross it off the list? Telluris is my only way of reaching out to the team."

"Okay. Assuming the theory, as crazy as it sounds, is true... You've been talking to Jax, Hansa, and Harper, right?" Derek asked, and I nodded. "You know them well enough to test them. Ask the right questions, the next time you talk, and confirm it's really them. If someone is posing as Jax, for example, surely they won't know *everything*, absolutely everything, about him, right? An impostor is not impossible to spot, no matter how crafty they are. Give it a shot. Dig deep into your memories, find a moment you shared with Jax, away from everyone else, and bring it into the conversation. See what he says. In the meantime, Corinne, Viola, and Phoenix are hard at work dealing with the first issue."

I had to admit—I was glad to have called Derek over. Most importantly, I was thankful to have him in our lives. His experience, his wisdom, and his ability to see past the "crazy" labels made him a powerful influence, and a true eye-opener. I couldn't help but smile.

"Thank you, Derek. Not just for your insight, but also for your ability to drill me, without regard for whatever might sound... insane."

Derek sighed, running a hand through his dark hair. "It's the least I can do. Part of my family is on Neraka right now. And there is nothing I won't do for family. Even if that means finding reason in the middle of crazy."

He had a point. Sure, it sounded ballistic to think that Telluris was compromised, and that it hadn't been Jax I'd spoken to. But it was what my instinct was trying to tell me. And yes, I did feel better just by voicing that thought.

All I had to do was wait for my next Telluris chat with Jax so I could put the theory to the test. Best case scenario, it was nothing. Worst case, Telluris was compromised, and I was in touch with impostors and had no other way of reaching out to my team —my friends, my *family*.

My skin crawled, so I shoved the thought away.

One question. The right question. That was all it was going to take for me to put this issue to rest. And if Jax gave me the wrong answer, well, at least I'd finally know what the hell was wrong with Telluris in the first place.

READY FOR THE NEXT PART OF THE SHADIANS' STORY?

Dear Shaddict,

Thank you for reading A League of Exiles!

The next book in the series, **ASOV 57: A Charge of Allies**, releases **March 2nd, 2018**!

Visit www.bellaforrest.net for details on ordering your copy.

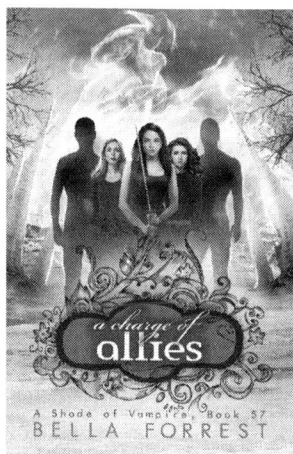

See you soon!

Love,

Bella x

P.S. Join my VIP email list and I'll send you a personal reminder as soon as I have a new book out. Visit here to sign up: **www.forrestbooks.com**

(Your email will be kept 100% private and you can unsubscribe at any time.)

P.P.S. Follow The Shade on Instagram and check out some of the beautiful graphics: @ashadeofvampire

You can also come say hi on Facebook: www.facebook.com/AShadeOfVampire

Made in the USA
Lexington, KY
24 February 2018